Chaos Comes To Kent

by

Jann Rowland

One Good Sonnet Publishing

By Jann Rowland
Published by One Good Sonnet Publishing:

PRIDE AND PREJUDICE VARIATIONS

Acting on Faith
A Life from the Ashes (Sequel to *Acting on Faith*)
Open Your Eyes
Implacable Resentment
An Unlikely Friendship
Bound by Love
Cassandra
Obsession
Shadows Over Longbourn
The Mistress of Longbourn
My Brother's Keeper
Coincidence
The Angel of Longbourn
Chaos Comes to Kent

PRIDE AND PREJUDICE VARIATIONS
Co-Authored with Lelia Eye

WAITING FOR AN ECHO

Waiting for an Echo Volume One: Words in the Darkness
Waiting for an Echo Volume Two: Echoes at Dawn
Waiting for an Echo Two Volume Set

A Summer in Brighton
A Bevy of Suitors
Love and Laughter: A Pride and Prejudice Short Stories Anthology

THE EARTH AND SKY TRILOGY
Co-Authored with Lelia Eye

On Wings of Air
On Lonely Paths
*On Tides of Fate**

*Forthcoming

This is a work of fiction based on the works of Jane Austen. All of the characters and events portrayed in this novel are products of Jane Austen's original novel or the authors' imaginations.

CHAOS COMES TO KENT

Copyright © 2017 Jann Rowland

Cover Design by Marina Willis

Published by One Good Sonnet Publishing

All rights reserved.

ISBN: 1987929624
ISBN-13: 978-1987929621

To my family who have, as always, shown
their unconditional love and encouragement.

CHAPTER I

$\mathscr{C}$haos. A simple, yet profound, concept, and one which is open to a wide variety of interpretation. For example, a cook in a large estate might consider the ebb and flow of the kitchen to be nothing more than the bustle of preparation, while one not familiar with the demands of a busy kitchen would think it nothing more than confusion and chaos. Similarly, one who did not know the dance steps and had never been to an assembly might find the commotion overwhelming, but to a young woman with a penchant for dancing, the smooth movement of dancers and people across a floor was an intricate pattern, pleasing to the eye.

However, while situations might be interpreted differently by disparate people, what happened in Kent in the spring of the year of our Lord eighteen hundred and twelve could not, under any circumstances, be considered anything other than chaos. But to understand the events of that spring, one must understand the history of what led to the commotion in question.

In Hertfordshire, there lived a family of minor gentry, typical of most families of their station in that it was peopled by those of different tempers and characters. What set them apart from the rest of those in the neighborhood was not the fact that they had been gentry for generations, nor was it the fact that Longbourn—the family estate—was the largest in the district, though in truth it was by no means a great estate. (There was one other larger, but it had not been inhabited for some time, other than for a brief period the previous autumn.)

What set this family apart was the fact that there were five female children, without a male to inherit, and as such, the estate was to devolve to a distant male relation to whom none of them had ever been introduced. As the wife—an attractive lady who, unfortunately, was not gifted intellectually—had no head for economy, there was very little put aside for their eventual support, should the master pass on to his heavenly reward before his daughters were settled in marriage. This possibility, of course, rendered her anxious about her future, which anxiety manifested itself in a nervous disposition and a determination to see her daughters married as soon as may be.

It was the unknown cousin who set the events in motion, though he had no idea what was about to be visited onto his doorstep; had he known, he doubtlessly would have kept his quill in its holder and his ink dry. Mr. Bennet—the master of the estate to which his cousin, Mr. Collins, was heir—had received a letter the previous autumn. Therein, Mr. Collins had proposed a meeting between the two branches of the family to heal the breach created by a longstanding dispute between Mr. Bennet and Mr. Collins's late father. Sadly, the engagement had fallen through, as an unexpected matter had risen, requiring Mr. Collins's presence in the parish where he was the rector and preventing his journey.

As was his wont, Bennet had not bothered to inform his family of the man's letter, thinking to himself that knowledge of the man's failure to attend the family could in no way affect them. Besides, Mr. Bennet, a man educated and delighting in all forms of knowledge, loathed the disruption to his home which would have ensued should he inform his wife of the detested cousin's olive branch. As the tumult at Longbourn was already almost unbearable, increasing the noise was not something he would willingly do.

In the spring of the next year, however, he received another letter from his cousin—they had been corresponding throughout the winter—with a proposal which he was tempted to reject without further thought. In the end, however, his hand was stayed when he considered the potential benefits. What decided him was the possibility of amusement which, to one who enjoyed the follies of others as much as a connoisseur might enjoy a fine wine, was nigh irresistible.

Thus, he found himself seated at the dinner table, his wife and five daughters in attendance, watching them as they ate and chattered among themselves. The two youngest, silly and ignorant, were discussing a recent party with their mother, laughing and speaking in loud voices of the officers who had been there, no doubt whispering of who was handsome and who was not or who filled out their coat better than the rest. His middle daughter, Mary, awkward and plainer than her sisters—at least to her own eyes, as Bennet had always thought Mary to be pretty in her own right—interjected moralistic observations on the proper deportment of young women during any perceived lull in the conversation, no matter how slight, in the hopes of being heard. It was obvious to Bennet that nothing short of a blast of cannon fire would succeed in diverting the attention of his wife and youngest daughters from so important a subject as the militia officers.

On the other side of the table, his eldest daughters—Jane and Elizabeth—the two jewels of his family, sat speaking quietly to each other. Bennet was not certain how each could induce the other to hear over the cacophony of voices on the other side of the table, but it seemed like the girls had long learned to simply ignore the piercing voices as their own conversation flowed uninterrupted. It was into this maelstrom of feminine voices that Bennet interjected his own.

"Mrs. Bennet," said he. "I have some news which you might find of interest."

Mrs. Bennet paused in mid-sentence, looking at him down the length of the table with seeming confusion; Mrs. Bennet was likely thinking of her husband's aversion for society, wondering what news he could possibly possess to which she herself was not already privy. It was clear to the Bennet sire that she considered simply continuing to speak with her youngest daughters, but apparently there was enough in his countenance to warrant her curiosity.

"News, Mr. Bennet?" asked she. "Whatever can you possibly mean?"

"Just that I have received a letter with a proposal that I dare say *most* of us will find agreeable, though Kitty and Lydia might not agree."

"Then, by all means, let us reject whatever this proposal is," said Lydia. The youngest, most spoiled daughter, was nothing if not determined. The very notion of pulling her away from her flirtations would be odious to her. Not for the first time, Bennet wondered if he should take the girl in hand rather than simply laughing at her excesses. The very thought of the uproar such a step would bring caused him to shy away from even considering it.

"Shall you not hear what I have to say before you reject it out of hand?" asked Bennet in a mild tone.

"Why should I, if it is as objectionable as you say?"

"Ah, but I did not say it was objectionable. I only said you and your sister might not find it as agreeable as the rest of us." Bennet directed a piercing look at his youngest, one which he used on those occasions he thought he could direct his daughter a little and still escape unscathed. "You should learn to think a little before you speak, Lydia, for words spoken in haste only serve to make one appear foolish."

Though Lydia sniffed in disdain, she had the presence of mind to keep her feelings on the subject to herself. It was a rare enough occurrence that it was notable, and Bennet did not question his good fortune.

"Well?" asked his wife in a testy tone. "What is this news for which you have interrupted our conversation?"

"Just that we have been offered the possibility of amusement and a change of scenery, Mrs. Bennet, an offer which does not often come our way."

That piqued his wife's interest. "And who has made this generous offer?"

"My cousin, Mr. William Collins," replied Bennet in an offhand manner, knowing the commotion which must unavoidably ensue.

Mrs. Bennet did not disappoint.

"Mr. Collins!" wailed she, in a voice which would make a banshee shriek with envy. "What could that odious man possibly have to say that we would wish to hear? What could he possibly have to offer us, other than a life bound to the hedgerows after you die?"

As always, Bennet was amused at his wife's single-mindedness. "I will attempt to refrain from taking offense to your conviction that I shall soon be in my grave, Mrs. Bennet."

"Oh, you and your clever comments!" snapped his wife. "You know perfectly well to what I refer."

"Indeed, I do, Mrs. Bennet, for you have often repeated yourself." Bennet held up the letter he had laid by the side of his plate. "Perhaps before you convict the young man of the serious crime of being my heir and brand him as the worst of all men, you should hear what he has to say for himself. I am quite sure you would consider him in a different light, should you only hear his thoughts on the subject most dear to your heart."

Though Mrs. Bennet was incapable of ascribing any pure intent to the detested man, once again her interest was aroused. "It is clear you wish to share the man's letter with us, Mr. Bennet, so I will not object to hearing it."

"Your charity does you credit, Mrs. Bennet." He could not quite suppress the sardonic note in his tone. Then opening the letter, Mr. Bennet began to read.

Hunsford, near Westerham, Kent
February 1, 1812

I was pleased to receive your last letter, sir, in which you explained the recent doings of your estate. I count it a rich blessing that we have managed to end the impasse between our two households, restoring a most agreeable discourse between us. It appears the estate is profitable, which I must own to some appreciation for the future security it will provide, though that security must needs be brought about by the eventual demise of your excellent person. I must assure you that I am quite comfortable in my current circumstances and, God willing, you will yet enjoy many years in your home with your excellent family.

"You have corresponded with Mr. Collins?" demanded his wife, aghast at the very notion.

"Of course, I have," replied Bennet with a shrug. "The man is my heir, after all—should I not foster better relations with him and hope he will be inclined to mercy, should I, as you so often like to state, end in my grave early?"

It appeared his wife had little to protest when he put it in such a manner.

"How long have you been writing to him?" asked she, a suspicious glint in her eye.

"Since the autumn," replied Bennet. "He wrote after Michaelmas last year, suggesting a visit to us to renew our acquaintance."

"Then why did he not come?"

"He was not explicit in his reasons for cancelling the engagement, but I understood it had to do with some matter of parish business which arose. Now, if I might be permitted to continue?"

Mrs. Bennet nodded, albeit reluctantly, and Bennet turned back to his letter.

My reason for replying to your recent letter with such alacrity is because I have been beset by a most agreeable notion, which I believe must also be acceptable to you. For you see, it gave me immeasurable grief to be forced to cancel my visit last year, as I was in a state of keen anticipation to make the acquaintance of you, your wife, and your daughters in person. The olive branch I suggested was not an idle suggestion, for I fully intend to make whatever restitution in my power to grant to your excellent wife and daughters. The opportunity to admire them, so cruelly denied, has filled my mind these last months, and I wish to correct that unfortunate deprivation.

My thought was to replace my previously proposed visit with an invitation to you and your excellent family to visit me at my parsonage in Kent. It is a pretty home, situated in the middle of a garden which, by the time you might arrive, would be showing the signs of the first bloom of spring in this most beauteous of all counties, and is by no means lacking in the necessary room to accommodate you all. Thus, we might meet in person, and I might show you all the wonders of Kent during your stay here. Alas, as the parish remains busy and the concerns it spawns, plenty, I will be unable to depart for some time to attend you in Hertfordshire.

I am pleased to report that my patroness, the honorable Lady Catherine de Bourgh, to whom I have related in full my intentions, approved of them whole-heartedly, suggesting that she, in her boundless condescension, would visit the parsonage directly upon your arrival to make your acquaintance. What rapturous munificence, for the lady is, as I have mentioned, the daughter of an earl, and a great personage in Kent. For her to condescend to pay such attentions to those of lower spheres is a testament to her goodness and liberality, as I am certain you must apprehend. She is charity itself, bestowing her boundless wisdom and assistance upon all within reach of her influence. We are blessed, indeed, to have her among us.

Please send me news at your earliest convenience of your willingness to attend me in my home, so that I can begin preparations to receive you. I propose that you come in the bloom of spring, so that you may see Kent in all its glory. Perhaps the first week of March would be agreeable? Then, if possible, I would ask you to stay at least two months complete in order to allow for certain developments to unfold.

I await your answer with bated breath.

Yours &c,
William Collins.

When he had finished reading, Bennet set the letter down on the table and looked with expectation at his wife. He was not disappointed.

Elizabeth Bennet, most like her father in wit and humor, listened to him read his cousin's letter, though she could not decide how best to react. The man's language was so flowery and absurd, she was sure it portended some pomposity of manner, some great arrogance, which seemed to be coupled with the man's utter lack of anything resembling sense. His open reference of her father's ultimate demise was highly indecorous in polite society, and his veneration of his patroness—a woman Elizabeth fully expected to discover was nothing more than a meddling crone—suggested almost open worship. And this from a minister of God, no less!

Furthermore, his blatant hints toward his expectation of an olive branch, extended to one of the Bennet sisters could not be misunderstood. Elizabeth had no pretensions when considering the subject of marriage. She understood she possessed little other than her person to induce a man to make her an offer of marriage, and her disposition was such that she could be as happy married to a parson as a duke, as long as she loved and respected him. Given the multiple absurdities in Mr. Collins's letter, she doubted respect was possible for such a man.

Unfortunately for Elizabeth's ears, her mother seemed to miss the inferences in the man's letter, instead choosing to focus on her long-held grievance with his position as the next master of Longbourn.

"What hubris, Mr. Bennet, to think that *we* would wish to visit his dingy little parsonage!" screeched Mrs. Bennet. "You may write back to him, refusing his generous offer, and any other he might choose to make."

"Oh, aye," said Lydia. "I would not wish to go to Kent, even if Mr. Collins lived in a palace. Not when the officers are still in Meryton."

"I will ask you, Mrs. Bennet," said Mr. Bennet, "not to dictate my response to my cousin."

Mrs. Bennet blinked, and the chagrin in her countenance suggested that she only now realized that she had overstepped her bounds. It was all Elizabeth could do not to shake her head; had her mother truly listened to what the letter said without prejudice, Elizabeth was certain her response would have been quite the opposite.

"As for you, Lydia," said Mr. Bennet, turning his attention on the youngest sister, "I will thank you to hold your tongue as well. *If* I decide we are to visit my cousin, we will visit him. I care not for the officers, and I dare say you can do without them for the space of a few weeks."

Lydia glared back at her father, but Kitty leaned over and said in a whisper: "If we are gone for some time, it will only make the officers faint with longing for our society."

The notion seemed to please Lydia, little though she appreciated the prospect of being without the officers' company for an extended period. She held her tongue, however, which was about all the rest of the family could hope for.

"Mrs. Bennet," said Mr. Bennet, "I believe you have not apprehended the potential benefits of accepting Mr. Collins's invitation. He has spoken of an olive branch extended to us, and at the very least, if he is known to you, I would think he would be less likely to arrange for your residence in the hedgerows as soon as may be upon my demise. Furthermore, there is a possibility of tying him even further to our family, which would almost certainly negate the prospect of your ever seeing the inside of one of those insidious bushes completely."

"Of what do you speak, Mr. Bennet?" asked his wife, frowning in her lack of understanding.

"Just this, Mrs. Bennet," said Mr. Bennet, once again lifting the letter from the table. He once again read over the pertinent passages, emphasizing Mr. Collins's words about olive branches, restitution, and admiration.

When comprehension finally came to Mrs. Bennet, it was akin to the dawn breaking over the hills, illuminating all in its path with the renewal of day.

"Oh, what an excellent thing, Mr. Bennet!" exclaimed she. "I had not understood his reference at first, but now that you have explained it, it makes perfect sense, indeed."

"I am happy to have been able to affect this transformation of your feelings," was Mr. Bennet's sardonic reply. "May I assume, therefore, that you have decided to relax your stricture against my intention to respond in the affirmative concerning our willingness to attend to Mr.

Collins in Kent?"

"Of course, you may!" said Mrs. Bennet, completely missing the irony in his voice as was her custom.

"But, Mama!" cried Lydia, still not giving up. "The officers!"

"The officers will still be here on our return, my love. And Kitty's suggestion is a good one—no doubt they will pine for you in your absence, and what is better than to make a man love you and increase his yearning by suspense?"

"What can be better, indeed?" echoed Mr. Bennet. Elizabeth could easily discern that though her father had enjoyed the scene, he was quickly tiring of it and longed to return to his library.

The meal continued in a relatively subdued fashion, for though the matter had been decided, not everyone in the family was in raptures over the possible amusement. As Elizabeth knew from her father's maps that Westerham was some distance from London, there would not be much in the way of amusement for young ladies of Kitty and Lydia's ilk, though they certainly did not understand that fact yet themselves. Elizabeth had no objection to it, and she thought a change of scenery would be good for her dearest sister after her recent disappointment.

Her mother was, it seemed, already scheming to ensure that Mr. Collins did his duty by them and offered for one of her daughters. It was no surprise that not all her daughters were created equal, as evidenced by the muttering Elizabeth could hear, something her mother often did, and in a voice louder than she realized.

"We must do all we can to ensure we catch him, for then I shall never be required to leave Longbourn. Jane could certainly succeed, of course, but she is too beautiful for the likes of a parson, and my Lydia too lively. One of the middle girls will suffice. Kitty and Lizzy are handsome enough, and Mary might not be a complete disappointment, as she is pious enough for a parson's wife. Yes, Lizzy, Mary, or Kitty will do nicely."

As important as Elizabeth thought it to respect one's parents and obey them, for her part she appreciated her mother's sentiment, but was determined to decline her portion of the benefits. With nothing more than his letter, Mr. Collins had proven his unsuitability to be her husband, and she had not the least intention of accepting a proposal should he deign to make one.

As it happened, Elizabeth had the opportunity to speak with her father later that evening to hear his thoughts on the recently discussed subject, and she was not at all surprised by his comments.

"Oh, I think it is quite clear that Mr. Collins is a fool to the highest degree," said her father when she raised the subject in his book room. "That and the fact that his patroness promises to be equally absurd suggests it will be an enjoyable visit, indeed."

"Papa," said Elizabeth, her tone faintly admonishing, "is it for nothing more than the enjoyment of laughing at a stupid man that you have agreed to attend him in Kent?"

Mr. Bennet had the grace to look a little shamefaced; indeed, Elizabeth was the only one of his family who was allowed such liberties, though she knew her disapproval had no real effect on his character.

"Well . . . not entirely." Mr. Bennet paused and attempted to smile at her. "It would be beneficial to be acquainted with the future master of the estate, would you not agree?"

"I would, Papa," said Elizabeth.

"Then it is settled. He might even be an acceptable husband for one of you; he is sure to be easily led, after all. I have many letters from the man, all proclaiming his character with every word he has committed to paper. In fact, with her own brand of pomposity, I suspect that Mary might do quite well with him."

"And his parsonage?" asked Elizabeth. "I am certain that this Hunsford is likely a greater house than our own parsonage, but will Mr. Collins have the wherewithal to house seven additional people in his home?"

"He assures me that is the case." Mr. Bennet chuckled. "In fact, I suspect he has had this invitation in mind for some time now, for he has shared the details of his home with me several times. It is not the size of Longbourn, of course, but it sounds like it is quite comfortable. I would suggest that Mr. Collins is almost lonely in his present circumstances, if I did not suspect that he spends a large part of each day paying homage to his patroness."

"Then I suppose there can be no objection. Though Kitty and Lydia will complain, I do not doubt it is a good thing that they will be removed from the influence of the militia. Their behavior is becoming so objectionable that I fear for our reputations."

"Their characters are well known in Meryton, Lizzy," said Mr. Bennet, his tone faintly reproving. "I doubt their actions would ruin your reputation, unless one of them actually managed to entice one of the officers into her bed."

"Papa!" exclaimed Elizabeth. "Do not speak such things!"

"It is hardly likely, Elizabeth. These officers are eager to flirt with empty-headed young ladies, but there is not a man among them who is not wary of the consequences of being forced into a marriage with a girl who can bring him little wealth. Do you think Denny or Wickham, in all their elevated opinions of themselves and obvious desire for a life of ease, would waste their attentions on girls who cannot supply them with such benefits? Of course not, as Wickham has amply proven with his pursuit of Mary King. And even Kitty and Lydia, silly and flirtatious as they are, would not stoop to such levels of behavior."

"That is not the point, Papa. Jane and I do what we can to curb their behavior, but you know Mama sees nothing wrong with it. They must be corrected, or they will bring us all ridicule. What will this Lady Catherine think of them?"

"I suspect she will be too caught up in her own munificence to pay them much attention."

As it was a lost cause, Elizabeth decided surrender was the only option. "I hope so, Papa."

The preparations for the family's departure began and the sense of anticipation, which always manifest itself before a journey, settled over them all. Even Kitty and Lydia, who were, as expected, unexcited about the prospect of leaving their friends and — more importantly — the officers behind, began to show at least a hint of curiosity for what their journey into Kent might bring.

Elizabeth was not looking forward to the journey itself, truth be told. The Bennet family possessed only one carriage, and though it was a serviceable conveyance, it was not truly comfortable for a journey any longer than the distance between London and their aunt and uncle's residence on Gracechurch Street near Cheapside in London. This sojourn was to take them much further, as Hunsford was as far away from Gracechurch Street as Gracechurch Street was from Longbourn. It was truly a blessing that they would stop and stay with Aunt and Uncle Gardiner for one day, for spending a full day in a coach with her silly sisters and mother, seven people seated on seats which were not even truly designed to hold six, would test her equanimity to its limits.

Due to necessity, Mr. Bennet's valet and the one maid who would accompany them on their journey, would travel by post and would arrive a day before the family themselves. The top of the carriage would be stuffed with their trunks and possessions and as the amount of luggage they meant to take accumulated, Elizabeth wondered if the slightest gust would not tip the vehicle over.

One evening, a little more than a week before their scheduled departure, Elizabeth had the opportunity to speak with her eldest sister, Jane, concerning the upcoming amusement. In addition, she was able to settle herself concerning Jane's state of mind.

"You have been quiet about our upcoming journey, Sister," said Elizabeth as they braided each other's hair in preparation for retiring.

"I am not against it, Lizzy," replied Jane. "In fact, I am convinced that a bit of diversion will help my overall state of mind."

"Oh?" asked Elizabeth. "Is there some part of you that still pines after Mr. Bingley?"

An expression of mild exasperation came over Jane, as cross as Elizabeth had ever seen her sister. "I have asked you not to speak of Mr. Bingley," said Jane.

"I realize that, dearest. Though you might prefer not to speak of the man, I would appreciate the benefit of having my fears for your equanimity eased. Shall you not share with me what is in your heart?"

Jane sighed. "I would never wish to unsettle you, Lizzy. The truth is, though I will own that I was heartbroken by Mr. Bingley's defection, I feel that I am much recovered. Staying in Kent for some weeks can only help, in my opinion."

"I still believe, if you had gone to London with Aunt and Uncle Gardiner after Christmas, you might have been able to see Mr. Bingley again. At least, then, you would know if he does not care or if his sisters have been conspiring against you."

But Jane only shook her head. It was one of the few times in Elizabeth's memory where she and Jane had been at odds with differences of opinion. There were always times in which they disagreed, but this one had descended into an argument which had left them nursing grieved feelings against each other for a few days the previous winter.

"I will not chase after a man like a common barmaid, Lizzy. It is Mr. Bingley's responsibility to make his intentions known and to carry through with them."

"But a woman must give a man some encouragement. I would not have considered going to London to be chasing him. Rather it would have shown him, in a manner which could not be misinterpreted, that your feelings were engaged."

"And his sisters?"

Elizabeth grimaced. Jane's reminder was well stated, though it had taken Elizabeth quite some time to persuade her sister to her opinion of the Bingley sisters' perfidy. "Yes, you are correct, of course. His sisters *would* see it as a desperate woman chasing after their brother's wealth."

"That is why I did not go."

"It is likely for the best," said Elizabeth, waving the subject off with some irritation. "If Mr. Bingley is that inconstant, then he would not suit you. You would forever be fighting with Miss Bingley for control over your own home, and if he is ruled by her, you would have little assistance there."

"True," replied Jane. "Then we shall continue on as we were. I still have hope. Somewhere in the world, I believe there is a man who would suit me, and who would do everything in his power to assure me of his regard."

With a smile, Elizabeth gathered her dearest sister into a warm embrace. "I am certain there must be, Jane. And I am equally certain you shall find him."

CHAPTER II

heir preparations completed, the family soon departed for Kent. The journey was made in two easy steps, as originally planned, the first four and twenty miles to Uncle Gardiner's house where they stayed the night, and the final distance the next day. As Elizabeth had anticipated, the division of the journey into two days was the only thing which made it tolerable for all involved. Being the slightest of the sisters, Elizabeth, Mary, and Kitty sat on the forward-facing bench, with the more ample-figured Jane on the far side, which left Lydia to sit on the other bench with their parents. But even then, they were cramped almost beyond endurance, to say nothing of the constant chatter and laughter from Lydia and Kitty, with the willing encouragement of their mother.

At times, her father, exasperated with the continual noise and bother of certain members of his family, took himself to the top of the carriage to ride with the driver. But that was not a comfortable situation for either the driver or Mr. Bennet, and it would not be long before he once again entered into the carriage for as long as he could endure and the cycle repeated itself again.

At length, however, the miles of their journey to Kent fell behind them, and they turned onto a road which led toward a large estate in the distance. The signs of spring were evident everywhere they passed. The trees had only begun to show signs of their summer bounty on their bare branches, and the fields, to respond to the renewed warmth of the sun with wildflowers and green shoots of new growth. Elizabeth longed to sample the bounty which was laid out before her.

In the distance, Elizabeth could see a large building rising over a swell in the land, ruling over it like a monolith loomed over everything in its shadow. It was too far distant to obtain any details, but it was obviously a great estate manor, the house seeming to be many times larger than the house in which she had been raised. It was Rosings Park, the home of Mr. Collins's patroness, Lady Catherine de Bourgh. Elizabeth was not anticipating making the lady's acquaintance, given what she had heard about her vicariously through Mr. Collins's letters to her father.

On the other side of the road stood a strand of trees blowing in the breeze, and amidst that strand stood a much more modest abode, a country parsonage, it seemed, constructed of the usual stone and wood, its walls bleached, its roof steeply gabled. It was to this house the carriage driver finally turned off the road, easing the horses to a stop before the front door. And there, in front of the entrance, stood a man, dressed in black clothes and a clerical collar.

When the carriage was settled, the family busied themselves with descending from its cramped confines, and as such it was some few moments before Elizabeth was able to obtain any impression of the young man. Her father exited, and he assisted in turn his wife, then Elizabeth and her sisters, in the order of who was situated closest to the door. As a result, Elizabeth was the last of her sisters to debark, and upon doing so, she stood with her family, facing their host of the ensuing weeks.

If Elizabeth was aware of her most blatant failing, it was her propensity to judge on first impression, and the immovability of that judgment thereafter. She had attempted to correct that fault within herself, though she still fell back on it at times. That day, arriving in Kent and being introduced to the master of the parsonage at which she was to stay, Elizabeth could not help but be tempted to surrender to that vice.

Mr. Collins was not a handsome man; Elizabeth was prepared to forgive him of that flaw without reservation, as not all men were particularly handsome. He was tall but portly, his face round and pudgy, and his hair, greasy and lank, hung about his head like the mop fixed on the head of a scarecrow. Further interaction—colored, no doubt, by what her father had learned of his character—did not improve her impression of the man, for he bowed low to them all and expressed his gratitude and pleasure at their introduction with a plethora of words, fit for a Shakespearean comedy rather than the reunion of two long-estranged branches of a family.

"My dear Mr. Bennet," said he, his voice solemn and his air grave. "I am most happy to make your acquaintance and cannot state in language animated enough how pleased I am to have you all visit my humble abode. As my patroness, Lady Catherine de Bourgh, likes to say, 'Words cannot express the importance of family ties.' Our reunion must have been ordained from on high, for I feel such a sublime rapture at our meeting as to render me utterly without any means of expressing myself."

Having said this, Mr. Collins proceeded to give lie to his words, for he greeted each of the members of the Bennet family in turn, speaking in language almost obscene in its verbosity the same sentiments he had expressed to Mr. Bennet only moments before. The whole scene was so comical that Elizabeth could not help but make an observation.

"I can see you are happy to see us, sir," said Elizabeth when he had said some words to her. "In fact, if the sublimity of your feelings inspires you to such heights of rapture, then no loss of words can ever possibly take hold."

Her words brought Mr. Collins up short, and he stared at her, attempting to make sense of what she had said. In the end, he must have decided it must not matter, for he only said: "I believe you have the right of it, Cousin." It was clear from the slightly mystified distance in his eyes that he did not understand her words, and perhaps he even thought she was mocking him. She was, of course, but he did not need to know as much.

Mr. Collins turned and beckoned them into the house, and they followed, eager to go inside and rest from their journey. That, however, was not to be, as Mr. Collins, with the excitement of a small child, began to show them about the parsonage, noting everything of consequence—and many more things of no consequence—during a drawn-out tour of his home. No detail was too small. He waxed eloquently on the stairs, declaring them perfectly suited to his position as a parson; Mr. Bennet observed, in turn, that since they reached the second floor, he had no doubt they served their purpose. Mr. Collins showed them his parlor, which afforded a view of the garden in the back; his bookroom, from whence he told them he could easily see whenever Lady Catherine or her daughter, Miss Anne de Bourgh, should pass by so that he may hasten to make his obeisance; and each of the bedrooms in detail. He also informed them, with no trace of humility, that he was in a position to employ a woman of the village to come to his house and cook his meals and was even able to employ a maid and a manservant.

Every detail was lovingly pointed out with enough words to make a poet envious, and Elizabeth caught a distinct air of self-congratulation about him. He had obviously come into sudden prosperity at an earlier age than a man of his profession might have been able to expect, and it had gone to his head, leaving him with an inflated opinion of his own worth. As Elizabeth might have expected, her father seemed to enjoy every exaggerated statement, every boast, even though he must be as worn as the rest of them were.

At length, Mr. Collins was persuaded to show them to their bedchambers, though Lydia's often spoken "Oh, I am so tired!" might have had something to do with it. There were, it seemed, a dearth of chambers to be found, with only three available for their use, which necessitated Mary sharing with Elizabeth and Jane, while Kitty and Lydia had their own room. Elizabeth, who had slept on occasion with Mary as a young girl, knew her younger sister tended to move about a lot during the night and was not anticipating repeating the experience, especially when there would be three crammed into the bed!

"Now, I will excuse you to refresh yourselves," said Mr. Collins with magnanimous solemnity. "The maid has been instructed to provide wash water to all the rooms, so you may cleanse yourself from your journey. Dinner will be served in one hour. I look forward to receiving you all in the dining room."

Then with a bow, Mr. Collins turned and departed, leaving them all standing bemusedly in the hall. They looked at one another for a moment—even Mrs. Bennet seemed to sense that their cousin was a foolish man—before they separated to their chambers. But before Elizabeth could enter her room with her sisters, her father sidled up to her, and in a soft voice, said:

"He is delightful, is he not? I am anticipating our sojourn here quite keenly, I assure you."

"I think I will consider ways to make myself disagreeable," said Elizabeth, making a face at him. "I would not wish for him to fix his attentions on me as the companion of his future life."

Mr. Bennet grinned. "I suggest you simply continue to make statements that he does not understand. He will likely consider you unsuitable if he cannot understand you, though he will attempt to fool himself into believing that you simply do not make sense."

Elizabeth laughed. It was perhaps the most sagacious piece of advice her father had ever given her.

The family descended to the dining room at the appointed time. One of the first things Mr. Collins did upon their arrival was to install Mrs. Bennet as the mistress of his home during their time there, though as Elizabeth was to learn, it was largely an empty position: as he did not entertain, her mother would not take up any decisions for the man's house.

"I am well aware that under normal circumstances it would not be proper to have you all here, since I have no wife and, therefore, no mistress of my home. But I believe that as family, you, Mrs. Bennet, may act as such during your stay, so that the demands of propriety are met. I am all keen anticipation, I assure you, of my future happiness when I unearth the companion of my future life and she may take up the role in perpetuity."

Having said this, Mr. Collins's eyes roved over the five sisters, his gaze containing a particularly leering quality that Elizabeth found distasteful. The man was essentially correct in that it was permissible for a woman of the family to act as hostess for a bachelor, but with the question of whether their presence was at all proper, Elizabeth decided not to concern herself. Of more importance, Elizabeth's sense of her own perception into the characters of others was telling her that, in this instance, her first impression was no less than correct. The prospect of receiving this fatwit of a man's intimate attentions was likely to induce her to cast up her accounts.

They all went in to dinner, and it was soon served. The food was more than adequate, and Elizabeth acknowledged that his cook was, at the very least, competent. She did not think on the difference in cooking for eight as opposed to cooking for one, and the additional strain this must put on the poor woman. She assumed Mr. Collins had considered the matter.

It was not long after they had sat at the dinner table when Mr. Collins was diverted to his favorite subject, one Elizabeth knew instinctually he could speak of without cessation for hours, if allowed.

"We noted a large estate up the road as we approached, sir," said Mr. Bennet. Elizabeth considered his enjoyment of Mr. Collins's silliness almost unseemly and shot her father exasperated looks when he repeatedly threw fuel onto the fire of Mr. Collins's stupidity.

"Rosings Park," replied Mr. Collins in a tone which betrayed the danger of his falling into an ecstasy. "The home of my patroness, Lady Catherine de Bourgh. There is no greater estate in all the land, I assure you, Cousin. Even if the building were not already the cream of English estates, her ladyship's presence would elevate it to the edge of the divine."

"Indeed?" asked Mr. Bennet. "It is even more impressive than Blenheim or Chatsworth, is it? I am very much interested in seeing it, for a house which makes Chatsworth a mere hovel in comparison must be a sight, indeed."

It was unsurprising that Mr. Collins did not understand the irony in Mr. Bennet's tone, and it was equally evident that he had never seen the grand estate to which Mr. Bennet had referred. He only nodded his head in apparent agreement and said: "I see you are a discerning gentleman, Mr. Bennet, and you see things aright. Though there are many worthy estates in England, there are few which can claim the right to be compared with the jewel of Kent. I have told her ladyship of my appreciation for the elegance? of her home many times, I assure you."

"And I suppose she accepted your flattery as nothing more than her due?"

"But it is!" protested Mr. Collins. "And I would not call it flattery, precisely. After all, if praise is due, does not flattery merely become a statement of the truth?"

"That is an interesting question, indeed," said Mr. Bennet with a sage nod of his head. "Some might say that you are completely correct."

But even as Mr. Collins nodded his head vigorously, Mr. Bennet's eyes found Elizabeth's, and he winked. Elizabeth could only shake her head. It seemed like Mr. Collins blurred the lines between flattering for the sake of ingratiating oneself and giving a sincere compliment. If the first, then there was no way Mr. Collins was correct. The second, she was convinced, was quite beyond the man's capabilities.

The conversation wound on, and Elizabeth watched as her father subtly led Mr. Collins from one absurdity to the next. Many centered on his veneration for his patroness, but if that were the extent of the man's silliness, Elizabeth might have been able to forgive him. As it was, he had little understanding of proper behavior, a highly developed (and completely unwarranted) notion of his own abilities, and he showed a remarkable lack of understanding of his religion, to which priesthood he was duly ordained and its tenets, he was bound to promote. It was one of the most ridiculous spectacles to which Elizabeth had ever been witness.

Mrs. Bennet was not the most discerning of creatures. Despite her husband's words to the contrary, she was not entirely unaware of this fact herself. Brought up the daughter of a country solicitor who was, himself, the grandson of a gentleman, she had had little occasion to learn the social graces. It was only after her fortunate marriage to a landed gentleman that she began to understand that certain behaviors were required. She was also blessed with an impulsive disposition, one which resulted in her making comments before truly thinking about them.

But even with these deficiencies, Mrs. Bennet could see that her husband's cousin was far from a model of propriety himself. He was, in fact, more than a little silly, not attractive of countenance or manners, and almost seemed determined to make a spectacle of himself every time he opened his mouth. Mrs. Bennet did not know what to make of the man.

One truth she kept firmly in mind, however, was that Mr. Collins almost literally held their futures in his hand. Mr. Bennet was healthy and would, God willing, live for many more years. But one could never be certain. And should he die before his daughters were disposed of in marriage, their situation would instantly become pitiable. So, she forced any thought of the man's strangeness aside, knowing that should he choose to marry one of her girls, their future would forever be secured.

As it happened, Mrs. Bennet found herself near to Mr. Collins after dinner, and she was not certain it was not by the man's design. She had not spoken more than a few words to him since their arrival, as most of his attention had been on her husband. She was, therefore, surprised when he addressed her while the rest of her family were involved in their own conversations.

"I must own, Mrs. Bennet, the charms of your daughters are quite beyond what I had ever imagined."

The charms of her daughters was one subject which never failed to incite Mrs. Bennet's eloquence — especially when speaking with prospective suitors — so she set to her task with eagerness.

"They are good girls, Mr. Collins, if I do say so myself. And I have trained them all to be excellent mistresses. I am certain they will do any man credit." Mrs. Bennet paused, and then thinking that she could remove one of them from the man's consideration immediately, said:

"Of course, Lydia is full young and not yet ready for marriage. But my older daughters are ready to assume such a responsibility and are much admired, I assure you."

"I can see why, madam." Mr. Collins paused, and he looked from one of her girls to the next, and though Mrs. Bennet was prepared to approve of him for no other reason than to secure all their futures, she could not help but be a little wary of him. The look he bestowed upon them was nothing less than a leer.

"They all appear to be good girls, indeed. But it seems to me that the eldest Miss Bennet, in particular, must be admired by all."

The inflection in his voice suggested that there was some reason for Mr. Collins to speak of Jane, but Mrs. Bennet was quite used to men singling her out. And for good reason—Jane *was* admired wherever she went, being the most beautiful of her daughters.

But Jane was also the daughter on whom Mrs. Bennet had pinned most of her hopes for a good marriage. And why would she not? Any man would be fortunate to secure such a sweet, angelic girl as a wife. But Mrs. Bennet had never seen Jane as a parson's wife. Her attributes were such that she was entitled—in Mrs. Bennet's mind—to expect so much more in a marriage. Perhaps she might even aspire to be married into the nobility! If Mr. Collins would not be moved, Mrs. Bennet would relent. But perhaps he might be persuaded to one of the other girls.

"Indeed, Jane is admired," said Mrs. Bennet. "But I must tell you that a young man of the area has been paying her attentions, and I should not wonder if an engagement is forthcoming."

It was not a falsehood—not an explicit falsehood, in any case. Mr. Bingley *had* paid her the most exquisite attentions, though his failure to return still vexed Mrs. Bennet beyond all endurance. Mr. Collins did not need to know that those attentions had ceased more than three months earlier. Besides, as a man who was as far from handsome as a man could be, Mr. Collins could not expect the most beautiful wife.

"Oh, that is unfortunate," said Mr. Collins, and Mrs. Bennet could sense some real regret in his voice. "I would not wish to intrude upon a pre-existing attachment."

"I am certain you would not," murmured Mrs. Bennet. "Perhaps one of my other daughters might be an acceptable substitute? My Lizzy, next to Jane in both beauty and seniority, is intelligent and agreeable. I dare say she would bring much to any parson, for she has cared for Longbourn's tenants for some years now."

The look which Mr. Collins bestowed on Elizabeth was far from what Mrs. Bennet was hoping to provoke. In fact, the man looked on her with something akin to distaste.

"I am certain your daughter has many sterling qualities, Mrs. Bennet," said he, though his tone did not substantiate his words. "But in the brief time I have known her, she seems to display a hint of . . . impertinence in her manner which I do not find entirely seemly. I do not think her penchant for clever comments would at all please her ladyship."

That was a statement which Mrs. Bennet could well understand, for had she not warned Elizabeth of that very failing many times in the past? Now that she had heard an eligible man's opinion, Mrs. Bennet felt vindicated.

But she was not one to revel in her victory. If Mr. Collins did not wish to contend with Elizabeth's cleverness and she did not wish to give him Jane or Lydia, why she still had two daughters available.

"Then if Elizabeth is not to your taste, perhaps Mary would suit? Mary is not so clever as her elder sister, but she is capable. Furthermore, she is knowledgeable concerning the Bible and possesses a streak of morality which I believe would do a man of the cloth quite well, indeed."

When Mr. Collins turned a critical eye on Mary, Mrs. Bennet was certain he was about to reject her as well. "Miss Mary has struck me as pious and knowledgeable. But she is not . . . Well, perhaps her attributes are not quite so fine as her sisters'?"

Mrs. Bennet grimaced, knowing to what he was referring. Mary, plain and awkward, would no doubt have difficulty attracting any man, even one who was not . . . Well, Mrs. Bennet was young enough to remember attraction to a handsome man, and Mr. Collins certainly did not fit that description. She cast about for something to say that would change his mind, when the man himself solved her problem.

"On the other hand, it is said that beauty is only skin deep." Mr. Collins gazed at Mary for another few moments, apparently pondering, before nodding his head slowly, his decision made. "Yes, I believe Miss Mary will do very well, indeed. Lady Catherine would surely approve of her piety, and if there is any lack of accomplishment in the matter of managing my house, I am certain Lady Catherine would be happy to see to her education."

"I assure you, sir," said Mrs. Bennet, offended he would even suggest such a thing, "that Mary is well trained and capable. You need not fear for that."

"I am sure you have taught her to the best of your abilities," said he, returning his attention back to her. "But you must understand that Lady Catherine has the most exacting standards, and since she has imparted some of them to me, I cannot but acknowledge her ladyship's primacy in this matter."

In truth, Mrs. Bennet did not see, and it was only by the force of her will that she did not snap at the man for his stupidity. Only the necessity of keeping his good opinion kept her from telling him that he could look somewhere else for a wife if he was concerned about their upbringing.

Mrs. Bennet watched her host as the night wore on. Soon, he took himself to where Mary was sitting on a sofa, watching her younger sisters with her typical disapproval. They began to converse, and as their discussion continued, Mr. Collins became more animated. As for Mary, though Mrs. Bennet had never truly been able to understand her middle daughter, she appeared to have no aversion to speaking with him.

In all, Mrs. Bennet was satisfied. If all went well, she thought she would soon obtain the first of her long-desired sons-in-law.

The next morning, the parsonage was graced with the presence of Mr. Collins's patroness, to whom he eagerly introduced his family when she indicated a desire to know them. She was a tall woman, perhaps a little older than Mrs. Bennet, with an aristocratic bearing, dark hair beginning to grey, and a posture which spoke of a woman accustomed to having her own way and aware of her position in society. What Elizabeth did not expect was how the woman would greet them all with apparent civility, inquiring after their journey and accommodations in a manner which could only indicate an unfeigned interest.

"How good of you to visit, your ladyship," said Mr. Collins when the pleasantries had been exchanged. "And your excellent daughter? I hope that Miss de Bourgh is well?"

"Indeed, she is, Mr. Collins," said Lady Catherine. "You will all meet her anon, as I intend to have you and your family to Rosings for dinner one night very soon."

"Thank you, your ladyship," said Mr. Bennet, even as Mr. Collins exclaimed: "We are all in your gracious debt, your ladyship. I could not have imagined such condescension as this, the very day after my humble family's arrival."

Lady Catherine turned a pointed look on Mr. Collins, a look he seemed to understand, as he immediately ceased his flattery and fell silent, though his adoring gaze never wavered. Seemingly satisfied with his silence, Lady Catherine turned to Mr. Bennet.

"I understand you are from Hertfordshire, Mr. Bennet."

It was clear that her father did not know what to make of the lady, but he replied readily enough. "We live some few miles north of London, your ladyship, not far from Luton and Stevenage."

"Ah yes, of course. Then you must live just west of the Great North Road."

"That is correct." Mr. Bennet paused. "Are you familiar with the area?"

"Not in particular, I must confess. But my brother is the Earl of Matlock and his estate is in Derbyshire. Thus, I have traveled that road many times."

Their conversation continued on such subjects for some moments, and her ladyship made every attempt to include all the Bennets in it, though there were times that she directed pointed looks at Lydia and Kitty, when their giggling strained her forbearance. It was not long, however, before Lady Catherine turned to Mrs. Bennet, and the conversation was carried on primarily between the two of them. Though Elizabeth might not have been able to credit it, it seemed like the two ladies found a measure of rapport with each other.

"It is difficult," said Mrs. Bennet, after they had been talking together for some moments. "I have five daughters all unmarried, as I am certain Mr. Collins has informed you. Through no fault of ours, the estate is entailed away from my daughters, and I must ensure they are all married as expeditiously as may be arranged."

"You have my apologies, madam," said Mr. Collins, intruding upon their conversation. "I am keenly aware of being the means of injuring your excellent daughters, though unwittingly, and I . . ."

"Yes, yes, we all understand that," said Lady Catherine. Mr. Collins immediately put a hand in front of his mouth, as if speaking a word over Lady Catherine might bring a penalty of death. "No one is accusing you, Mr. Collins. Mrs. Bennet's concerns are valid."

"Of course, I was not condemning Mr. Collins," said Mrs. Bennet, though the glare she snuck at the man seemed to bely her words. "But it is hard, as the estate is not large, and consequently, my girls do not have much fortune to their names."

"I sympathize with you, Mrs. Bennet. I have only one daughter to see married, and though she can be a difficult girl, I cannot imagine what I might feel if I had *five* to care for."

"Exactly." Mrs. Bennet turned to her husband and regarded him, and Elizabeth was forced to confess her mother's expression bordered on smugness. "You see, Mr. Bennet. Lady Catherine understands me perfectly."

"Indeed, she does," replied Mr. Bennet, looking perplexed.

"Then perhaps we should put our heads together and see what we can do to ensure they marry well, Mrs. Bennet."

Eyes alight with pleasure, Mrs. Bennet nodded eagerly. "I would be happy to accept the assistance. I am certain your ladyship knows many eligible gentlemen who are in need of wives."

Lady Catherine smiled faintly and then changed the subject. The two continued their conversation for some time, and the longer Elizabeth listened to it, the less she was able to understand it. Her mother, she had long known, was not blessed with an excess of intelligence, but it was evident that Lady Catherine was not similarly afflicted. But for some strange reason, she seemed to enjoy Mrs. Bennet's company, and she spoke with her for some time with perfect ease and even a certain level of eagerness.

At length, however, the lady changed the subject, and Elizabeth was convinced she had some purpose in mind when she spoke again.

"And how do you find Mr. Collins's parsonage?"

"It appears to be a comfortable enough home," was Mrs. Bennet's diplomatic reply.

The lady shook her head in what seemed like impatience. "It is, indeed. When it was built, my husband took care to ensure it was constructed with care and with attention to detail. I doubt there are many parsonages in Kent which are as solidly built. But would you not consider it a little small to house a family of seven in addition to Mr. Collins?"

His surprise evident, Mr. Bennet interjected: "I suppose it is. But we are quite comfortable, I assure you, and quite grateful to my cousin for his invitation."

"And I was ever so happy to make it, Cousin," interjected Mr. Collins. "For I assure you that no one has more appreciation for family than Lady Catherine, and I have endeavored to emulate her opinions in every particular."

Once again Lady Catherine turned an exasperated eye on Mr. Collins, and he subsided. "It is to your credit that you feel that way, Mr. Bennet," said she. "But I cannot think that living in such confined quarters is easy. I have given some thought to this matter, and if you are willing, I should like to extend an invitation for you to stay at Rosings."

Elizabeth gaped, wondering if she had heard the lady correctly. She could see that her father was in a similar state.

"Indeed, we have plenty of room at Rosings, for there is only Anne and I in residence, and I dare say we would be happy to have the company, for rarely do we receive visitors. And even should you stay there, you will still be close enough to visit your cousin whenever you please."

"Lady Catherine!" exclaimed Mr. Collins, some sort of rapture seeming to have fallen over the clergyman. "Words cannot express how awed we are to be the recipients of your gracious condescension, your boundless generosity. Truly, the nobility you display with your every action is beyond comprehension."

Lady Catherine once again turned her gaze upon Mr. Collins, and he stammered, and his speech trailed off.

"It is no great matter, Mr. Collins," said she, keeping her eyes upon him. "I am quite happy to extend the invitation, and I suspect that given the relative sizes of our homes, the Bennets would be far more comfortable at Rosings than they are here."

It was obvious that Mr. Collins was reluctant to contradict his patroness, but he plucked up some courage and said: "Your generous offer is most appreciated, your ladyship. But my cousin and his family are not . . . Well, let us simply say that they are quite happy to stay at Hunsford with me."

"How say you, Mr. Bennet?" asked Lady Catherine, ignoring Mr. Collins. "It would be no trouble to host you and your family. I am quite happy to have you stay with me."

"It *is* a little cramped, to be sure," said Mr. Bennet slowly. "But we did come to visit with Mr. Collins. We would be poor guests, indeed, if we removed to your house immediately after our arrival."

Lady Catherine nodded with evident approval. "I understand, Mr. Bennet. Then perhaps some of your family might come to Rosings, to allow those who stay more comfortable accommodations? You and your wife might remain at the parsonage, for example, and your daughters stay with me. I insist, Mr. Bennet; it shall be for the best."

"Your ladyship is most kind," said Mrs. Bennet, interjecting when Mr. Bennet hesitated. "I believe we would be happy to accept your kind offer. Perhaps Jane and Lizzy might stay with you? And perhaps Kitty and Lydia? As Mr. Bennet has stated, we would not wish to deprive our cousin of our presence so soon after our arrival, but if Mr. Bennet and myself stay, that should be sufficient. And Mary would be more comfortable at the parsonage I am absolutely certain."

Elizabeth almost looked skyward at her mother's blatant manipulation, but Lady Catherine only smiled.

"Excellent thought, Mrs. Bennet. In that case, I shall send over a carriage to convey your daughters to Rosings. And you must all come and dine with us on the morrow."

"I am certain we shall all be excellent friends!" cried Mrs. Bennet.

Thus, to Rosings Elizabeth and her three sisters were to go, though Elizabeth could not make any sense of what had happened. But there was no time to think on it, as there were trunks to pack once again. Consequently, she dutifully climbed the stairs to her room to prepare. She could not help but wonder what else this visit had in store for her family.

CHAPTER III

*R*osings Park was, as Mr. Collins had informed them time and time again, a very great estate. Situated on a small rise and surrounded by beautiful fields which would turn golden with their bounty in the summer, Elizabeth was hard pressed to think of a more idyllic scene. Here and there strands of trees stood, including a more substantial woodland to the south of the house, which promised delights she was eager to savor. And though the back gardens were a little too formal for Elizabeth's taste, they were lovingly maintained and extensive, promising a peaceful retreat when the surrounding woods were not available due to inclement weather.

The house itself was large and built of costly materials, as evidenced by the marble staircase which assaulted the sisters' eyes as soon as they entered the house. It only improved from there, as they were shown to a dizzying array of rooms, and from thence, to their bedrooms on the second level. And as their guide to the house's interior, Lady Catherine showed them with evident pride in her home, but no trace of condescension or arrogance Elizabeth might have expected the great lady to display.

"Your bedchambers will each be connected to a sitting-room between," said the lady as she showed them to their rooms. "I have arranged for Miss Elizabeth and Miss Bennet to have adjoining chambers, as well as Miss Kitty and Miss Lydia to have their own. I trust that meets with your approval?"

Though she could not imagine emulating Mr. Collins in anything, in this instance, Elizabeth was not about to gainsay her ladyship. She wondered if it would be better for her and Jane to share sitting-rooms with their younger sisters to provide a check on them. But in the end, she decided that they would be well taken care of in this instance.

"That is quite acceptable, your ladyship," said she, when none of her sisters spoke. Indeed, they appeared quite as overwhelmed by the grandeur as Elizabeth felt herself.

"I do apologize for the décor," said Lady Catherine, as she led them into the rooms. "I have not replaced the furnishings here since my marriage, as though they are not quite to my taste, they are still in good condition. It would be wasteful to replace them when they are still serviceable, and I am attentive to frugality in this instance. The walls and colors have been refreshed periodically as fashions change, but those updates are nothing more than cosmetic in nature." Her ladyship paused and smiled. "As I stated, we do not often have visitors at Rosings, so the rooms are not often occupied."

"They are lovely rooms," replied Elizabeth, though she could see to what Lady Catherine referred. The rooms were bright and airy, and the colors were done in soft pastels and were pleasing to the eye. But the furnishings were heavy and overly ornamental, of a fashion of many years gone. But as she said, they were solid and well crafted, and if they were used as seldom as the lady suggested, there truly was no need to make changes.

When they later descended to the first floor to attend their hostess, Elizabeth noted that the principle rooms were decorated in a much more modern fashion, with furnishings more clearly fine, but of less gaudy ornamentation than what they had seen above stairs. Lady Catherine clearly understood her wealth and power and surrounded herself with luxuries accordingly. But what she chose was elegant, without proclaiming her wealth in a loud voice. Again, it was not something Elizabeth might have expected from the lady.

It was in the sitting-room that the Bennet sisters once again attended Lady Catherine, and there they were introduced to her daughter. And no two ladies who were so closely related could be so dissimilar. Lady Catherine was, as Elizabeth had noted, a tall woman, her form healthy and filled out. She was not the most beautiful woman Elizabeth had ever seen, but she was handsome, and her kindly expression rendered her all the more attractive because of it.

Miss Anne de Bourgh was obviously cut from a different cloth, however. She was a small woman, her body thin and wanting curves, her dress was too large for her and was made of a heavy fabric, which Elizabeth thought must be uncomfortable in the warmth of the room, and of colors which further subdued her pale complexion. When she was introduced to the Bennet sisters, she nodded her head only slightly, her nose seeming to be assaulted by some foul reek. It was clear that whatever haughtiness of manner Elizabeth might have expected from the daughter of an earl was instead gathered in the person of the granddaughter.

"We are pleased to make your acquaintance, Miss de Bourgh," said Jane when they had all sat down together. "Mr. Collins has told us much of you."

The look Miss de Bourgh returned suggested that she was quite aware of the parson's foolishness. "Quite," was all she said.

"You have a beautiful home," said Elizabeth, trying to draw some reaction from the young woman. "The house is delightfully situated, and I would imagine that there is much beauty to be discovered in the woods."

When Miss de Bourgh only sniffed and did not respond, Lady Catherine took up the office, but not before shooting a reproachful look at her daughter. "You are a lover of nature, Miss Elizabeth?"

"Oh, all Lizzy does is walk all day long," said Lydia with a flippancy that embarrassed Elizabeth. "Sometimes I think all she does is walk or bury her nose in a book."

"You walk, do you?" asked Miss de Bourgh, her eyebrow quirked in something resembling contempt.

"Walking is very beneficial exercise," observed Lady Catherine, though this time her admonishing glance included both Lydia and her daughter. "I am certain there are many beauties to be found on the grounds of Rosings, and I would invite you to do so at your leisure. And if you would like to view them from a higher vantage, we have a mare or two which I will sometimes take to visit tenants. You are welcome to use them."

"Thank you, Lady Catherine," said Elizabeth, "but Jane is the rider. I have always preferred to use my own two legs."

"You do not ride at all?"

Once again Lydia interjected into the conversation. "Lizzy was thrown from a horse as a child and is now deathly afraid of them."

"That is not precisely the truth," said Elizabeth, glaring at her younger sister. "I *did* fall from a horse when I was young, and as I broke my arm, it took some time before I was able to attempt it again. I am not afraid of horses and I am able to ride if necessary, but I enjoy the exercise walking provides, which I dare say riding would not."

"Indeed, I must agree with your thoughts about walking," said Lady Catherine, eying Lydia with clear disapproval. "At times, however, there are locations which can only be reached with ease if one rides. Perhaps once you become more familiar with Rosings, you will find it useful to ride on occasion."

"Your ladyship is all generosity," said Elizabeth. "I would be happy to do so, if the situation arises."

"Excellent!" said the lady.

The conversation continued for some moments, though Miss de Bourgh did not say much, and the conversation was mostly carried on by Elizabeth and Lady Catherine, with Jane's assistance, and the occasional comment, almost always interjected by speaking over someone else, by Elizabeth's younger sisters. The more comments they made, the more severe Lady Catherine's expression became.

After some length of time, Elizabeth indicated her desire to explore some of the back gardens of Rosings, and Jane agreed to accompany her. Miss de Bourgh left without stating her intentions, but Elizabeth suspected that she simply wished to be away from such uncouth company. But before Lydia and Kitty could rise to depart, Lady Catherine bid them stay with a softly spoken word.

"Miss Kitty, Miss Lydia, you will oblige me for a moment. There is something of which I would speak to you."

Elizabeth and Jane shared a glance at Lady Catherine's imperious demand, proving the lady could be commanding when she felt the need. Neither said anything, however, content to simply excuse themselves for their walk. But when they left the room, Elizabeth turned an amused eye on her sister, quirking her brow and inviting Jane to speak first.

"What do you suppose she means to say to them?"

Elizabeth chuckled. "I know not, but I would dearly love to hear it. I did notice her countenance become positively forbidding as evidence of our sisters' manners presented itself."

"Then I wish her well. Lord knows we have never had any luck."

To that, Elizabeth could only agree.

Lady Catherine de Bourgh considered herself a congenial lady, one who was easily pleased, and one who treated all and sundry with respect and consideration. Indeed, she had been governed in this behavior by her younger sister, Anne, who had been a model of gentility throughout the course of her life. Anne had been so gentle, so beloved by all who knew her. Lady Catherine missed her exceedingly, hardly a day passing that she did not think of her sister.

Jane Bennet reminded Lady Catherine of Lady Anne Darcy: they were both beautiful, both had the most genteel manners, and they even shared some of the same mannerisms. Having the girl here in her house might have caused Lady Catherine to feel the pain of loss for the sister, gone these twelve years, but instead she chose to observe the woman and delight in the echoes of her lost sister, though in truth, they looked nothing alike.

But if there was one thing that Lady Catherine could not abide, it was poor behavior of ignorant girls who were not sensible of their own place in the world — girls who were not sensible of their vulnerability. Anne had always been a trial, not because of any overt poor behavior, but because she insisted upon comporting herself as if she were the daughter of a duke rather than a baronet; Sir Lewis's family was ancient and respected, but not of the nobility. Lady Catherine had done her best with her daughter, and she had helped other young women improve their manners from time to time when called upon. Her brother had her to thank for helping amend the behavior of his youngest daughter, who had been quite wild, indeed.

But nothing had prepared her for Lydia Bennet, and to a lesser extent, her sister Catherine. The two girls simply had no knowledge of propriety, a discovery which was even more shocking because their two eldest sisters were the very models of gentility and excellent breeding. They laughed and giggled between themselves when others were speaking, broke in to the middle of the conversation with loud and sometimes embarrassing statements, and they seemed not to understand how they must defer to their elder sisters.

Lady Catherine was not about to stand for it. Any young lady who stayed in her house would act with propriety and restraint. She would see to it.

As the two young girls in question resumed their seats at Lady Catherine's request, she studied them with a critical eye. They were comely girls, but so all the Bennet sisters were. Given the way they carried on, however, she suspected that they frittered away their time in frivolous pursuits and were rarely required to think serious thoughts. She also suspected their accomplishments were nonexistent.

"Miss Kitty, Miss Lydia," said Lady Catherine, knowing that she would need to handle them delicately, "I have asked you to stay because I would like to learn more of you."

"Of course, Lady Catherine," asked Miss Kitty. "What would you like to know?"

At least one of them was able to display a hint of manners when the situation demanded it.

"I merely wish to understand what your interests are, what accomplishments you have. As young ladies who are still not out, you must have something to fill your time. I wish to understand, so that I might arrange for this in the best way appropriate."

"Not out?" demanded Miss Lydia. "Whatever can you mean?"

"Miss Lydia," said Lady Catherine, immediately understanding the situation, "you might be out in your small society near your home, but you are certainly not ready for real society like that in London."

Miss Lydia looked ready to protest, but her sister elbowed her and she subsided.

"Regardless," continued Lady Catherine, "there is not much society in this neighborhood — one must go to Westerham to partake of society, and Anne and I rarely do. As such, you will need something to occupy your time."

"You did say that it would be tedious in Kent," ventured Miss Kitty. Her hesitance made it obvious who was the dominant sibling. "If we do not have something to do, it will be quite dull here."

But Miss Lydia just rolled her eyes. "The sooner we can return to Meryton and the officers, the happier I will be."

"Officers?" asked Lady Catherine. "Is there a company of militia stationed near your father's home?"

"Oh, yes!" said Miss Lydia, her eyes sparkling with admiration. "They are ever so handsome and so very fond of me. Several of the men have had nothing but praise for my manners and my skill on the dance floor."

Miss Kitty appeared like she longed to say something, but she held her tongue. Lady Catherine watched the two girls, her suspicions confirmed. But lectures could wait. For now, it would be best to ensure the two girls turned their energies to more useful activities.

"You are accomplished at dancing then? That is a good skill for a young woman to possess. What other activities do you enjoy?"

Miss Lydia turned a blank look on her, but Miss Kitty, after some few moments of thought, ventured in a timid voice: "I like to remake my bonnets from time to time with bits of ribbon and lace."

"And do you draw or paint? Do you play the pianoforte, or do you have skill in other languages? Or perhaps embroidery is more to your taste?" Perhaps it was a little abrupt of her, but patience was not a virtue Lady Catherine possessed, and their constant silliness was wearing on her composure.

"I do like to draw, though I do not do it often," said Miss Kitty.

Miss Lydia only snorted. "Why would I wish to do such things? I want to have fun, not sit in front of a boring pianoforte like Mary does all day."

"There are many reasons why one would wish to undertake such activities," said Lady Catherine, keeping her tone reasonable. "One provides enjoyment for others when playing and showing her works of art. Besides, gentlemen appreciate our efforts to become accomplished, and their appreciation often brings additional attention."

That bit of information drew Miss Lydia's attention, and she perked up, almost as a dog would upon catching the scent of a juicy bone. Then her countenance soured, and she appeared almost cross.

"But one must practice to become proficient at such things," cried Miss Lydia. "And practicing is ever so dull!"

"Were you not required to practice to learn the steps of a dance?"

"Yes, but I *enjoy* dancing!"

"Then perhaps, if you practice some other activities, you would find that you enjoy them too."

Miss Lydia blinked, as if she had not thought of such a thing before. "But Lizzy and Jane, and especially Mary, spend their time in such tedious pursuits. I have no wish to become as tiresome as they."

"I believe you simply need to adjust your thinking, Miss Lydia," said Lady Catherine, feeling the silly girl's protests fraying the edges of her endurance. "No one can know what brings them pleasure unless they actually attempt it. From what your sister has said, I believe she would enjoy drawing, if she was ever given the chance. Is that not true, Miss Kitty?"

The girl gave her a shy smile. "I believe I might, your ladyship."

Lady Catherine knew that the girl was easily led, her disposition far more flexible than her younger sister's. She already felt a fondness for Miss Kitty, who was, she thought, often lost in the company of her more vivacious and confident siblings.

"Then it behooves you to attempt to make something of whatever talent you have been given." Lady Catherine turned back to Miss Lydia. "But what you say is also correct. If you do not enjoy drawing and have little aptitude, it does not make much sense to spend your every waking moment in an activity which brings you little pleasure. You had much better try to find something that *does*."

The girl appeared set against anything which gave the appearance of forcing her into something she did not wish, so Lady Catherine thought her approach was as likely to have success as any. Younger siblings were often more rebellious than their elder, especially younger sisters who were forced to wait for the elder to be married. Of course, from what she had heard, Mrs. Bennet had allowed all her girls to come out, not an unusual circumstance in country society, so that was not quite applicable. But unless Lady Catherine missed her guess, she suspected that Miss Lydia had a burning desire to outstrip her sisters in any way possible. That energy she could turn to something beneficial for the girl.

"Perhaps," said Miss Lydia, her tone carefully noncommittal.

"Here is what I suggest," said Lady Catherine. "My daughter's companion, a Mrs. Jenkinson, has been with us for many years, and she is well versed in many of the subjects we discussed. For you, Miss Kitty, I will ask her to instruct you in drawing and painting, and perhaps in a few other subjects you might find interesting." Lady Catherine smiled at the girl. "She is quite talented with a pencil and brush, as I recall."

For her part, Miss Kitty smiled, and Lady Catherine thought she caught a hint of eagerness in her manner. "I would like that."

Then Lady Catherine turned back to Miss Lydia, the more difficult of the two. "As for you, Miss Lydia, I will ask her to introduce you to a range of activities so that you may discover something you enjoy. When you do, she will instruct you, or if it is something in which she does not possess any ability, we can arrange with your father to employ someone who does. Is that acceptable?"

Though Miss Lydia made a great show of thinking the matter over, Lady Catherine knew she had convinced the girl, if only for the present.

"I suppose I could agree to that," said Miss Lydia at length.

"Excellent. I shall speak with Mrs. Jenkinson directly."

What Lady Catherine did not tell either girl was that she would also have a word with her daughter's faithful companion about the behavior of the two girls, though she knew Mrs. Jenkinson would instantly recognize their wildness. Finding them accomplishments that they enjoyed was only part of the battle. They would be less likely to misbehave if they thought the instruction they were about to receive pertained to those subjects which interested them.

*   *   *

As promised, those at the parsonage arrived for dinner that evening. Elizabeth watched as her mother entered on her father's arm—Mary being escorted by Mr. Collins—with wide eyes and a disbelieving expression of shock on her face. Mrs. Bennet had not, so far as Elizabeth was aware, travelled widely, and she likely had not seen many residences of the rich. As such, she likely would not have had any true notion of just what wealth could bring.

"You have a marvelous home," said Mrs. Bennet with breathy enthusiasm once they had all taken their seats and the three remaining Bennets had been introduced to Miss de Bourgh. For once, Elizabeth thought her mother's tone held nothing but appreciation rather than an avarice—Elizabeth did not think her mother was of a grasping disposition, but her eagerness often made the observer think she was.

"Thank you, Mrs. Bennet," said Lady Catherine. "I am proud of it, and of my husband's heritage, though he was not titled. Rosings is the product of many years of arduous work by his forebears, and its current prosperity a testament to the many people who work to make it a success."

It was clear the affinity between the two women had not waned since the previous day, and soon they were talking with one another, with animation from Mrs. Bennet, and more restraint from her ladyship. It was not long, however, before Mrs. Bennet turned her attention to her daughters.

"I hope you girls are behaving and not causing her ladyship undue trouble?"

"They have been excellent houseguests, Mrs. Bennet," said Lady Catherine. "I am very happy to have them with us."

Anne's quiet snort suggested that she did not share her mother's sentiments, but Lady Catherine only ignored her daughter.

"I had some instruction today with Mrs. Jenkinson, Mama," volunteered Kitty, her manner tentative.

"Instruction?" asked Mrs. Bennet, clearly befuddled.

"Yes, Mama. Mrs. Jenkinson was teaching me how to draw properly. I think I will enjoy it very much."

"Your daughter expressed an interest in it," explained Lady Catherine. "Since Mrs. Jenkinson is quite talented, I asked her to help Miss Kitty along. Mrs. Jenkinson reports that she shows a great deal of promise."

Her parents showed the same amazement that Elizabeth had upon hearing the news.

"Drawing, is it?" asked Mr. Bennet, regarding his second youngest. "That is quite remarkable, Kitty. I was not aware you had any interest."

Blushing at the unaccustomed attention, Kitty said: "I have done a little drawing in the past, but I have always been too . . . busy to give it much attention. I believe I would like to learn more."

"And you, Lydia?" asked Mr. Bennet, turning his attention to his youngest.

"Oh, I have no interest in drawing," said Lydia with an airy wave. "A tedious activity, I should say."

Kitty flushed in anger, but before any indignant words could be exchanged, Lady Catherine inserted herself into the conversation. "You are simply different from your sister, child. Did you and Mrs. Jenkinson find anything that interests you?"

"She said that with my exuberance I might learn to ride," said Lydia, seeming to understand that she had said something she ought not. "She also showed me a few exercises on the pianoforte in her room. I believe I might find them tolerable, though I should not like to play the mournful dirges Mary prefers."

"I play many things," said Mary. "A little solemnity would not go amiss in you, Lydia."

"That is good to hear," said Lady Catherine, again speaking to avoid an argument. "You are welcome to use the pianoforte in the music room. I rather treasure the memory of my sister learning to play when I was young."

"Do you play yourself, your ladyship?" asked Elizabeth.

"I do not." Lady Catherine gave her an amused smile. "I confess I have little aptitude. I appreciate music, and I can be coaxed to sing on occasion, but the scales seemed to tie my fingers up in knots, and I was never able to become truly proficient. My sister, Anne, was a marvelous performer."

Lady Catherine appeared to be caught up in memories of her sister, who Elizabeth assumed had passed, as the look in her eyes became distant and contemplative. But she was interrupted before long by Mr. Collins's ill-timed entrance into the conversation.

"I am certain that had you learned, you would not have been anything but a true proficient, your ladyship. Indeed, I cannot imagine there being ten others in all of England who can boast the taste, the innate sense of what is good, which you possess. It is hard that we have been deprived of such inspiration. We must console ourselves that you have used your talents to become great in other matters, for we would be bereft without your graciously bestowed guidance."

"Thank you, Mr. Collins," said Lady Catherine, "though such praise is not warranted. I am naught but a woman, one who does her best regardless of the situation."

Mr. Collins opened his mouth, no doubt to once again treat them all to his curious brand of continuous blandishments, but Lady Catherine looked at him pointedly, and he subsided. Clearly, she did not appreciate his ubiquitous praises as much as he would have liked. It was a situation which mystified Elizabeth. Lady Catherine clearly saw Mr. Collins for what he was, and yet she had installed him in his situation. Surely her ladyship must have seen the man's faults upon first meeting him. If so, why had she given him the living?

They were called in to dinner soon after, and Lady Catherine proved that her table was as fine as her estate. And through it all, Mr. Collins kept up his monologue of compliments directed at Lady Catherine, Miss de Bourgh, the meal, and anything else which crossed his mind at the time. Nothing was beneath his ability to flatter, and he made use of the full range of his vocabulary. Lady Catherine, though she often rolled her eyes or shot the man exasperated glares, in the end did nothing to stop him. How he managed to be so voluble when he ate more than any other two people was a mystery, but there it was.

After dinner, it seemed like Mr. Collins had eaten so much that his tongue was stilled, and a lassitude settled over him; and the rest of the company was grateful for it. That evening, two interesting conversations took place, and Elizabeth was close enough to both that she overheard, though the second she could hardly have missed.

Lady Catherine continued in her interest in Mrs. Bennet, and during the course of the evening, Elizabeth thought their friendship was forged. Mrs. Bennet was her usual vociferous self, and Lady Catherine seemed content to allow her to speak, venturing only a few comments when she thought it most likely the other woman would hear her.

"I am grateful to your ladyship for allowing my daughters to stay with you," said Mrs. Bennet after they had been speaking for some time. "I dare say they will enjoy themselves while they are here, and I hope you will have some small benefit from their presence."

"I am quite happy to have them, Mrs. Bennet," assured Lady Catherine. "They are good girls. Your youngest will have activities to occupy themselves, which I believe might have been a problem at the parsonage."

It was clear Mrs. Bennet did not quite understand the thrust of Lady Catherine's comment, so she ignored it. "I am glad Mary decided to stay with us, however. We have high hopes for her and Mr. Collins, you understand."

Mary blushed as she overheard this comment, but as she was carrying on a—mercifully quiet—conversation with the man himself, she did not respond to her mother.

"Mr. Collins and Miss Mary, is it?" asked Lady Catherine, though more to herself. She allowed her eyes to rest on the couple and fell silent in contemplation.

"I believe so," said Mrs. Bennet. "Mr. Collins wished to focus on Jane, but I do not see her as the wife of a parson. Mary is a much better choice."

The nod with which Lady Catherine indicated her agreement was slow, but the lady's conviction seemed to be growing as she considered the matter further. "I believe you might be correct, Mrs. Bennet. Miss Mary appears to be a sensible, pious sort of girl. Mr. Collins will benefit from both of those qualities in a wife."

"I am glad your ladyship agrees."

Lady Catherine turned a smile on Mrs. Bennet. "Of course, once the courtship progresses to a more formal agreement, Miss Mary will, of a necessity, be required to be removed from the parsonage. It would not be proper at all for her to live in the same house with the man who is courting her."

Though once again puzzled, Mrs. Bennet readily indicated her agreement. "I will be guided in this matter by your superior understanding."

With a nod, Lady Catherine changed the subject, and the conversation turned to other matters. It was at this point that Miss de Bourgh began to speak, and Elizabeth found her words to be far more interesting than Mary's courtship.

"Did you know, Miss Bennet, my cousins are to come to Kent to visit?"

"Are they?" asked Jane, to whom the question had been posed.

"Yes, they are." There seemed in Miss de Bourgh's manner some great conceit, as if her cousin's coming was a compliment to her in particular. "The will be here the week before Easter and are scheduled to stay at least three weeks. I am anticipating their coming very much."

"The visit of dear relations is always agreeable," replied Jane. "I hope to make their acquaintance while they are here."

"That can hardly be avoided, my dear," said Lady Catherine. "They will stay at Rosings, so an introduction is inevitable."

"They are great men, you see," said Miss de Bourgh, apparently intent upon making herself the center of conversation again. "My cousin, Colonel Fitzwilliam, is the second son of an earl, while my other cousin, Mr. Darcy, is the proprietor of a great estate in Derbyshire."

"A colonel!" exclaimed Lydia at the same time Elizabeth blurted out: "Mr. Darcy?"

Miss de Bourgh chose to ignore Lydia, instead turning a suspicious eye on Elizabeth. "Do you know my cousins, Miss Elizabeth?"

"Last autumn my family made the acquaintance of a Mr. Darcy from Derbyshire," replied Elizabeth. "He travelled to Hertfordshire with his friend, Mr. Bingley, to stay with him at Mr. Bingley's leased estate near my home. Can he be the same man?"

A sudden grimace overtook Miss de Bourgh, and she appeared to be tasting something sour. "Yes," said she, though the words almost seemed to be expelled with great reluctance, "that is he. Though I have told him time and time again that he should not associate with such men as Mr. Bingley, he has not taken my advice."

"There is nothing wrong with Mr. Bingley, Anne." Lady Catherine's tone was reproving. "He is an amiable gentleman, one seeking to establish himself in society, which is a credit to him."

"He is naught but new money," replied Miss de Bourgh. Her nose had climbed even higher in the air, and Elizabeth had to stifle a laugh at the woman's blatant pride. She then turned back to Elizabeth and said in a voice filled with self-congratulation: "Darcy returns to see *me*, you see. For we have been engaged for many years, and I expect him to formalize our engagement this year."

"Formalize an engagement that already exists?" asked Elizabeth, baffled at the other woman's assertion.

"It is a strange sort of engagement, Miss Elizabeth. My mother and his planned our union from the time when we were in our cradles. Darcy has simply had other matters to attend to before we could meet at the altar. But he is dutiful and so very fond of me, and I do not doubt that our union shall come to fruition this year."

Elizabeth was about to say something when she happened to catch sight of Lady Catherine out of the corner of her eye. The lady had grimaced and was shaking her head, and Elizabeth was certain it was in response to her daughter's declaration. Was Miss de Bourgh perhaps wishing for something that did not exist? This talk of a cradle betrothal was odd, especially since Lady Catherine did not seem to believe in its existence.

"Then I wish you the best in it," said Elizabeth, deciding that it would best promote harmony to simply agree with the woman. Besides, it would not be good manners to contradict her when she knew nothing of the situation.

"Thank you, Miss Elizabeth," said Miss de Bourgh, her nose firmly in the air. "I do not doubt we shall do very well together. Breeding always runs true. My cousin and I are descended from the same noble line on our mothers' side, and our union shall create one of the wealthiest dynasties in all England."

Miss de Bourgh's self-congratulations did not finish there—in fact, the woman went on at some length about her expectations, her certainty that her cousin was as committed to the marriage as she was herself, and the power she would wield once she finally became Mrs. Darcy. It smelled very strongly of wishful thinking, but Elizabeth knew it was not for her to attempt to disabuse the woman of her fantasies.

It was not long before Elizabeth grew tired of Miss de Bourgh's conversation, and at the first opportunity she turned to Jane who was nearby. "What do you make of this news that Mr. Darcy and his cousin are to come?"

"It sounds like a longstanding engagement, Lizzy." Jane turned a piercing look on Elizabeth—she did not do it often, but on occasion Elizabeth thought her sister was looking straight through her. "Surely you are not bothered by the news that Mr. Darcy will come here. You cannot still hold a grudge against him, I am certain."

With a shake of her head, Elizabeth said: "Indeed, I do not, Jane. I will own that I was annoyed with Mr. Darcy for his words about me at the assembly, but I have learned to be philosophical about it, despite his rudeness."

"He was the model of propriety thereafter," observed Jane.

"That he was," replied Elizabeth. Then she laughed. "In fact, I distinctly remember an occasion at Sir William's party not long after the assembly, when Mr. Darcy made up for his prior refusal and asked me to dance."

"He did?" asked a surprised Jane. "You never told me of it!"

"At the time, I did not think much of it. If you recall, Kitty and Lydia drew some of the officers aside to dance, and since they were laughing and carrying on, I thought to have a word to prevent them from exposing us to ridicule. But as I approached them, Sir William intercepted me and recommended me as a partner to Mr. Darcy, and he obliged by requesting my hand."

"It is clear you refused him," said Jane. "I do not remember you dancing with him, and surely Mama would have spoken of it."

"I did not think his application was serious," said Elizabeth, thinking back on the event. "He did so only at Sir William's suggestion, and you know how Sir William is. We received word soon after that Mr. Darcy had departed Netherfield for London, and he never returned."

Elizabeth paused, thinking of the man she had known for only an abbreviated time, and then turned back to Jane feeling more than a little mischievous. "You know, I always wondered what might have happened had Mr. Darcy been at Netherfield when you fell ill and I came to nurse you. At the time, as you know, I harbored few charitable feelings about him—we might have argued the entirety of the five days!"

"I doubt that, Lizzy," said Jane, though she smiled at Elizabeth's playfulness. "Mr. Darcy is far too well bred to argue with a lady."

"*If* he even considered me a lady," replied Elizabeth.

The two girls laughed and turned to other topics. But inside, Elizabeth continued to consider the matter of Mr. Darcy. She had not thought of the man in months and her feelings for him at this point were dispassionate. He had struck her as a proud man at their first meeting, but Jane was correct that he had behaved with perfect propriety thereafter. He could hardly disapprove of the Bennet sisters—at least openly—when they were guests of his aunt's. She was not sure what his coming would bring, but she could at least look at the prospect with mild curiosity.

Chapter IV

$\mathcal{T}$he first few days of the Bennet sisters' stay at Rosings Park passed away in peace, and the sisters settled into their unaccustomed surroundings. Elizabeth was treated to her every expectation of finding serenity and beauty on Rosings' grounds, and she took every opportunity to partake in them. The sisters — particularly Jane and Elizabeth — were careful to attend to their hostess in gratitude for her generosity in hosting them. Kitty and Lydia appeared immersed in their own activities — not once had Elizabeth suspected that Lydia would take to the pianoforte, of all things, though she knew that Kitty had sketched on occasion — so her worries for their behavior were largely put to rest when they were so carefully overseen by Mrs. Jenkinson. And that Sunday when they had attended church, Mr. Collins proved that his style of sermonizing was as ponderous as she had expected.

"Yes, it is beautiful, though I own it myself," said Lady Catherine one day when Elizabeth complimented her on her home. "Have you given any thought to my suggestion of riding to see some of the more distant sights? I would be happy to accompany you."

"Not yet, your ladyship," replied Elizabeth. "There is still so much beauty to be explored in the immediate area of the house that I do not feel any need to range any further away at present."

"In the immediate area of the house?" repeated Lady Catherine, raising an eyebrow. "The servants have informed me that you will often leave the house and will not return for an hour or two after. Surely you are ranging further than the back garden."

"And has your ladyship set the footmen to watch me wherever I go?" asked Elizabeth, tilting an eyebrow at Lady Catherine. By now she felt secure enough with Lady Catherine's character that she felt her ladyship would not be offended by a little archness in her manner.

As she expected, Lady Catherine only laughed. "Not to spy on you, of course. But the footmen have been asked to keep an eye out, for you must own that it is somewhat unusual for a young woman to walk out by herself. If Rosings were not such a peaceful location, I might even be concerned for your safety."

Surprised, Elizabeth said: "But I have walked the paths near my father's estate for some years and never experienced any difficulties. Surely Kent is not much different."

"You are correct. We live in a peaceful land. But you must own that there are still bandits aplenty and others of less than high moral character. I would not expect to find them in such a location as this, but one can never know.

"Regardless, I did not mean to censure you for your habits. Walking, as you have noted, is quite beneficial, and I have come to understand that you are an active sort of person." Lady Catherine paused and looked at Elizabeth through serious eyes. "I visit tenants on occasion, and I would be happy for your company, if you would consent to it."

"I would be happy to, Lady Catherine," said Elizabeth. She was pleased the lady thought enough of her to suggest her attendance.

"Excellent. Now, if you have some moments, I should like to speak with you."

"You have something particular to say?"

Lady Catherine shook her head. "More, I would wish to understand more about you and about your knowledge of my nephew, as you have mentioned that you have already made his acquaintance."

"Yes, I have," said Elizabeth. For all that Lady Catherine was an amiable and helpful sort of woman, she was also rather forthright, and Elizabeth suspected she would have no trouble demanding that which she wished to know.

"And how did you find him? Darcy is a good man, but sometimes he is a little aloof in company."

"I did find him so," said Elizabeth, speaking slowly, attempting to put her feelings—her past feelings—for Mr. Darcy in a diplomatic way. "He is clearly a capable man, and we did hear some information of his position in society. But he never displayed himself to be a man who would indulge in frivolous conversation or speak unnecessarily."

Lady Catherine shook her head. "I dare say that Darcy did not display himself to best advantage, given what you are telling me." When Elizabeth tried to protest, her ladyship only put up a hand. "I can see you are trying to be diplomatic about Darcy's behavior, but I am well acquainted with his ways. His father was a good and generous man, and he taught his son to be likewise. But for all Robert Darcy's struggles in society, I believe his son experiences even more difficulty, in part due to my sister's early death."

"I did not wish to give you the impression I was censuring your nephew, Lady Catherine," Elizabeth hastened to say. "Yes, he was aloof, and at times he appeared to consider himself above his company. But I do not think anyone in Hertfordshire thought any true harm of him."

"That is good, for he is truly the best of men." Lady Catherine paused and regarded Elizabeth for a moment, her expression knowing. "You will pardon me if I am overstepping, my dear, by I sense there is something you are not telling me. Did you have difficulty with my nephew in particular?"

"No!" exclaimed Elizabeth. "Mr. Darcy was everything that was gentlemanly."

"You do not need to dissemble. Darcy somehow manages to offend nearly everywhere he goes. In fact, when I mentioned his name to your mother the last time I spoke with her, she said something to the effect that you were not good enough for him. Now, what did he say?"

Cheeks blooming with embarrassment, Elizabeth searched for a way to put Lady Catherine off without relating the entirety of the incident at the assembly, but the lady looked at her in such a way as to make evasion impossible. Knowing the lady would hear all and would likely apply to her mother if Elizabeth was not explicit, she sighed and nodded her head.

"During the assembly at which I first made Mr. Darcy's acquaintance, I was sitting out a dance, as gentlemen were scarce and I was in want of a partner. Mr. Darcy was standing nearby when his friend approached him and demanded he dance. Through the course of their discussion, when Mr. Darcy refused and Mr. Bingley insisted, he made a comment which, at the time, offended me."

"And what was that?"

"He told his friend that he had no intention of dancing with a young woman who was snubbed by other men, and that I was not nearly pretty enough to induce him to overlook such a slight."

Elizabeth raised her chin and dared Lady Catherine to find fault with her for saying as much, but the lady only shook her head. "Oh, Darcy," said she, "you truly do have a talent for saying the worst things without thinking about them in advance. I have never heard of such incivility."

"I believe he was out of sorts that evening," said Elizabeth. "I never had a reason to find fault with him after, though the aloofness I mentioned remained unaltered. He was not in Meryton long before he returned to London."

"Yes, I heard of his abbreviated stay with his friend." Lady Catherine paused and then shot Elizabeth a grin. "Part of his reason for leaving was to see his sister, who had suffered a disappointment not long before, and part was because he simply cannot abide Miss Bingley."

Elizabeth laughed. "That I can well imagine, though I am sorry to hear of Miss Darcy's misfortune. I hope she is recovered."

"To a great extent, I believe she is." Lady Catherine paused and shook her head. "I wished for Darcy to bring his sister when he and his cousin visit, but for some reason Georgiana finds me intimidating. She prefers to stay in London with her masters rather than spend Easter in Kent."

"Then that must be the reason for Mr. Darcy's behavior. After he left, I thought about what happened for some time, and I decided there was no reason to cling to my offense. It has been some time since I thought of him at all until your daughter mentioned that you were expecting him."

"He and his cousin will be arriving the Monday before Easter. I hope you will not be made uncomfortable by his coming."

"Not at all!" protested Elizabeth. "At the very least, I can state that Mr. Darcy is an intelligent man, and I have no doubt he will add much interest to our party. If I *was* made uncomfortable, it would be my responsibility to remove myself to the parsonage. He is your nephew, after all, whereas I am nothing but a cousin of your parson."

"Excellent," said Lady Catherine. "I believe meeting Darcy in more familiar surroundings will show you another side of his character. I anticipate the company very much, indeed."

They then parted, but Elizabeth found herself thinking about Lady

Catherine's interrogation for some time after. The news that Mr. Darcy was coming did not affect her at all, though she would own to a little curiosity about whether he would behave differently from the manner he had last autumn. Of the prospect of meeting Colonel Fitzwilliam, Elizabeth was curious—she had never met a member of the nobility, other than Lady Catherine herself, of course.

But in the back of her mind, Elizabeth wondered about Lady Catherine's questions. She seemed to have some . . . interest in the matter of her opinions about Mr. Darcy, though Elizabeth could not think of what it could possibly be. In the end, she decided that it was nothing more than wishing to ensure that harmony would continue to exist in her home when her nephews arrived. That decided, Elizabeth resolved to think on it no more.

Lady Anne Darcy had died more than twelve years earlier, and Lady Catherine had never felt such anguish, such heartrending grief as when her sister had slipped away in the night. No two sisters could have been so close as they, and though marriage, children, and responsibilities had separated them more often than not, their bond had never weakened, never faded. The barrage of letters passing back and forth between the two estates had persisted through the days of their marriages, as the sisters had exchanged confidences, news, and even the occasional bit of gossip through mail. Even the death of her dear husband had not affected Lady Catherine to the same degree as losing her sister had.

When the pain of her loss had finally settled into the dull ache of longing, Lady Catherine had decided that she would take up her niece and nephew's cause, to be as a much mother to them as she could be. She loved her brother's children too—Colonel Fitzwilliam, in particular, was a favorite due to his irrepressible spirits and good humor—but her sister's children were all she had left of the woman herself. Perhaps it was not laudable, but for that fact alone she favored Fitzwilliam and Georgiana.

Lady Catherine could not be prouder of how Anne's children had grown to be a credit to her. Darcy was a good man, a conscientious master, and a tower of strength, both within the family and in the community in which he lived. It was true that he also tended toward arrogance and standoffishness, and, at times, he could be positively rude, but it was the heart that mattered, and Darcy's heart was the largest Lady Catherine had ever seen. And Georgiana, though she was still shy as a mouse, was beginning to show signs of confidence, which

Lady Catherine was certain would blossom, making the girl a beautiful woman, beloved by all. Yes, they had made her proud.

But there was something missing. Darcy was now eight and twenty and unmarried. Lady Catherine was convinced that should he marry the right woman, he would be happy, and his sister would have a woman near her own age to guide her, not only in society, but in life. Well, Lady Catherine knew she had found that woman, and she meant to make certain Darcy did not allow the chance at happiness pass him by.

Consequently, she had sent a note that morning to the parsonage, requesting Mrs. Bennet attend her at Rosings. The woman was desperate to marry her children to eligible men, and Darcy and Fitzwilliam both were all that was eligible. It was fortunate that the children were so well suited and that their interests coincided so perfectly.

As Mrs. Bennet sat across from her, Lady Catherine thought about how to best approach the matter. If she went about it the wrong way, the woman would no doubt begin proclaiming the matches for all the world to hear, no doubt ruining everything in the process. Mrs. Bennet, kind soul though she was, was not the most discerning. Lady Catherine knew she would have to make sure the woman attempted subtlety. Darcy could be obstinate when he thought he was being directed, and she had no doubt Miss Elizabeth was his match in that regard. Fitzwilliam and Miss Bennet would be easier to manage, which was useful, as Lady Catherine was certain they were also well suited. There was no point in Miss Bennet's waiting for that Bingley fellow, for he was simply still too young and green to take a wife, particularly one as gentle as Miss Bennet. Mr. Bingley was naught but a puppy, and that harpy of a sister of his would rule them both with an iron fist should they marry.

A stray thought crossed Lady Catherine's mind, and she grinned to herself, hiding her smile behind a sip of her tea. Her brother would no doubt call her a matchmaker should he discover what she intended to do. But matchmaker was such a gauche term, and one which did not convey the full import of what she meant to accomplish. Lady Catherine would not forget that the young people possessed the power of choice with respect to their own lives. But she hoped they would see what she had seen.

"I wish to speak of your daughters, Mrs. Bennet," said Lady Catherine at length.

"They are behaving, are they not?" said the woman with a hint of worry.

"No, you need not concern yourself." Lady Catherine smiled to put the woman at ease. "In fact, they have been model guests. With just myself and Anne for most of the year, I often long for some other feminine company. I am glad they have agreed to stay with us."

"Then how may I help you?"

"I merely wish to understand your opinion on several matters."

"Of course," replied Mrs. Bennet.

"First, what is your opinion of my nephew, Mr. Darcy? Miss Elizabeth has informed me that you met him in Hertfordshire."

Mrs. Bennet stared at her through suddenly wide eyes, akin to the look of a hare being stalked by a fox, and her response was atypically hesitant. "Well . . . Mr. Darcy, he . . . Well, I am not certain . . ."

"You may speak frankly, my friend," said Lady Catherine. "Your daughter has told me something of his time in Hertfordshire."

An expression of complete affront came over Mrs. Bennet. "Mr. Darcy was very disobliging—very disobliging, indeed. He was nothing to his friend, Mr. Bingley, who was everything agreeable and friendly. And Mr. Darcy slighted my Lizzy, you know. I do not doubt she had plenty to say of the man."

"In fact, Miss Elizabeth seems to have allowed the matter to rest in the past. She claims to have no injuries to resent."

Once again, Mrs. Bennet seemed shocked.

"And as for Mr. Bingley, I can well believe that he was everything charming, but so he is with everyone. Furthermore, according to Darcy, he tends to fall in love often, falling *out* of love with equal frequency."

Mrs. Bennet gasped. "Are you saying he is inconstant?"

"I am saying he is young and inexperienced, Mrs. Bennet. Compare Mr. Bingley to my nephew Darcy, for instance." Mrs. Bennet made a face, but she did not interrupt. "Darcy has had the responsibility of his estate since he was two and twenty, and he was brought up to know his duty. He is a gifted master, knowing instinctively what is required in any situation. All his tenants and his servants consider him the best of masters. If he has a failing, it is a tendency to an excess of gravity and difficulty speaking with those he does not know. But *that* deficiency might be corrected, at least in part, by a vivacious wife, can it not?"

The only response Lady Catherine received was a blink. She smiled to herself, for she knew she had enticed the fish to the riverbank. Now it was time to bait the hook.

"Then let us speak of Mr. Bingley. He is an amiable man, at ease in any company, and a great favorite among all the ladies. But he is almost five years younger than Darcy, he has never had to see to an estate, never had to do anything other than draw the interest of his fortune to support himself. He has never had to do any work, never had to fend for himself, has never been required to make decisions when matters depended on him. Even when they were in Hertfordshire, I have it from Darcy that he himself was obligated to meet with Netherfield's steward in Mr. Bingley's stead, as the man was often engaged in other activities. Darcy was only in Hertfordshire to assist his friend in learning how to manage his estate, yet Mr. Bingley took little interest. Now, which of the gentlemen would you rather have responsible for your daughter's welfare."

In truth, Lady Catherine felt for Mrs. Bennet. She was essentially a simple woman, for whom a truth was a truth that could not be disputed. She had clearly held it as an inviolable opinion that Darcy was a man of mean temperament, and Mr. Bingley was amiable. Lady Catherine understood she was upending the woman's opinion of the world. Fortunately, she knew exactly how to make it better.

"I do not say this to criticize Mr. Bingley, but it is clear that he has not yet attained that soberness of mind which comes with maturity and experience. Darcy is clearly the better catch, Mrs. Bennet. Mr. Bingley is a good man, and some day, I believe he will be a good husband to some young woman. But that time is not now.

"Both of my nephews are good men, both are independent, and both have much to offer to a wife. As I said, Darcy will improve in company with the right wife. My other nephew, the colonel, has no need, as he is already at ease in any society, but his life may be fulfilled if he takes the right wife. I believe that each of my nephews will find exactly what they require in your two eldest daughters."

For a moment, Lady Catherine was worried that Mrs. Bennet might not have heard her, let alone understood what she was trying to tell her. But then a slow smile settled over her face.

"Are you suggesting that your nephews might be induced to marry my daughters?"

"I merely suggest that there is a possibility that they might suit. If we point out their relative merits, I am certain they will do the rest themselves."

Mrs. Bennet actually clapped her hands in her excitement. "Of course! You may speak to your nephews, and I shall deal with my daughters."

"Exactly. But gently, Mrs. Bennet." Lady Catherine shared a secret smile with the woman. "They must not think they have been directed by meddling relations."

"Of course," replied Mrs. Bennet, her eyes alight with the fire of determination. "If all goes well, we shall be connected twice over!"

"We need only to gently guide them, my dear Mrs. Bennet. Everything else will fall into place."

The discussion continued for some time, and Lady Catherine attempted to stem the tide of Mrs. Bennet's exuberance. In the end, she knew that the woman's daughters were aware of her character, so if she said some things which were not precisely decorous, they would likely not think much of it. Her enthusiasm must be kept from Darcy and Fitzwilliam, however, for they would almost certainly dig in their heels, should they be aware of the machinations occurring about them.

In all, it was a good start, she thought. Fitzwilliam and Darcy would be happy—that was all Lady Catherine wanted. If Mrs. Bennet would not be quite the most desirable relation, at least she was good hearted, and with a little guidance, she would still be acceptable. The happiness of the young people was the paramount consideration.

While Lady Catherine and her mother were plotting Elizabeth's future happiness, she herself was enjoying a constitutional which had taken her some ways into the woods behind Rosings. They were perhaps even more beautiful than the groves near her home in Hertfordshire, though Elizabeth would be hard pressed to own it. There was something about her home which demanded her allegiance.

In the time since the Bennet sisters had been staying at Rosings, Elizabeth and her sisters—or at least Jane, for she did not think Kitty or Lydia cared two figs—had attempted to come to know Miss Anne de Bourgh better. It would be a much more comfortable situation if the woman was at least polite to them, even if they never became friends.

But it was all in vain. Though Miss de Bourgh displayed a veneer of polite manners, Elizabeth was able to discern the woman's barely concealed contempt for everything Bennet. A query would bring about a sneer, and a kind comment, a sharp retort. Soon, knowing she would eventually lose her temper if she persisted, Elizabeth decided to leave the woman to her own devices. It did not follow, unfortunately, that Miss de Bourgh was equally willing to ignore the Bennets.

That day when Elizabeth returned to the house after her walk, she soon came across Miss de Bourgh and was greeted with the woman's usual frosty scorn.

"I see you have been out walking again," said she, her voice fairly dripping with contempt. "How quaint."

"As you see," said Elizabeth. "I cannot imagine why you are surprised. I did not hide the fact that I am fond of walking."

But Miss de Bourgh only ignored her words. "I prefer my phaeton," said she. "It allows me a better view than I might have if I walked, and it allows those who work the estate to see me and know I am their mistress."

"Perhaps," said Elizabeth, wondering at Miss de Bourgh's pride. "But it is not very beneficial in terms of exercise. I walk as much for the benefits as the love of nature."

"It only proves to me your common upbringing," said Miss de Bourgh as she turned away. "Those of higher society would not care to walk when there are other means available to them. I pity you, Miss Bennet, as you have nothing to recommend you, and will almost certainly never attract a man to you. *I*, on the other hand, already have my future secured."

And with those final words, Miss de Bourgh was gone. Elizabeth could only shake her head. To think the woman considered *walking* an activity for no one but commoners! Elizabeth had never heard such a ridiculous thing in all her life. Perhaps Miss de Bourgh was more than a little eccentric. Elizabeth was certain there were many of the upper echelons of society who were more than a little peculiar.

CHAPTER V

The days following were much the same for the Bennet sisters at Rosings Park. Lydia and Kitty found their time occupied by various activities, many of which seemed designed to force them to grow and become something more than they were at present. Lady Catherine was never overt in proclaiming what they needed to do to become accomplished young ladies, and her methods were effective as a result, for surely young ladies as ungoverned as Kitty and Lydia would have found reason to protest otherwise. Elizabeth even found Kitty with a book of Shakespeare in her hands, and her sister confided in her that though she had not enjoyed Hamlet when she had attempted to read it, she found the comedies much more to her taste. Lydia steadfastly refused to read anything other than a novel, but as her behavior was better and she was attending to those things she did with at least some determination, Elizabeth did not see fit to take her to task over her reading material. Nor did Lady Catherine, it seemed.

Jane and Elizabeth enjoyed their time as well. Elizabeth walked with Jane accompanying her on occasion, and they kept Lady Catherine company at other times, while pursuing their usual activities. Elizabeth found that Lady Catherine was not only kindly, but also intelligent and well read. She found she had as much pleasure from debating literature with the lady as she had ever had with her father. The only blight on their pleasure was the continued insolence of Miss Anne de Bourgh. The woman continued to sneer at any Bennet she came across, and though Lady Catherine admonished her several times to be more tolerant of their guests, it was all for nothing; the woman had decided to be displeased, and displeased she would be.

There was still much congress between the Bennets staying at Rosings and those remaining at the parsonage. Mrs. Bennet came to Rosings almost every day and sat with Lady Catherine, and a stranger friendship could not be imagined. Her mother was not changed much, and Lady Catherine was a quite different personality, but still they talked and laughed, and perhaps even plotted, for all Elizabeth could not understand of what they could conspire. Mr. Bennet also came from time to time, but his purpose was to visit Lady Catherine's library and borrow books, which she allowed willingly. As for Mary, her unofficial courtship with Mr. Collins seemed to be proceeding apace.

"It is the most amusing spectacle," said Mr. Bennet, chortling with delight when Elizabeth asked him about it. "Clearly the man has no notion of how to make love to a woman. He simpers and preens and makes love to my daughter by venerating his patroness and boasting of his enviable situation at all hours of the day. I dare say if he was as effusive in his praise of Mary as he is of his patroness, he would have proposed, been accepted, and been married by common license by now!"

"And Mary?" asked Elizabeth, having expected no less of Mr. Collins. "How does she bear his effusions?"

"I know not. Mary seems to listen carefully to what he is saying, but she never displays any hint of what she is feeling." Mr. Bennet paused for a moment. "Of course, even should he compliment Mary, I doubt we would see much of a reaction from her. She is as inscrutable a young lady as I have ever seen. Your mother, though she initially stayed to ensure that the courtship between them proceeded without impediment, now considers them as good as engaged. I am certain you have noticed that she now spends more time at Rosings than she does at Hunsford."

"And you, Father?" asked Elizabeth. "How are you enjoying yourself?"

"I am quite pleased. I have the run of Lady Catherine's library, which is almost as extensive as my own and contains many works I have not read. Mr. Collins provides almost continuous amusement, and I could not wish for more. Should he suggest we extend our visit, I am of mind to oblige him!"

Of Mr. Collins himself, Elizabeth saw relatively little. He seemed to have some sort of disinclination for her that Elizabeth could not quite explain, but she was not about to question her good fortune. Lydia and Kitty, of course, could find nothing pleasing about Mr. Collins and were content to remain at Rosings. As for Jane, she was attentive and polite as ever whenever Mr. Collins did appear, but Elizabeth was certain Jane did not wish to be in the man's company any more than Elizabeth did herself.

When they had been at Rosings for some two weeks, Mr. Collins invited the four Bennet sisters at Rosings to the parsonage one evening for dinner. He delivered the invitation in person, noting: "You are my family, after all, and I should not like to completely cede your company to my patroness, though I know staying at Rosings to be an experience highly edifying and much better than anything my poor parsonage could provide. Still, I would see to my duties as your host, if you will."

"Of course, we will attend," said Jane, with nary a hint of exasperation for the man's interminable speech.

"Anne and I will have a quiet dinner together," added Lady Catherine. "I shall call for the carriage to convey you to Hunsford and back at the appropriate time."

What followed was, unsurprisingly, a long soliloquy from their cousin on the gracious condescension of his patroness. Though the Bennet sisters were each grateful in their own ways, such barefaced flattery was beyond their ability to withstand, so they busied themselves with other pursuits.

It turned out that Mr. Collins had a specific reason for inviting them that evening, and it concerned the arrival of Lady Catherine's nephews, who were to come the following Monday.

The dinner was excellent; as Elizabeth had noted before, the woman who cooked for Mr. Collins knew her business and provided him with excellent meals. The family sat at his table, partook of his food, and, in general attempted to ignore the constant flow of words which tumbled from his mouth. Mr. Bennet watched him with amusement as he normally did, but there were also several other conversations carried on around the table. Elizabeth was certain that Mr. Collins was not even aware that he was not the sole focus of their attention.

It was when they had been seated at the table for some time that the tenor of the man's voice suddenly changed, and he regarded them with something akin to sternness. Of course, sternness in such a silly man was all relative, and to Elizabeth, the only thing he accomplished was to give the impression of being constipated.

"I do have a matter of which I would like to speak with my cousins staying at Rosings. For, you see, I have it on good authority that Lady Catherine's nephews, Mr. Darcy and Colonel Fitzwilliam, will soon be arriving at Rosings to stay with her ladyship."

"Yes, we have heard of it," replied Elizabeth. "In fact, I believe you may have been there when Lady Catherine informed us of it herself."

"Well am I aware of it," said Mr. Collins. The look he pinned on Elizabeth was colored with more than a hint of distaste—Elizabeth found she could bear his contempt cheerfully. "In fact, I suggested to Lady Catherine that for the length of her nephews' stay my young cousins return to the parsonage. Alas, she is as generous as she is accommodating, and she would not hear of it. And as I will not contradict her ladyship, there is nothing to be done—you shall remain her guests while her nephews are present."

"What are you saying, Mr. Collins?" asked Mrs. Bennet. "Are you suggesting that my girls do not know how to behave toward Mr. Darcy?"

"Of course not, madam. But I believe there is some cause to take care while they are in residence. It would not do to offend such great men."

It appeared to Elizabeth that her mother wished to say something to the parson, for her mouth opened several times. In the end, however, she kept her silence, though it appeared she was sorely pressed.

"I believe you worry for naught, Mr. Collins," said Elizabeth. "You forget that we have already met Mr. Darcy. By all accounts his cousin is an affable man."

"I have not forgotten it, Cousin. But I believe I must still insist upon your good behavior. Lady Catherine, in her infinite good humor, allows a certain . . . informality of manner. She is everything that is pleasant and agreeable, of course, and though I have never met them, I must assume that her nephews are the same.

"But Colonel Fitzwilliam is not only a worldly man and a member of our illustrious military forces, but Mr. Darcy is a man of high stature, sober, respected, and deferred to by all. Though my cousins, in general, show manners which are commendable, there is, at times, a decided want of propriety among you, not to mention a certain impertinence which Mr. Darcy must inevitably find intolerable."

"I dare say he might," said Mr. Bennet with a straight face. "But you might be surprised, Cousin. Mr. Darcy always struck me as a competent man, but he might not be the paragon of virtue you seem to think he is. In fact, I am quite certain that Mr. Darcy possesses the capability of behaving atrociously and perhaps even insulting those who are undeserving of his contempt."

Elizabeth was forced to raise a hand to her mouth to stifle her laughter and, in the process, refrain from spitting her peas all over the table. She turned a severe glare on her father, but he only winked at her.

For his part, Mr. Collins regarded Mr. Bennet with something akin to horror, before he began to shake his head violently. "Surely you are jesting, Cousin. Mr. Darcy is descended from the noblest stock in the kingdom, his assets vast, his understanding profound. He could never behave in such a manner, I am absolutely certain."

"You may be surprised, Mr. Collins," replied Mr. Bennet. His smirk never wavered, but he refrained from commenting further.

"No, I absolutely cannot fathom it," denied Mr. Collins. "Mr. Darcy does not possess the capacity for such things, and should my cousins carry on in their usual fashion, I am certain they will give him grievous offense."

Mr. Collins again attempted his stern glare with them. "I will have your solemn promise. You will treat Mr. Darcy with deference and respect, you will not do anything to draw attention to yourselves, and you will rein in your impertinence while he is present."

"We shall not offend Mr. Darcy," said Elizabeth, speaking for her sisters. She was not of mind to say anything else to the man, for he was beginning to irk her with his insistence.

"That is well. Now, allow me to instruct you of what is proper when confronted by a man of Mr. Darcy and Colonel Fitzwilliam's standing."

What followed was a long and often nonsensical account of what Mr. Collins considered to be appropriate behavior. He spoke with great verve and intensity, warming to his topic and continuing well past what any other person would consider necessary. His advice was often contradictory—how were they to offer the man compliments if they followed Mr. Collins's advice to not speak at all in Mr. Darcy's presence?—and he often repeated himself, making it seem like he was saying something new by simply rearranging his words. Within five minutes of this new oratory, Elizabeth had decided to simply stop listening to him—she would certainly end up strangling the silly man otherwise. Her sisters had chosen to do the same.

"Do you suppose Mr. Collins has ever met a man who would require a person to behave in such a way?" asked Elizabeth of Jane when he had gone on for some time. "I have difficulty believing even the Prince Regent would be so conceited."

"I doubt Mr. Collins has ever met anyone of any standing other than Lady Catherine," replied Jane.

"Aye. That is what makes it all that much more puzzling. Lady Catherine surely does not require such obeisance. Why would he think it would be acceptable?"

"I believe part of it to be his upbringing," said Mr. Bennet, from where he sat by Elizabeth's side. "His father was miserly and had not much idea of any social graces. I suspect he dominated his son and instilled this obsequiousness. Then he was likely taken advantage of in his seminary, which set his character in stone."

Elizabeth acknowledged what her father was saying, but it was still mystifying. Mr. Darcy had been aloof, cold, and arrogant when he had lately been in Hertfordshire, but he had not been nearly so proud as Mr. Collins suggested. And with Lady Catherine present, Elizabeth could not imagine he would behave that way when they met him again the following week.

"It is best to simply humor Mr. Collins, I suppose," said Elizabeth. "If he oversteps at Rosings, I am certain Lady Catherine will put him in his place."

"That would be a sight to see," agreed Mr. Bennet.

"Well, he is useful for one thing." Mr. Bennet and Jane both looked at Elizabeth askance. She grinned at them and replied: "I shall have plenty of which to write to Charlotte tonight. I am certain she will be excessively diverted at our cousin's absurdity."

The laughter they could not hold in finally drew Mr. Collins's attention. He did not say anything, but his glare was reproachful, and he clearly suspected them of conspiring to ignore his dictates. Elizabeth did not care enough to disabuse him of it.

It was only by the slimmest of margins that Mrs. Bennet had been able to hold her countenance when Mr. Collins had blathered on about his idea of proper behavior. What notion could a parson possibly have about proper behavior? Lady Catherine considered Mrs. Bennet's daughters good enough for her nephews; what could Mr. William Collins possibly have to say about it if her ladyship approved?

For perhaps the first time, Mrs. Bennet wondered about this

courting business with Mary. Mr. Collins had proven himself to be a fool—should she really wish to promote a closer connection with such a man? If her girls were to marry Mr. Darcy and this Colonel Fitzwilliam, should Mary not be able to find a better match than her husband's odious cousin?

All the ill feelings Mrs. Bennet had felt about Mr. Collins, even long before she had ever met him, were returning, and she wondered if she should not direct Mary away from him. Mary was a good girl; surely she would agree and obey her mother.

But in the end, Mrs. Bennet decided to say nothing. Part of her decision was based upon the fact that she thought it difficult for plain and pious Mary to attract a man, so it was likely for the best that she allowed the courtship to play out. She had also noted Mary looking at the man with displeasure when he attacked her sisters. It was entirely possible Mary would rebuff Mr. Collins should he decide to come to the point. In the meantime, Mary could provide a distraction for Mr. Collins while Lady Catherine's nephews courted Mrs. Bennet's eldest daughters. Once those marriages were settled, Mrs. Bennet could take some thought to whether to allow Mary's courtship to continue or end it so the girl could attempt to find some other match.

When dinner ended, Mrs. Bennet left the dining room with the other members of the family to sit in the parlor for a short time before her daughters were to return to Rosings. There was no separation of the sexes—there had not been any night since they had come to Kent, and Mrs. Bennet knew the reason why. The thought cheered her, making her feel a sort of savage glee to know that her husband could not abide the man alone. It vindicated all her dislike of him.

The parlor was a dingy little room, in Mrs. Bennet's opinion—the wallpaper was dark and dull, the furniture was situated all wrong, the windows looked out in the wrong direction, and it was not nearly so large as their sitting-room in Longbourn. She supposed that it was only a parsonage and, as such, could not match the comfort of even a small estate, but she could not find herself at ease in such surroundings either. But it was what they had available, so there they went.

It was fortunate, indeed, that Mr. Collins took himself to a sofa and sat beside Mary, speaking with her exclusively and not sparing a word for any of her other daughters. Mary, Mrs. Bennet watched closely, attempting to see if she could discern anything of the girl's feelings. But Mary had always been adept at hiding herself—she was almost as reticent as Jane. Whatever she thought of Mr. Collins, she spoke to him civilly, and seemed to focus her attention on him to the exclusion of all others.

This worked to Mrs. Bennet's favor. It was time to begin putting the plan that she and Lady Catherine had devised into action, and there was no time better than when Mr. Collins was inattentive to what was happening around him.

"Jane, dear, as your cousin has stated, Mr. Darcy is to come soon."

"Yes, he is, Mama. I anticipate renewing our acquaintance."

"You do?" Mrs. Bennet could own to a little surprise; Jane had been so focused on Mr. Bingley, that she had seemed hardly aware of Mr. Darcy.

"Of course," replied her eldest earnestly. "He struck me as an intelligent man, though his manners *were* a little unfortunate."

"I believe he is," said Mrs. Bennet, though she had no idea if it was true. "Your society at Rosings is likely to become more interesting." Mrs. Bennet then turned to Elizabeth. "This Colonel Fitzwilliam is, by all accounts, an amiable man. I am certain it will be a relief for you to have someone of like temperament available to keep you occupied."

Elizabeth smiled. "I will be happy to make the colonel's acquaintance, Mama. Lady Catherine has given him quite the flaming character."

"Excellent," said Mrs. Bennet. She had half expected Elizabeth to contradict her for no other purpose than to be contrary. With such an auspicious beginning, she felt she could almost begin to plan the weddings and the trousseaux.

But she would be patient, as Lady Catherine had suggested. Until Elizabeth was engaged to Colonel Fitzwilliam and Jane, to Mr. Darcy, she would need to continue to nudge her girls in the direction they needed to go. For today, it was enough to have sown the seeds of her daughters' future happiness.

When the Bennet sisters arrived back at Rosings, Lady Catherine was waiting for them in the sitting-room, though her daughter had returned to her room for the night. Kitty and Lydia excused themselves a little later, leaving Elizabeth and Jane alone with the lady, where they made polite conversation for some time.

"And how was your dinner at the parsonage, my dears?" asked Lady Catherine.

"The dinner was excellent," replied Jane.

"It seems like the woman Mr. Collins employs is quite skilled," added Elizabeth.

"Mrs. Green is a gem," replied Lady Catherine. "Her children have grown and left, leaving only herself and Mr. Green. And as Mr. Green benefits from being able to eat at the parsonage every day with his wife, it is a beneficial arrangement for all.

"But come, I expect you were happy to dine with your parents again. Though you came to Kent to stay with Mr. Collins, you have not actually been much in his company."

"A very little of *his* company will do," muttered Elizabeth. When she saw that Lady Catherine had heard her, she colored in embarrassment.

"Mr. Collins is an . . . unusual man, is he not?" said Lady Catherine. "Can I assume he outdid himself this evening?"

"He had many . . . instructions for us," said Jane. Though Elizabeth had not noted it before, it seemed like Jane was a little disturbed by all Mr. Collins had said. It was not surprising, therefore, that Lady Catherine saw it as well.

"Instructions? Of what sort, Miss Bennet?"

"Oh, my apologies, Lady Catherine," said Jane, feeling her own embarrassment. "I should not have spoken."

"No, I would hear what you have to say." Lady Catherine reached out and touched a hand to Jane's arm. "You have no need to fear of my reaction. As we have already discussed, I know how Mr. Collins can be."

Elizabeth sensed that Jane would not respond, so she took the office upon herself. "Dinner tonight was a long dissertation from Mr. Collins concerning how we should behave when your nephews are present."

"Oh?" asked Lady Catherine. That one innocuous-sounding word conveyed a depth of meaning, from annoyance to amusement.

"Apparently, while your ladyship allows a certain 'informality of manner,' in Mr. Collins's opinion, your nephews are great men who demand respect."

"He thinks so, does he?" It was clear that the lady was quite annoyed with Mr. Collins. Elizabeth could well understand the sentiment, for she could not remember a time in his company since they had met where she had *not* been annoyed with him.

"I think he simply wishes to ensure we make a good impression," said Jane.

Elizabeth snorted. "You are far too apt to think the best of others, Jane."

"What do you think his reasons were, Miss Elizabeth?" said Lady Catherine.

"I am certain I cannot say, though I suspect that he actually believes what he told us."

"You are undoubtedly correct." Lady Catherine shook her head. "But you must not believe him. You have met Darcy, and though your impressions were not the best, I believe you know enough of him to understand that he does not consider himself above his company."

Privately Elizabeth was not at all certain of that, but she would not contradict her hostess and insult her nephew.

"As for Colonel Fitzwilliam, you will see within moments of his arrival that he is a most amiable man. Neither would expect such deference, and neither would expect either of you to be anything other than what you are."

"Mr. Collins was most particular in attacking Elizabeth's impertinence," said Jane quietly.

"And I own to a certain level of impertinence," said Elizabeth. "Quite happily, in fact."

"I prefer to think of it as archness," replied Lady Catherine with a warm smile at Elizabeth. "And I doubt Darcy would label it as impertinence either. Perhaps I should speak with Mr. Collins."

"I doubt it would be of any benefit," replied Elizabeth. "And no doubt he would castigate us for misrepresenting what he said."

"Not if he values his comfortable position," said Lady Catherine. "But I shall be guided by you in this matter. If the man gives you further distress, please inform me so that I might take action."

Jane and Elizabeth both agreed and the subject was dropped. Soon the three ladies bid each other good night and returned to their rooms.

CHAPTER VI

"So, Cousin, you have been rather tight-lipped ever since we received word of our aunt's guests. I understand they are known to you?"

Pulled from his thoughts as he was—deep thoughts at that—Darcy started at the sound of his cousin's voice. When he turned to regard Fitzwilliam, the man sat across from him on the rear-facing seat, his manner expressing an entirely unwarranted level of enjoyment. It was always thus with Fitzwilliam, especially when he thought he had the least chance of eliciting some response from Darcy by making sport with him.

"They are known to me," replied Darcy in the vain hope that Fitzwilliam would take the hint and be silent. And vain such a hope turned out to be.

"Well, out with it then! What can you tell me of them?"

"They are a family of minor country gentry, nothing of any consequence."

"Then why do they have you out of sorts?"

Darcy's scowl meant nothing to Fitzwilliam, obviously, for he only grinned all that much wider.

"I am not out of sorts. I am merely disinclined to their company."

"I should have known," replied Fitzwilliam. "For surely a family of pleasant and pretty young ladies would not be agreeable to *you*."

"It is not the fact that they are ladies. It is the fact that the youngest two are silly and improper, and the mother is hardly better. I only knew them for a brief time, but never once did I see the father take his family in hand."

"And the elder daughters?"

Darcy shook his head; it was the elder daughters—one of the elder daughters—who was responsible for Darcy's being so out of sorts. He had left Netherfield above five months earlier, had only been there for a matter of fewer than three weeks, and still she haunted him. And yet the sound of her laugh was as clear in his memory today as it had been then.

"The elder daughters are restrained and proper, though I do not remember the middle girl well. The eldest is one of the most beautiful young ladies I have ever seen, while the second, though not so pretty as her sister, is still handsome, as well as being playful and easy in company."

"Oh ho!" cried Fitzwilliam. "This visit promises to be quite interesting then, not that visiting Aunt Catherine is a trial." Fitzwilliam leaned forward and slapped Darcy on the shoulder. "So, which of these sisters is the cause of your odd behavior?"

With a weary shaken head, Darcy indicated the conversation was over, and he turned to look out the window. Though he esteemed Fitzwilliam more than almost anyone else in the world, it was at times like these that his cousin could be so tiresome.

"Then I shall discover it for myself. I am certain Aunt Catherine would be pleased to help me ferret out your secrets." When Darcy did not respond, Fitzwilliam continued: "For myself, I would wager it is the playful one. You know beautiful ladies aplenty in London, and none have ever caused such a reaction. Surely she must be more agreeable than Anne."

Darcy shook his head; Fitzwilliam had the right of it. "She becomes more insistent each time we visit, and nothing our aunt tells her has any effect."

"So, tell her you will not marry her," said Fitzwilliam, shrugging with unconcern.

"You know I have tried. My words are no more efficacious than our aunt's are."

"Then I suggest you be more persuasive. If you continue to defy her, I would not put it past her to attempt a compromise."

Darcy snorted at the suggestion. "You think I do not already know that? The last two times we visited, I ensured my door is locked and that I was never in a room alone with her." Darcy shot a look at his cousin, which he had seen so many times directed at him. "You do not think I stayed with you because I enjoy your company, do you?"

Fitzwilliam guffawed. "What about keys? Are you not concerned that she has obtained the keys to your room to use when you lower your guard?"

"Lady Catherine has seen to it that the keys are locked away and cannot be obtained by our cousin. And for good measure, Snell always searches out the housekeeper to ensure that she has not . . . misplaced a set. The woman is loyal to Aunt Catherine and would never hand over the keys just because Anne asked for them."

"It appears your battle plan is well-drawn, Darcy. Just remember that the best laid plans are only good until first contact with the enemy."

"Do we now refer to our cousins as enemies?" asked Darcy softly.

"When they are determined to rule our lives and ensure their wishes take precedence over ours, then there is little choice."

"True," said Darcy. "Very true.'

And Darcy fell silent and returned his attention to the passing countryside. For once, Fitzwilliam was silent, allowing him to brood.

When Mr. Darcy and his cousin entered the room after they had refreshed themselves from their journey, Elizabeth was treated to a spectacle easily the equivalent of something her mother might have authored. Only this time, the insanity originated from one who was accounted to be among the highest society had to offer, the granddaughter of an earl, no less.

The gentlemen had no sooner entered the room when Miss de Bourgh stood and approached Mr. Darcy, a predatory glint in her eye. "Darcy! You have finally come for me!"

For his part, Mr. Darcy regarded Miss de Bourgh as if she was a dangerous animal. "Anne," said he with a curt bow. "I trust you are well?"

"I am well now that you are here." The woman actually fluttered her eyelashes at her cousin, and Elizabeth was forced to cough to stifle a laugh. Miss de Bourgh shot her a sour look, but Elizabeth affected not to see it. It mattered little, as she soon turned back to her cousin and sidled up to him.

"Shall we go to another room for our long-overdue conversation,

Cousin? I am certain you are as impatient as I."

"Come now, Anne," said the other man, subtly stepping up next to Mr. Darcy and allowing him to back up a little, so that he could step in between them. "Do you not wish to greet your favorite cousin?"

"Fitzwilliam," said Anne shortly. "I am certain I may greet you after other, more important matters are dealt with."

"But then we would be rude to your mother's guests. You forget I have not yet been introduced to them."

"Of course, you have not," said Lady Catherine, standing and glaring at her daughter. "Let us observe the proprieties, Anne."

Observing the proprieties seemed like the last thing Miss de Bourgh wished to do, but she turned and strode back to the sofa, throwing herself onto it, where she sat, arms crossed, a petulant pout displayed for all to see.

"Hello, Aunt," said Colonel Fitzwilliam. "I can see you are quite well. I am happy to see you."

"I am well, Fitzwilliam. Thank you."

The three exchanged the greetings of family long sundered, and then turned to the Bennet sisters who were waiting, in some cases, impatiently. Lydia seemed to be inspecting Colonel Fitzwilliam, likely attempting to imagine the picture he would present were he wearing his red coat.

"Now, Aunt, if you will introduce me to these lovely young ladies, I will be much obliged."

"Of course, Fitzwilliam," said Lady Catherine, a smile on her face which seemed to suggest that she knew some great secret to which no one else was privy.

"Nephew, may I present Miss Jane Bennet, Miss Elizabeth Bennet, Miss Catherine Bennet, and Miss Lydia Bennet. They have agreed to stay with us while their parents and middle daughter, Miss Mary Bennet, are staying at the parsonage with their cousin, Mr. Collins. Miss Bennets, this is my nephew, Colonel Anthony Fitzwilliam, the second son of my brother, the Earl of Matlock."

"Ladies," said the colonel, bowing to them all. "I am pleased to make your acquaintance."

Though his words were directed at them all, Elizabeth thought she detected more than a hint of admiration for Jane, and for her part, Jane seemed to sense it and was far from displeased. Elizabeth turned a critical eye on the colonel, noting that while a handsome man, he was not Mr. Darcy's equal. But he was tall, and broad shouldered, possessing of dark, wavy locks, and moved with grace and an economy of motion. After Jane's disappointment with Mr. Bingley, Elizabeth was wary of any man paying attention to her dearest sister. But should Colonel Fitzwilliam take an interest in Jane, Elizabeth decided she would have no objections. There was something about the colonel which spoke to maturity.

"A colonel!" said Lydia as she stepped up to him and curtseyed, looking at him with more brazen confidence than a girl of only sixteen years should possess. "I am happy to make your acquaintance, sir, for I have only ever met one colonel."

"And he is old and tired and commands only the regiment at Meryton," said Kitty with a giggle.

"Ah, but if he commands a regiment in Hertfordshire, then he is naught but a militia colonel." Colonel Fitzwilliam grinned at them. "I, on the other hand, am a colonel in the regulars, and though I have been in the army for some years, I do not consider myself to be old and tired."

"Oh, Fitzwilliam, do not encourage them," said Lady Catherine. "Come, girls, let us at least attempt to adhere to propriety."

"I believe propriety is alien to them," said Miss de Bourgh *sotto voce*.

"I think she is hardly one to speak," said Elizabeth in an aside to Jane.

It appeared, however, that Mr. Darcy had overheard her words, for he turned to her, and though he did not say anything, his eyes seemed to express mirth. Uncertain, Elizabeth smiled tentatively at him, which seemed to prompt him to speak.

"Miss Elizabeth. I see you have not lost any of your wit."

"I hope not, Mr. Darcy. A woman may age and her face lose those qualities which drew young men to her in her youth, but I would hope the mind remains as sharp as it ever was."

Mr. Darcy laughed, the first time Elizabeth had ever heard him give voice to his mirth. "It is not above five months since I saw you last. Surely you have not become old and decrepit in such a short time."

"I hope not," replied Elizabeth. "I am sorry, Mr. Darcy, but we were led to understand that you left Meryton to attend to your sister. I hope she is well?"

"Yes, very well, indeed."

"I wish you would convince Georgiana to attend us here," said Lady Catherine.

"Perhaps later in our stay she might be persuaded. At present, she is much engaged with her masters and preferred to stay with Aunt Susan in London."

Lady Catherine harrumphed and allowed the subject to drop. They sat down and conversed for several minutes, and Elizabeth watched as the sitting-room descended into controlled chaos. Kitty and Lydia, though chastened by Lady Catherine's admonishment, were not ready to cede the attentions of the colonel to anyone else. Lydia continued to badger him, asking for stories of his experiences. The colonel only showed her a mysterious smile and chatted happily with her.

Mr. Darcy sat with Jane and Elizabeth, and though he was not verbose, he was at least more vocal than he had been in Hertfordshire. As for the de Bourghs, Lady Catherine sat watching of them all like a queen on her throne, joining each conversation to interject a comment or two and then sitting back and watching them. Miss de Bourgh said nothing, though the scowls she directed at Jane and Elizabeth told them clearly that she wished for Mr. Darcy's full attention. That changed about fifteen minutes into their visit, when something Lydia said drew the colonel's close attention.

"I am sorry, Miss Lydia, but did you say you know a Mr. Wickham?"

"Yes, we all do," said Lydia, continuing with blithe unconcern. "He is frightfully handsome, though not nearly so interesting as Denny or Carter."

As Lydia continued to speak of her acquaintances in the militia, the two gentlemen shared a look with their aunt. Then Mr. Darcy turned to Elizabeth, and she sensed something odd about his mood. "Mr. Wickham joined the militia? Mr. George Wickham?"

Elizabeth nodded. "He arrived in Meryton not long after you left. I am sorry, but you are acquainted with him?"

"As much acquainted as I ever wish to be." He paused, and then he turned his gaze upon Elizabeth, and there was something penetrating in it, though Elizabeth thought it was not directed at her. "Did Mr. Wickham . . . Did he mention a connection with me?"

Though surprised, Elizabeth was able to answer: "Nothing of which I am aware. He is quite the charmer, it seems, as half the ladies were in love with him not five minutes after he arrived. I do not know him well, though Kitty and Lydia might know more of him."

A tension seemed to drain from Mr. Darcy's shoulders at that moment, a tension Elizabeth had not even noted. With concern and compassion, Elizabeth reached out and touched his arm.

"Am I to understand that yours is not a happy association with Mr. Wickham?"

"As perceptive as ever, Miss Elizabeth. No, it is not a happy association. Mr. Wickham is not who he portrays himself to be, and many have discovered that to their detriment."

"I understand that he began courting a Miss Mary King after the New Year."

Mr. Darcy shook his head. "Can I assume she has some fortune to tempt him?"

Not surprised that Mr. Darcy should guess this much, Elizabeth nodded. "She recently inherited it from an uncle, I understand. She has been staying with some relations in Meryton for the past several months, so I am not much acquainted with her."

For a brief moment, Mr. Darcy fell silent. Then he seemed to shake off his mood, giving Elizabeth the image of a dog shaking the water from its coat, and he turned back to Elizabeth. It was as if he had made the decision not to allow disagreeable memories to plague him.

"I would not talk of Mr. Wickham, Miss Elizabeth, for he is not an agreeable subject. Perhaps we could defer such talk to another time?"

Elizabeth agreed readily, and they began speaking of other things. Though the conversation was general between them all, Elizabeth had never been so entertained in Mr. Darcy's company. Mr. Bingley had on one occasion said something to the effect that Mr. Darcy was more open and comfortable in society with which he was familiar. Now that Elizabeth had seen it, she was certain that he had only spoken the truth.

"Fitzwilliam," said Darcy, beckoning his cousin to join him.

After spending some time in Lady Catherine's sitting-room, Darcy had remembered that the other Bennets were staying at the parsonage and thought it proper that he and Fitzwilliam pay their respects as soon as may be. Lady Catherine had waved them off, wishing them a pleasant visit, before going to attend to some matter of the estate. Of course, Anne could not be roused to pay a visit to such an objectionable location, so Darcy and Fitzwilliam had left with the Bennet sisters for the short walk to the parsonage.

Miss Lydia and Miss Kitty, as Darcy remembered she was called, seemed disinclined to give up Fitzwilliam's company, but he bowed to them and said a few low words, and then allowed himself to fall back to where Darcy was walking. Miss Bennet and Miss Elizabeth were leading the way, and aside from the need to speak to his cousin, Darcy was desperate for a distraction to keep him from staring at Miss Elizabeth's form.

"I must say, Cousin," said Fitzwilliam as he fell into step with

Darcy, "she is not what I would have expected from you." Darcy shot a look at Fitzwilliam, but he was watching the ladies and not paying attention. "I might have thought you would gravitate to a woman more like her sister, at least in looks. In temperament, she almost seems a little too . . . spirited for you."

"It only proves you do not know me nearly so well as you think," replied Darcy. "But none of that now. I think it might be prudent for you to write a letter to the colonel of the militia company in Meryton. He should know some of the more salient facts concerning one of the men under his command."

Fitzwilliam's responding grin bared his teeth, and Darcy was reminded that for all his jovial nature, Fitzwilliam was a fierce enemy when crossed. "Just the thought I had, old man. Miss Lydia was kind enough to share the name of the colonel of his regiment with me. Tonight I shall compose a letter to him, and I will be sure to leave none of the important points out."

"I am certain he has run up debts."

"I am certain he has. I take a great amount of pleasure in the thought that our friend George will finally be called to account for at least some of his actions."

Though he nodded, Darcy did not reply. A part of him remembered the engaging Wickham as a young boy, how they had played together, the fun they had shared, and his father's regard, though Wickham had become increasingly unworthy of it. Then he remembered all the times he had cleaned up Wickham's messes, and the tears his sister had shed, and he wanted Wickham to pay for his crimes. It was best to just leave it in Fitzwilliam's hands. Darcy himself was too conflicted to act with impartiality.

The parsonage loomed in the distance, and soon they had entered therein. Mr. Bennet and his wife were just as Darcy remembered them—indifferent and silly in turn. Miss Mary was still quiet and watchful, not saying more than three words together. Mr. Collins, however . . .

"Mr. Darcy. Colonel Fitzwilliam."

The man spoke in a solemn and awed voice, and when he bowed, he bent over so low that Darcy was afraid he would tip over and fall onto his head. When he rose, he fixed them with an expression of utter vacant servility.

"We are so greatly honored to make the acquaintance of such august personages that words simply fail to give meaning to our feelings. You are very welcome, indeed, sirs, and I cannot imagine that my humble abode has ever seen such illustrious visitors as those who grace it at present. Of course, Lady Catherine de Bourgh, your aunt and my beloved patroness, has also graced these halls, so I must exclude herself from my observation, given how gracious and condescending she has been to assist me in my poor home."

It seemed all that Fitzwilliam could do to hold in the hilarity Darcy was certain was bubbling under the surface. For himself, Darcy wondered what had ever possessed Lady Catherine to grant the living to such a buffoon.

"Thank you, Mr. Collins," said Fitzwilliam. "I have heard much from our aunt, but I am afraid reality does not do you justice."

Mr. Collins preened at this perceived compliment, but Darcy was hard pressed to hold in his laughter. Nearby, Miss Elizabeth's eyes danced with mirth, though she gave no outward sign of it.

They sat down, and Darcy was treated to the oddest visit he had ever experienced. Mr. Collins's ability to flatter was positively indefatigable, as the words spilled from his mouth like water over a fall. Nothing was beneath his notice; he even praised the color of Darcy's hair, as if it was something Darcy could control!

"Your cousin is quite . . . singular," said Darcy in a low tone to Miss Elizabeth. "If I had not been informed of it, I could never have imagined he was a relation."

Miss Elizabeth laughed. "It is a distant connection, and one who was unknown to us for many years. My father and his had some disagreement when they were young, which has only recently been healed."

"Your father seems to take some pleasure in his company."

Once again she laughed. "It is only because he finds his brand of ridiculous behavior diverting."

Darcy did not know what to make of that statement, but he noted that Mr. Collins, though he still spoke, was glaring at Miss Elizabeth. For her part, Miss Elizabeth affected to take no notice, though she seemed to understand what had offended him. Though Darcy would have liked to call the man to order, he remained silent, knowing it was not his place to do so.

Though he had only been in her presence again for a few moments, Darcy felt as much danger from this vibrant country miss by his side as he ever had. In the autumn, when he had left Hertfordshire, his stated reason for doing so was to rejoin his sister, who was in poor spirits. He had also told himself that he wished to be away from his friend's sister, who had started grating on his nerves mere moments after his arrival. Renewing his acquaintance with Miss Elizabeth exposed all his pretensions and forced him to acknowledge that which he had not wished to acknowledge.

As they sat in the parlor, Darcy watched the scene with a critical eye. Mrs. Bennet, as he had noted before, was still noisy, her society still a trial, but able to look at her from a different perspective, Darcy could see there was little harm in her. Miss Bennet was as serene and beautiful as ever, and even Miss Lydia and Miss Kitty seemed to have improved a small measure. The most unfathomable member of the family was Mr. Bennet. He could see the man was aware of his family's shortcomings, but to take no action to correct them was a grave oversight, in Darcy's opinion. Surely an intelligent man would act to curb their excesses.

But the true gem, in his opinion, was still Miss Elizabeth. She was effortless, even with the irksome Mr. Collins in attendance, and in the sometimes unruly company of her family, though he supposed she must be easy in *their* company, if only because of her long association. When she spoke, she did so with joy and laughter, and she made others around her smile for the simple reason of her presence. He was as drawn to her as he ever had been. He could not imagine how anyone could resist!

But there was one who was apparently able to resist. Through his long monologues and ponderous speech, Darcy noticed that Mr. Collins kept his eyes on Miss Elizabeth, and though Darcy originally wondered if it was the eye of a suitor, unable to take his eyes from the lady of his affection, the tightness in Mr. Collins's eyes soon revealed it to be disapproval. To what the man objected Darcy could not say, but the longer they sat there the more apparent it became.

"Your cousin seems to be watching you carefully, Miss Elizabeth," observed Darcy to Miss Elizabeth at one point.

"Yes," replied she in the same low tone Darcy had used. "He seems to be offended by my very existence."

"Do you not know why?" asked Darcy, frowning.

Miss Elizabeth turned her expressive eyes on him, filled to the brim with amusement. "Mr. Collins considers me dreadfully impertinent, Mr. Darcy. It is shocking, do you not think?"

Before Darcy could respond, the sound of Mr. Collins's voice interrupted them. "You are very kind to pay attention to my cousin, Mr. Darcy, but you do not need to feel obligated. Elizabeth is . . . well, we shall simply say that her forward nature and tendency to laugh at everything sometimes bring her trouble. She would do well to assume a demure demeanor, for others would respect her more."

Unable to believe what he had just heard, Darcy only stared at Mr. Collins. Fitzwilliam was equally surprised, though he seemed to be feeling a hint of dark amusement, and even Mr. Bennet, who laughed at all and sundry, seemed to be taking offense at Mr. Collins's words.

"On the contrary, Mr. Collins, I find your cousin to be charming. There is nothing of her manner which is improperly forward or lacking in any way."

The look Mr. Bennet bestowed on Darcy at that moment was filled with speculation, but Darcy paid the man little heed. Mr. Collins, though he frowned — directed at Miss Elizabeth rather than Darcy himself — said nothing further. But he did not stop watching Miss Elizabeth the entire time they were there.

Later, those staying at Rosings took their leave, with promises that Lady Catherine had charged Darcy to make, of an invitation to dinner on Easter Sunday. Mr. Collins's effusions on the subject were predictable and highly redundant, and Darcy did not feel the need to pay any attention to the man's blathering. Soon, they departed, the youngest leading the way, their elder sisters following, while Darcy and Fitzwilliam brought up the rear.

"We have fallen in with an interesting bunch, have we not?" said Fitzwilliam. "But though the Bennets are, indeed, a disparate group of characters, I cannot quite make Mr. Collins out."

"Obsequiousness mixed with pomposity," replied Darcy. "It is not a usual combination, but we have met others who were similar."

"Yes, but none of them take it to the extremes the excellent parson does. I dare say there are not ten people in all of England who can match Mr. Collins for the sheer brilliance of his absurdity." Fitzwilliam glanced at Darcy. "I thought you might deliver a beating upon the man for what he said to Miss Elizabeth."

"If she is disposed to laugh at him, why should I bother? As you said, he is ridiculous, so his opinion cannot signify."

"True. I commend you for your choice, Darcy. She is in every way exquisite."

"I have made no choice, Fitzwilliam."

"Oh, I believe you have. You simply must acknowledge it. For my part, though I consider Miss Elizabeth to be everything that is delightful, I find my eyes drawn to her elder sister. Now there is a woman unlike any other. I find myself wishing to know her better."

The sharp look Darcy directed on his cousin went unnoticed, for Fitzwilliam was otherwise engaged. Should Fitzwilliam turn his attention on Miss Bennet, Darcy wondered what would happen should she be reintroduced to Bingley, who had been paying her an inordinate amount of attention before Darcy departed. He could not imagine Bingley truly enamored of her, considering how he had left Hertfordshire without a backwards glance—of course, that might have been the doing of his sisters, too. It would be an interesting scene, indeed, should she meet him as a relation by marriage of Darcy.

CHAPTER VII

As they did every year when they visited their aunt in the spring, Darcy and Fitzwilliam spent some time assisting her with the estate. Lady Catherine was capable of directing the estate toward prosperity and making decisions as astutely as any estate master. But the times being what they were, the assistance and direction of a man did wonders to smooth any ruffled feathers among the tenants or those who had dealings with the estate.

In addition, Darcy reviewed her books to provide his aunt with any opinions she might request, and he and Fitzwilliam surveyed the estate while present. In general, Darcy did not find much to criticize—his aunt had been managing the estate for some time and knew what was to be done. Those times Darcy offered his advice, her ladyship had often already taken the action that he had suggested.

"Thank you, Darcy, for visiting and taking an interest in such matters," said Lady Catherine one morning not long after they had arrived. "Not many young men would give of their time so freely when there are other amusements to be had."

"It is no trouble, Aunt," replied Darcy. "Fitzwilliam and I enjoy the time we spend with you."

"Then you should come more often." Darcy did not think he had reacted to her suggestion, but she burst out into laughter anyway. "Do not concern yourself, Darcy. I understand Anne is a trial, and doubly so when we visit Pemberley. I appreciate your attention all the same."

"I can deal with Anne," said Darcy. "She is determined, but I am more so."

Lady Catherine shook her head with rueful exasperation. "I wish she would come to her senses, but she is convinced you will offer for her."

"Perhaps you should take her to town to be introduced to other men."

"She will not go. She declares she is quite content to stay at Rosings until you 'come to your senses.' I am at my wits' end."

There was nothing more to be said, so Darcy held his tongue. Anne was a blight upon their coming, a source of frustration and stress, but Darcy would not avoid his aunt because her daughter was objectionable.

In watching them, he was struck, as he often was, by how different mother and daughter were: Lady Catherine kind and generous to all, quick to laugh, though perhaps too eager to share her wisdom; and Anne the opposite—arrogant, proud, and at times insufferable, especially to their guests. For their part, the youngest Bennets ignored her—a rather erudite decision by them—while Miss Bennet accepted the abuse with patience, and Miss Elizabeth laughed at her. In Darcy's opinion, Anne would benefit by learning to laugh the way Miss Elizabeth did.

Anne was a constant source of annoyance. The girl followed him about with that predatory look in her eye, and if he was not careful, Darcy knew she would attempt some sort of compromise. She tried to be coquettish, but the result was not what she expected.

"Shall we not talk of our future," said she to him the day after his arrival. "I am certain you have been waiting to speak with me."

"On the contrary, there is nothing particular of which I feel the need to speak."

"Oh, Darcy, I know you do not truly feel that way." She reached forward and attempted to lay a hand on his arm, but Darcy only shifted, making his movement appear natural but preventing her from achieving her objective nevertheless. "We have much to recommend us to each other. Shall we not come to an agreement?"

"I do not know to what you refer," said Darcy. "I am happy with our relationship as it stands now."

Though Anne was quite obviously displeased with his response, she only redoubled her efforts. She would follow him from room to room, speaking to him without cessation, making allusions to their future felicity, which were subtle only to her, and generally ensuring his time in Kent was miserable. She was worse than Miss Bingley in many ways, which was saying quite a lot.

The only thing that made the situation tolerable was the sight of Miss Elizabeth's amusement. His cousin's unsubtle attempts at wooing were a source of hilarity for Miss Elizabeth, and her grin rarely disappeared when Darcy was present. But far from displeasing Darcy to be a source of her entertainment, it further endeared her to him.

She took to interfering with Anne's machinations whenever possible. On a day when his cousin's attentions had become so intolerable that Darcy was considering the relative merits of strangling her, Miss Elizabeth rose and announced her intention to walk in the back gardens, which itself was not remarkable. But as she stood, she turned a look on Darcy so casual, and yet so pointed, that he immediately offered to accompany her.

"Oh, Darcy, you do not need to walk the gardens," said Anne, her tone petulant, a dark hatred for Miss Elizabeth in her eyes. "Miss Elizabeth may walk as she knows nothing better. Why do we not ride the area in my phaeton? It will be so much more delightful."

"A walk is just what I need now, Anne. Perhaps we might ride in your phaeton another time."

Anne pouted, but she said nothing further. Thus, Darcy found himself walking the back gardens with the enchanting young woman who was rapidly beginning to consume his thoughts once again.

"I thank you for your suggestion, Miss Bennet," said Darcy after they had quit the house.

"Suggestion?" asked she, her eyes shining with repressed mirth. "I cannot recall having said anything, Mr. Darcy."

"Not in words, you did not. But I fancy that sometimes a more profound understanding is exchanged with no more than a glance. I knew there was an invitation in your gaze the moment you looked at me, and I was more than happy to accept."

"Then you have caught me out. I had observed how uncomfortable your cousin made you and thought a little fresh air would do you good."

"Indeed, you are correct, Miss Bennet."

When the attempted compromise was put into motion, Elizabeth did not know whether to be annoyed with the woman for trying to enforce her own desires upon an obviously unwilling man or simply laugh at her for her ineptitude. Surely Miss de Bourgh did not even understand what constituted a proper compromise, which Elizabeth was forced to own was entirely fortunate for Mr. Darcy.

The day after their walk in the gardens, Elizabeth had gone to the library to look at Lady Catherine's collection of books, for she had exhausted the few volumes she had brought herself. It was while she was engaged in looking at the bookshelves that the door opened behind her, and Mr. Darcy stepped in. He appeared surprised to see her, but he hesitated only a moment before he stepped forward to greet her, leaving the door wide open behind him.

"Miss Bennet," said he with a bow. "I was not aware that you are a connoisseur of the written word."

"I was taught at my father's knee," replied Elizabeth after returning his greeting. "A more dedicated bibliophile you would have difficulty finding."

"A man after my own heart, then," said Mr. Darcy. He stepped forward to the shelf Elizabeth had been examining. "I believe this is Lady Catherine's history section. I was not aware you read such a wide variety of works."

"What wide variety do you call it?" asked Elizabeth, directing an arch smile at him. "As far as I am aware, we have never discussed reading before."

"Then perhaps we should rectify that deficiency."

Elizabeth agreed and they spent the next hour in pleasant conversation. Elizabeth was interested to discover that while their tastes were by no means the same, there were still some opinions they shared, particularly in the area of poetry and the works of Shakespeare. She enjoyed histories, and while he did too, she preferred the history of antiquity, while Mr. Darcy preferred that of England and France. And while Elizabeth laughingly owned to reading a novel on occasion, she teased his predilection toward farming treatises.

"What dusty, dull accounts those must be!" exclaimed she. "Much as a farmer must feel after a long day of tending his fields."

"I do not deny that," replied Mr. Darcy, his complacency indicating he took no offense to her sportive words. But as a gentleman farmer myself, does it not follow that I should understand my tenants' concerns?"

"You are correct, of course," replied Elizabeth.

They continued to speak for a little longer when they began a discussion of a work they had both read, until they disagreed on one of the lines it contained. Certain she was correct, Elizabeth stood to retrieve the book, which was situated in a bookcase along the wall behind the door. It was while she was obtaining the volume to prove her point that she heard a rustle of skirts.

"Fitzwilliam, there you are," purred a voice. "I have looked all over the house for you."

"Anne," replied Mr. Darcy, standing and executing a courtly bow.

At once Elizabeth realized that Miss de Bourgh had not noticed her presence, hidden as she was by the open door, and she stepped out a little way to see what the woman wanted. Elizabeth recognized the determined gait of her walk, and had she been able to see Miss de Bourgh's eyes, she was certain a predatory glint would have been reflected in their depths.

"Finally, I have found you without that Bennet woman present. She must be trying to capture you, Fitzwilliam. You should avoid being in her company so often."

"There is nothing objectionable about Miss Bennet's behavior, Anne. She is propriety itself."

Elizabeth noted the stiffening of Miss de Bourgh's back. "I do not know what you see in that hoyden. I do not know why my mother insists on housing the Bennet sisters in such superior circumstances. They are naught but minor gentry, completely unsuited to mingling with those of us of a more exalted sphere."

"They may surprise you, Anne," replied Mr. Darcy, though in a voice so quiet Elizabeth was forced to strain to hear him. "The eldest Miss Bennets in particular are all that is good."

She was almost able to hear the frustrated grinding of Miss de Bourgh's teeth from where she stood by the door. What happened next was almost so fast that Elizabeth could not follow it. Miss de Bourgh stepped toward Darcy, and though there was nothing in her way, she feigned tripping over something, and Mr. Darcy, by reflex, reached out a hand to steady her. She caught his arm, and drew herself to him, attempting to wrap herself around his torso and cling onto him. At the same time, she said in a seductive sort of voice:

"Oh, Fitzwilliam, I thought we would never be alone like this together. I believe we must marry, since you have compromised me so thoroughly."

But Mr. Darcy stepped back, causing her to lose her balance, and she threw out a hand to steady herself on the corner of a sofa. "I do not know of what you refer, Anne. I only steadied you when you stumbled. I have no more intention of proposing now than I had this morning."

"You must!" said Anne, though the purr had become more of a growl. "Our reputations shall both be ruined if you do not. We are alone. *Alone!* It is the very definition of compromise!"

Though Elizabeth was bursting with the need to laugh at this ridiculous scene, she noted Mr. Darcy's pleading expression and took pity on him. She was sorely tempted otherwise, however.

"You are not alone, Miss de Bourgh."

Once again Elizabeth's composure was put to the test. At the sound of her voice, it seemed like Miss de Bourgh jumped three feet in the air, and she was reminded of a cat's propensity to land on its feet when Miss de Bourgh spun around to face her. When she saw who it was, her eyebrows furrowed in fury.

"You!" screeched she. "Why are you here spying on us?"

"I should think that is what you wished. Would you not wish for your 'compromise' to be published to every corner of Kent?"

"I could not trust *you* to do it," spat Miss de Bourgh. "You wish to have Darcy for yourself!"

"Whatever it is that I wish for, I believe I have more refinement than to feign stumbling on nothing more substantial than air in order to fling myself into the arms of a man who will not have me."

"You know nothing," said she. "Fitzwilliam, throw this upstart from the room, so that we may begin planning for our nuptials. We must marry."

"Do not be ridiculous," said Elizabeth. "There was no compromise, for I was here the whole time."

Surprised, Miss de Bourgh turned an accusing glare on Darcy. "You will not own to compromising me, yet you are in a room alone with this Jezebel and allow her to sink her talons into you?"

"The door was wide open the entire time," said Mr. Darcy.

His tone had taken on a particularly distant and emotionless quality, which Elizabeth remembered from when he had been in Hertfordshire the past year. In a flash of insight, she realized that it was how he protected himself from unwanted attention and those with whom he was not familiar. In that moment, she understood him better.

"In addition," continued Mr. Darcy, "the footman has been stationed outside the entire time and can testify that nothing improper happened." Then Mr. Darcy turned a stern eye on his cousin, which Miss de Bourgh returned with seeming composure, though Elizabeth thought she detected a hint of nervousness. "Really, Anne, if this is the best you can do to try to compromise me, then I have worried for no reason these past years. In matters such as this, you are nothing more than a babe in arms, when compared to scheming misses of London."

Offended, Miss de Bourgh pulled herself up to her diminutive height and scowled at her cousin. "You will see, Darcy. One day soon you will come to your senses and propose to me." Miss de Bourgh turned a sneer on Elizabeth. "In that day, I shall laugh at this pretender."

Then with a swish of her skirts, Miss de Bourgh turned and stalked from the room. For a moment, the two left behind were silent. But Elizabeth could not hold it for long, and soon she burst into laughter, and though Mr. Darcy appeared surprised, he joined her quickly.

"Did she truly feign a stumble and hurl herself into your arms to compromise you?" asked Elizabeth between her peals of mirth.

"I believe she did," replied Mr. Darcy. "It surprised me as much as it did you."

"Oh, I suspected she would eventually make the attempt," replied Elizabeth. "I am simply surprised at her utter lack of anything resembling style."

"Style?" asked Mr. Darcy. His tone suggested a certain incredulous surprise, but Elizabeth was too amused to reign in her wit.

"Surely you have seen much better attempts in London. Would not an affected faintness be much more convincing? Or perhaps she could wait until you are seated and throw herself on your lap. Or the invented assignation in your bedchamber — would not arranging a servant to find her there a moment after you have walked into the room be that much more damaging to your reputation?"

By the time Elizabeth finished speaking, Mr. Darcy was laughing openly. "I did not know you were so versed in such arts, Miss Bennet. Should I be more concerned with what *you* might do rather than my cousin?"

"Oh, I think not," said Elizabeth, breezily waving his words aside. "I shall not make the attempt to entrap you." She paused and threw him a devilish smile. "But I can assure you that should I decide to do so, I would do it with much more panache than your cousin just showed. I can also promise that if I did, I would be successful."

Still chuckling, Mr. Darcy shook his head. "I dare say you would be, Miss Bennet. I have no doubt that you could do anything to which you put your mind.

"Now, I believe you were about to prove yourself incorrect about a certain disagreement we just had. Have you found the incriminating evidence, or were you holding that book in case you needed to defend my virtue by beating my cousin back with it?"

Elizabeth scowled at him. "It is, indeed, the book, and I shall prove you incorrect. But I would not use anything so clumsy as a book, when there is a fire poker easily at hand."

Had anyone been walking by the library at that moment, Elizabeth was certain they would have wondered at the laughter the two shared. She decided she would not concern herself for it. Miss de Bourgh's performance was comical, and Elizabeth did so love to laugh. She was coming to know Mr. Darcy all that much better, and if it took Miss de Bourgh's poorly conceived compromise attempts to speed things along, Elizabeth was quite willing to thwart them every day she stayed in Kent.

"She did what?" exclaimed Lady Catherine.

"As bold as brass," confirmed her nephew, "though perhaps the execution was more than a little clumsy. Miss Elizabeth and I laughed long about it."

There was a certain . . . something in Darcy's expression when he spoke of Miss Elizabeth. Lady Catherine could not quite put a name to it, but there was a tenderness and depth of regard that sent a thrill of satisfaction through her, even as her indignation toward her own daughter consumed her. Eventually, indignation won out, though she would own to more than a little smugness if pressed.

"I do not know what to do with her, Darcy. She does not listen to me and proclaims she knows exactly how it will be at any hint of dissent."

Darcy shrugged. "If her attempts continue to be this poorly conceived, then I have no doubt I have nothing to fear."

But Lady Catherine only harrumphed. "Perhaps that is so, though she should not even be making the attempt. She is . . ." Lady Catherine paused and sighed. "You are aware that she is a bit of a disappointment to me. I had hoped to bring her up as a credit to her namesake, your dearly departed mother. But she has grown more headstrong as she has grown older, and she listens to nothing I say. She would obey her father when he was still alive, but she is almost ungovernable since he was taken from us."

"Do not concern yourself, Lady Catherine," said Darcy. "I can handle her."

Lady Catherine looked at him warmly. He truly was a good man — the best of men, though the son of her dearest sister could hardly be anything else.

"If you were married, she would have no choice but to give up this hopeless dream," said Lady Catherine slyly.

"No doubt she would," replied Darcy. His tone was even, perhaps daring her to say something further, though whether he expected her to endorse Miss Elizabeth or make some comment urging him on, she was not certain. She chose the simple expedient of not doing as he expected.

"Then you had better get to it, do you not think?"

Anne pouted for the rest of the day and into the next, and Lady Catherine watched her daughter's performance with exasperation. Though she attempted to have a word with her concerning her behavior, Anne acted as if nothing untoward had happened and refused to confess to it, even when Lady Catherine told her of her sure knowledge. Eventually, she decided nothing was to be gained by continuing to harp on the matter, and she allowed it to drop, though she continued to watch her Anne closely.

Never had Elizabeth been so annoyed by her mother's matchmaking schemes. Though the woman was ostensibly living at the parsonage, she spent a large part of every day at Rosings, and it seemed like she had decided how everything would be and was determined to act upon it. Case in point, the day after the compromise attempt, Mrs. Bennet arrived at Rosings and promptly proceeded to cause further insanity.

Elizabeth was happy for Jane, for in the past few days she had noted definite signs of Colonel Fitzwilliam's interest in her elder sister. The man was jovial and open, but in some ways he was as guarded as Mr. Darcy. He joked and laughed and spoke, and Elizabeth was certain that at least some of his tales of his experiences contained a grain of truth, but his manner was always flippant and happy and betrayed little of the inner person.

But this would change when he was in Jane's company. Mr. Bingley had often been like a puppy, as he had hung onto Jane's every word and had often simply stared at her, seeming enchanted by her pretty face or the sound of her voice. Colonel Fitzwilliam did not show any of these tendencies, but after a little time, Elizabeth began to see that he paid her more of his attention, gave deference to her opinions, and there was a certain admiration in his looks which bespoke a man developing a regard for a woman.

On a certain day, they were gathered in Lady Catherine's sitting-room, speaking and having tea. Miss de Bourgh was sitting to one side, glaring crossly while Elizabeth spoke with Mr. Darcy, and the younger Bennets were off to the side speaking quietly with each other. Lydia and Kitty had taken the colonel's apparent defection with an unlooked-for measure of philosophy. They laughed at his stories and enjoyed his witty repartee, but Elizabeth wondered if they ever truly saw him as a soldier, as they had never seen him wearing his red coat.

Into this scene of domestic harmony came Mrs. Bennet. She was welcomed and invited to sit, and for some time she sat with Lady Catherine speaking in an animated fashion. When Lady Catherine was called from the room by the housekeeper, Mrs. Bennet looked over the assembled. It was easy to see that her mother was not happy with the way the party was seated.

"Jane!" said she in that high-pitched voice she used when she was agitated. "Shall you not come sit here closer to the fire? I do so worry for your health."

"It is quite warm, Mama," said Jane, looking at her mother, perplexed. Indeed, she was correct, as, though there was a fire, it was small and had largely burned itself out.

"You must take care of yourself," insisted Mrs. Bennet. "Come, I insist."

Jane had always given into her mother's whims, and though Elizabeth thought she might refuse this time, eventually she gave a longsuffering sigh and allowed herself to be guided to where her mother indicated. This, of course, was where Elizabeth was seated close to Mr. Darcy. Jane smiled apologetically when her mother insisted Elizabeth give up her seat, but Elizabeth only shook her head, for she knew it was not in Jane's nature to resist. Then, in a move so transparent there was no chance anyone could misunderstand, Mrs. Bennet moved Elizabeth back to where the colonel was watching with amusement.

"Your mother is singular, is she not?" asked he in a quiet voice when Elizabeth had taken her seat.

"You have no idea, sir," said Elizabeth.

Elizabeth made polite conversation with the colonel, noting that Jane was doing the same with Mr. Darcy, but she was heartened by the looks she saw pass between Jane and the colonel on several occasions. For herself, Elizabeth esteemed Colonel Fitzwilliam greatly, knowing him to be a good and amiable man. But she longed to return to her conversation with Mr. Darcy, though she knew her mother would not appreciate it if she attempted to resume her previous seat.

"My Jane is an excellent girl," said Mrs. Bennet, suddenly speaking over them all. "She is beautiful, of course, but she is also the most gentle, patient girl in all the land. Did you know that she was ill not long after you left Netherfield, Mr. Darcy?"

"No, I was not aware of that, Mrs. Bennet," said he, looking at Jane, who appeared more than a little embarrassed.

"Indeed, she was. She was invited to dine with Miss Bingley and her sister, and she fell ill, necessitating a stay of five days."

"I hope you are very much recovered, Miss Bennet," said Mr. Darcy. He appeared not to know what else to say.

"I am quite well, thank you," said Jane. "It was naught but a cold."

"She will deny it, but I tell you she suffered a vast deal," said Mrs. Bennet. "But then again she has such a sweet temperament that even those of us who know her best would never know she is suffering! Personally, I believe it was some great neglect by those artful Bingleys which caused her to become ill. I cannot imagine why they would come to the neighborhood for only a few months and then depart, never to return, leaving Netherfield as empty as it had been before they came."

By this point, Elizabeth wished that the earth could open up and swallow her to hide her mortification. She almost pointed out that her mother had forgotten how it was on her orders that Jane had gone on horseback, become soaked through, and as a result fallen ill. But there was nothing she could do about it. Her only consolation was that Colonel Fitzwilliam was listening to Mrs. Bennet's words, and he appeared to be very interested in them. Would that his interest would survive being confronted by such a silly relation!

What Elizabeth failed to see was another gentleman's interest in another quarter, though her sister saw it as clear as day. Jane was mortified by her mother's unguarded behavior, though she often was. The fact that her mother meant well was little consolation in times like these. But then Mrs. Bennet's focus changed, and she turned and addressed Colonel Fitzwilliam.

"And do you know that my Lizzy would not have anyone attend to her beloved elder sister? She insisted on going to Jane the next day, though Netherfield is three miles distant and the horses were not available, as only she could nurse her sister back to health. And she sat with Jane, night and day for the whole of those five days, patiently tending to her, making her comfortable as best she could."

"Did she?" asked Colonel Fitzwilliam. He turned to Elizabeth, and

Jane was forced to stifle her laughter when he winked at Elizabeth. "That is very generous of you, Miss Elizabeth. Some young ladies would concern themselves with becoming ill themselves, but according to your mother you took no thought to your own safety."

"I cannot imagine that anyone would do less for a dear sister," replied Elizabeth.

Perhaps Elizabeth did not think so, but it seemed like there was at least one in the room who was impressed with this recitation of Elizabeth's intrepidity. Mr. Darcy was watching the scene with interest, and his gaze upon Elizabeth, unless Jane missed her guess, was filled with admiration.

"Yes, they are the best of girls," continued Mrs. Bennet, oblivious to the question of who was more impressed by the praises she was heaping on her daughters. "They are a great comfort to me and assist me a vast deal. Both can manage a house of any size and complexity, both care for our tenants, and both are devoted to family and friends. A man could do much worse with either of them as a wife."

Curiously, Jane felt much the same as her sister had only moments before, though she could not know it. But then Jane happened to look up at Colonel Fitzwilliam to see him gazing at her with admiration. And all her embarrassment and hesitation drained way, leaving only happiness in its wake. Mr. Bingley had made her feel flattered with his single-minded devotion, but Colonel Fitzwilliam's attentions were much more . . . mature in nature. With him, she felt valued and cherished, rather than just an object to be worshipped. Perhaps nothing would come of his attentions, but she was already certain that she wished for them. She wished for the more than she ever had from Mr. Bingley.

When Lady Catherine returned to the room, she noted that the seating arrangement had been changed. Whereas before it had been perfect, now the couples were in the wrong places, and she could not fathom how it had been brought about. She knew her nephews as well as her own daughter; surely Darcy had not taken an interest in Miss Bennet, nor Fitzwilliam, in Miss Elizabeth!

"I flatter myself in saying that I doubt there is a mother in all England who can boast two such handsome daughters. Do you not agree Mr. Darcy?"

"They are pretty girls, indeed," replied Darcy.

Lady Catherine looked on the scene critically, and as she watched, she became certain that the author of the change in arrangement had been perpetrated by Mrs. Bennet. What Lady Catherine could not fathom was exactly why the woman had seen fit to make the alterations.

Determined to watch what was happening so she might understand how to repair it, Lady Catherine sat down in her normal chair and kept a close eye on Mrs. Bennet. But whatever the woman was thinking, Lady Catherine could make no sense of it, for she continued to blather on about this and that, mostly concerning her daughters' unique qualifications to be the wives of men of fortune. Why she felt the need to say such things was quite beyond Lady Catherine's ability to understand. By her reckoning, Darcy and Fitzwilliam were already aware of the charms of the Miss Bennets! There was little more to be done than to smooth out some of the rough patches that may inevitably arise.

When the company finally separated after tea, Lady Catherine had all the satisfaction of seeing that the couples once again moved toward each other, though Mrs. Bennet did not seem to understand what was happening. In fact, she appeared akin to the cat who had gotten into the cream. Lady Catherine lamented that she had not more with which to work; Lady Catherine was fond of the woman, but sometimes she could be positively daft!

"Mrs. Bennet," said Lady Catherine once the others had all departed, "what happened? When I left the room, all was well, but when I returned, Elizabeth and Jane had changed seats."

"There is nothing of which to worry," said Mrs. Bennet. The dreamy smile on her face suggested that Mrs. Bennet had not even heard Lady Catherine's question. "Everything is proceeding exactly as planned."

Then Mrs. Bennet excused herself. "I must return to the parsonage, for your parson is dragging his heels, and I must push him along."

Lady Catherine watched her go, wondering yet again about Mrs. Bennet. Did the woman truly want Mr. Collins, of all people, as a son? Lady Catherine had thought of introducing him to one of the tenants' daughters, but she had stayed her hand, for she was not certain any girl she knew deserved to be pushed together with such a foolish man. And she was not at all certain that Mrs. Bennet's plan was identical to Lady Catherine's, but there was some piece of information she felt she was missing.

In the end, Lady Catherine put it out of her mind for the present. She could always question Mrs. Bennet if she was concerned the woman was about to make a fool out of herself. Besides, Lady

Catherine was certain that things were proceeding exactly as *she* had planned, and she doubted there was anything that could be done to change it now.

CHAPTER VIII

On Easter morning, the parties from Rosings and Hunsford met at the church for the Easter service. On this day, one of two days most holy to the Christian calendar, Elizabeth found it difficult to focus on what was being said.

The first part of that problem was, unsurprisingly, due to the person who was speaking them. In all, Elizabeth was satisfied with her relationship with Mr. Collins, for precisely the reason that there was little to be had. Mr. Collins came to Rosings almost daily to confer with Lady Catherine, but though he often came, Elizabeth found reasons to absent herself, whether it was by walking, staying in her room, spending time with her sisters or Mr. Darcy, or by simply leaving the room when the man arrived. Mr. Collins did not appear to repine the loss of her society.

But on that Easter morning, Mr. Collins's sermon was more ridiculous than ever before. The usual sermon on Easter was to talk about the rising of the Savior from the tomb, and the profound effect this event had on the world. But Mr. Collins, in his infinite wisdom, only spoke in a perfunctory manner about the Savior; rather, he reserved most of his remarks for an entirely different subject.

"And our Lord was entirely devoted to his duty," droned Mr.

Collins. The man's sermon making voice—though it was not all that different from his usual speaking voice—was entirely soporific, and Elizabeth was forced to fight to keep her eyes open and her mind from the oblivion of sleep. "Duty is a matter which must concern us all. There is duty to our God, duty to those above us in society, duty to our family. Let us not ever allow ourselves to fail in our duties, whatever they may be."

On and on the man went, expounding, exhorting, and at times almost begging, all on the subject of duty. He repeated himself over and over again, at times changing a word or two, revising the order, or simply restating word for word what he had already said. And the dissertation was so long that Elizabeth saw more than one member of the congregation nodding off from sheer fatigue, if not utter boredom.

Lady Catherine sat in her pew next to Elizabeth—Mr. Darcy sat on her other side—and Elizabeth could see that her ladyship was equally curious of Mr. Collins's choice of material. One glance at Miss de Bourgh, however, told Elizabeth that the woman was positively enjoying herself.

And it all became clear. Only a few days earlier, she had seen Miss de Bourgh standing with Mr. Collins in the entrance hall of the estate, after the man had finished speaking with his patroness. She had not considered it at the time, but the way Miss de Bourgh was preening and directing sly glances down the pew at Mr. Darcy—and less than subtle glares at Elizabeth—it was clear she had directed Mr. Collins to change the subject of his sermon.

Thus it went for some time, until Elizabeth thought she might simply sink into oblivion from the tedium, when a miracle occurred. Mr. Collins was restating something for what felt like the one hundredth time when Lady Catherine—her expression had gotten darker the longer the man rambled on—cleared her throat quite loudly. Mr. Collins fell silent and looked down at her, and noting her evident annoyance, he coughed, ran a hand under the white of his clerical collar, and brought his sermon to a close so quickly it was almost unseemly.

The assembled quickly dispersed—Elizabeth thought more eagerly than usual—and left the Rosings party outside the church speaking quietly. It was then that Elizabeth was treated to another spectacle involving Mr. Collins.

"I hope you enjoyed the sermon, Mr. Darcy," said the parson, stepping forward and confronting the man, though his form was a little hunched as usual. "I chose today's subject with the party at

Rosings in mind specifically."

Miss de Bourgh continued to beam, but Mr. Darcy only looked at the foolish man with something akin to contempt. "It was . . . curious, Mr. Collins. I attend Easter services every year and have done so many times in this very church. In all of them, however, the subject has been our Lord. Duty seems like a common enough subject that it may be spoken of on any Sunday."

"Perhaps you are correct, Mr. Darcy," said Mr. Collins, his darting glance at Miss de Bourgh confirming Elizabeth's earlier suspicion. "But I fancy I am inspired to know what is best for my congregation to hear on any Sunday, and I thought duty would be the most appropriate today."

It was clear that Mr. Darcy was not insensible to Mr. Collins's meaning, but at that moment Lady Catherine interjected into the conversation. "In the future, Mr. Collins, perhaps we should adhere to the usual practices of sermon making and speak of the subjects approved by the church?"

Though Mr. Collins could hardly have missed the displeasure in his patroness's tone, he only bowed and said: "Of course, your ladyship. Next Easter I am certain there will be no need to speak of duty. I flatter myself that my words today have planted a seed, one which will grow to bear beautiful fruit."

"Yes, Mr. Collins," said Lady Catherine, "you do flatter yourself."

The gentlemen nearby — particularly Colonel Fitzwilliam and Elizabeth's father — seemed to be choking on their tongues in an effort not to laugh, but somehow they managed it. For herself, if Elizabeth might have felt like laughing herself, had she not been quite annoyed with both Mr. Collins and Miss de Bourgh. Mr. Darcy only looked at Mr. Collins, much the same way that one might look at an ant when contemplating whether to step on it. The man himself just preened, not understanding his patroness's jibe.

"Now," continued Lady Catherine, "if you will all come along, we shall retire to Rosings."

"Of course, Lady Catherine!" exulted Mr. Collins. "Your ladyship is so kind to be continually thinking of us. I can imagine no greater privilege than to spend the day at Rosings, basking in the glory of your kind —"

The man would have continued in such a way all the way to Rosings, Elizabeth was certain, but he was silenced when Lady Catherine turned a glare on him. He dropped back and offered to escort Mary, who took his arm, though with a discernable lack of enthusiasm. Elizabeth had not seen her sister in several days; she wondered if Mary's interest in her suitor was waning as much as it seemed.

While Mr. Collins was thus engaged, Lady Catherine turned her attention back to those remaining. Elizabeth, standing beside Mr. Darcy as she was, noted the speculative look she bestowed on them all, and the nod she gave when everything was arranged to her satisfaction. Elizabeth suspected her ladyship of preferring her to pair with Mr. Darcy and Jane with Colonel Fitzwilliam, but as she was quite happy with the arrangement herself, Elizabeth did not make an issue of it.

They were just about to set out when her ladyship's attention was called by a tenant who was standing by the side of the path, and she turned to him and began speaking in hushed tones. Miss de Bourgh, who had been standing beside her mother, turned, and her eyes alighted on Mr. Darcy, a disturbing gleam shining from within. But before she could move, another decided to stamp her authority on the company.

"Jane, what are you doing?" Mrs. Bennet bustled up and grasped her arm, tugging her over to where Mr. Darcy and Elizabeth stood. "Mr. Darcy, if you would be so good as to escort Jane. She is not the walker that Lizzy is and will require your assistance."

"But, Mama, it is not far," gasped Jane.

"Nonsense, Jane. You will stay here and walk with Mr. Darcy."

The matter settled in her mind, Mrs. Bennet turned, and Elizabeth soon found herself the recipient of her mother's determination.

"Now, Lizzy, you will walk with Colonel Fitzwilliam." She all but dragged Elizabeth to the man and then simpered at him. "My Lizzy is an excellent walker. I am certain a military man such as yourself will find her exuberance charming."

Then Mrs. Bennet returned to her husband's side, her smugness covering her like an umbrella. Mr. Bennet, for his part, was watching the display and smirking, looking like he had never had so much fun in his life. At that moment, Elizabeth almost hated her father.

"Now, Anne," said Lady Catherine, her conference at an end, "shall we lead our guests back to Rosings?"

It was then that Lady Catherine seemed to notice that the situation was not as she left it. She seemed to decide there was nothing she could do, so she began to walk with her daughter, though Miss de Bourgh looked longingly back at where Jane was being escorted by Mr. Darcy.

"Tell me, Miss Elizabeth," said the colonel in a low tone when they had walked for some minutes. "Is my arm somehow insufficient for Miss Bennet's support? She has never complained about it before."

"Only the very best for my dearest sister, Colonel Fitzwilliam," said Elizabeth, arching an eyebrow at him. "At least in mother's eyes, there can be no compromise when it comes to Jane."

"Ah, cut to the quick!" said Colonel Fitzwilliam, putting a hand over his heart. "To think that I am merely second best. How shall I ever bear the shame?"

"Lizzy!" Elizabeth cringed at the sound of her mother's shriek. "Do not carry on with your impertinent ways! You are offending the colonel."

Colonel Fitzwilliam winked at Elizabeth, and he stopped and waited for Mr. Darcy and Jane, who were walking behind, to draw close. "Indeed, you are correct, Mrs. Bennet. I am offended. I am offended to be considered less than sufficient to escort your eldest daughter.

"But I am determined to improve myself, to show you that I am quite as capable as my cousin. And as Miss Elizabeth assures me that there is nothing lacking in me, I must insist on escorting Miss Bennet."

And stepping forward, the colonel offered his arm to Jane, which she took readily, though not without an apologetic look at Mr. Darcy. Elizabeth only glared at the colonel, knowing that her mother would interpret the scene as her offending the man. But before she could say anything, Mr. Darcy stepped forward and offered Elizabeth *his* arm, which she willingly accepted. They started off again, following Colonel Fitzwilliam. From behind her, Elizabeth heard what sounded suspiciously like a snort of laughter from her father, and her mother's huff of displeasure.

"Miss Elizabeth," said Mr. Darcy as they walked. "Is it naught but my imagination, or does your mother seem to be intent on pairing your sister with me and you with my cousin?"

"That would seem to be the case, Mr. Darcy," replied Elizabeth.

"How very unfortunate."

Elizabeth peered at him, wondering what he was saying. Mr. Darcy seemed to recognize, for he said: "It is just that I have no intention of allowing myself to be turned to Miss Bennet. She is a lovely woman, but I have no romantic interest in her."

"Oh?" asked Elizabeth. "Then I suppose Colonel Fitzwilliam will be vastly relieved by your confession."

"I am certain he already knows," replied Mr. Darcy. "I have made my preferences amply known."

Elizabeth colored but she stayed silent. It was not, after all, a declaration of any kind. But she could not help but feel warmed by it.

Luncheon was served soon after the party arrived at Rosings, and after, they separated for a time, each to his own preferred activity. Elizabeth walked out to the hedge maze in the back gardens and made her way to the center to think for a time, while the gentlemen retired to the billiard room—without Mr. Collins, of course. The parson stayed in Lady Catherine's sitting-room with Mary, and Mrs. Bennet and Lady Catherine sat in that same room chatting. Mr. Bennet retired to the library, and the younger girls went to their rooms, where they did whatever young ladies do when they have nothing to do on a Sunday afternoon.

Later that afternoon they all gathered back together once again, and it was there that they were all treated to a spectacle of Biblical proportions. Ennui had set in to a certain extent, and especially the younger girls were complaining for something to keep them occupied.

"Why do we not read one of Shakespeare's plays?" asked Lydia.

"Yes!" exclaimed Kitty, excitement coloring her voice. "We could read one of the comedies."

"Or perhaps Romeo and Juliet," suggested Lydia. Then she sighed. "It is so romantic that they love each other enough that each cannot live without the other."

"Yes, but who gets to play the star-crossed lovers who die in the end?" asked Mr. Darcy. Elizabeth shared a smile with him.

"How about Mr. Collins and Miss Elizabeth?" said Anne, not quite *sotto voce*.

Mr. Bennet raised his book to hide a chuckle, while Lady Catherine glared at her daughter with exasperation. For her part, Elizabeth only grinned at Miss de Bourgh's suggestion, prompting an even more sullen expression on the part of Miss de Bourgh.

"On the contrary," interjected Colonel Fitzwilliam, "we should read *A Midsummer Night's Dream*."

"At least you have your happy ending," replied Mr. Darcy. "But would you prefer the role of Lysander or Demetrius?"

"Either ends up with his lady love, so it would not matter," said the colonel. Elizabeth did not miss his steady gaze at Jane while he was speaking, and neither did Jane.

"But since Demetrius follows Lysander, intending to kill him, perhaps *A Midsummer Night's Dream* is not the best," said Elizabeth. The two gentlemen laughed, accompanied by Mr. Bennet's chuckle.

"Then what of *Much Ado About Nothing*?" asked Mr. Bennet.

"You would need to be Claudio and I would be Benedick," said Colonel Fitzwilliam, looking at his cousin.

Mr. Darcy frowned. "Why do you say that?"

"Because, old boy, I am further along than you are."

"I have been acquainted with the Bennets much longer than you have," replied Mr. Darcy.

"Perhaps, but you are still working your way through your feelings and the initial manner in which you met. I have no such reservations."

By this point Elizabeth was blushing fiercely, and she knew that Jane was in similar straits. Unfortunately, such literary references were not Mrs. Bennet's forte, and she broke in at exactly the wrong moment.

"You have no reservations, Colonel?"

"No, madam. None at all."

Mrs. Bennet stared at him, a slow smile slipping over her face. Mr. Bennet watched his wife, and Elizabeth was certain he was seeing the same thing as Elizabeth herself—Mrs. Bennet was quite mixed up as to who was paying court to whom. Unfortunately, Elizabeth's experience with her mother told her that she would not be easily persuaded to the right way of things

"Perhaps instead we should turn to opera," said Miss de Bourgh. "Then we could read *Così fan tutte*. I am certain the Miss Bennets would play the roles of Fiordiligi and Dorabella admirably."

"Anne!" snapped Lady Catherine, glaring at her daughter. All about the room, those who understood her reference were mimicking the lady's expression. Elizabeth was certain that her father was on the verge of castigating the woman, and her cousins appeared ready to throttle her.

"Do not say such things. Do you not recall that these people are our guests?"

Miss de Bourgh did not say anything in response, but her expression was mutinous as she looked away. Mr. Darcy, watching her as he was, appeared furious with her, though he did not speak directly to her to censure her.

"Perhaps it would be best to leave both play and opera alone," said he.

Lady Catherine eyed her daughter, and then turned her scrutiny to Mr. Darcy, before she nodded her head slowly. "I believe you may be correct, Darcy." She turned to Elizabeth. "Perhaps you would favor us with a few songs on the pianoforte, Miss Elizabeth?"

"Of course," said Elizabeth, "though I would not wish to excite your anticipation. You may have heard me from time to time these past days. I am not a proficient."

"What I heard sounded lovely," said Lady Catherine. Then she turned to Mary, who was eager at the suggestion that the pianoforte be opened. "I understand you play as well, Miss Mary. As I understand that your sister is not disposed to playing more than a few songs, perhaps you would allow her to play first, after which you may play to your heart's content."

For perhaps the first time in Elizabeth's memory, Mary did not immediately agree and hurry to the instrument. Instead, she paused for a moment and then said: "Your ladyship is too kind. I would be happy to play, but I will only play a few pieces like Elizabeth."

"That is acceptable," said Lady Catherine. She turned to Mr. Darcy as Elizabeth was rising, saying: "Perhaps you would care to turn the pages for Miss Elizabeth? Then when Miss Mary takes her turn, Mr. Collins may take up the office."

"Certainly," said Mr. Darcy.

At the same time, Mrs. Bennet gasped, clearly wishing she had thought of pairing Colonel Fitzwilliam with Elizabeth at the pianoforte. Elizabeth noted with amusement, as she looked through the music, that her mother glared at Lady Catherine, but the lady either did not notice, or took the simple expedient of ignoring her.

Within a few moments, Elizabeth, having chosen a piece of music she thought well within her capabilities, began to play. The music soothed as it washed over her, and though she thought she had suppressed her emotions well, she had been just as angry at Miss de Bourgh for her spiteful comment as any of the gentlemen. Focusing on the music allowed her to regain her composure and put the comment in perspective, namely that it was a tactless comment by a bitter and jealous woman.

As she played, she became ever more aware of Mr. Darcy's presence. The man was quick to turn the pages in the right places, proving that he was able to read the music, and she was allowed to play unimpeded. But the longer she sat next to him, the more aware she became of *him*. He was a large man, broad-shouldered, and as handsome as any man she had ever met, and he was doing her the singular honor of paying the most exquisite attention to her. Elizabeth was not certain what she felt for him at this stage of their acquaintance, but she knew she had never been indifferent to him. He had always provoked some response from her, negative in the beginning, but increasingly positive the longer she knew him. She could not imagine that it would not continue to become even more positive the longer they were acquainted.

"Miss Elizabeth," said he in a quiet voice when Elizabeth had begun her second song. "Please allow me to apologize for my cousin's mean-spirited words. I cannot tell you how mortified I was."

"Do not trouble yourself, Mr. Darcy," said Elizabeth. "I was not unaffected by them I confess, but *you* have nothing for which to apologize."

"Nothing I have done, of course. But her actions are motivated by jealousy as I am sure you know."

"Your aunt has mentioned something of it to me. I can hardly imagine a woman behaving in such a manner for the benefit of a man who does not favor her."

"And yet she does," replied Mr. Darcy. "I will be required to speak with her again, though the last time I did so it did not change anything. But I will not allow her to continue to insult you or your sister in such a way."

Elizabeth felt warmed all over by this new evidence of Mr. Darcy's regard. She turned to him and allowed her gaze to inform him of her returning regard. It was apparent that he received her message, for he smiled at her, and then reached up to turn the page yet again.

They sat thus until Elizabeth finished playing the second piece. When completed, she gracefully excused herself from the pianoforte, noting with some amusement that though Mary had refrained from imposing upon her hostess, she was still eager to play. Elizabeth squeezed her sister's hand as they neared each other, and stepped aside for Mary to go to the pianoforte.

When she turned, she was confronted by the sight of Mr. Collins, standing tall — though with that ever-present hunch in his shoulders — glaring at her. "It seems, Cousin that you still have not learned your place."

"Her place is secure, Mr. Collins," said Mr. Darcy, stepping forward to confront the man. "*You* should remember *yours*. Miss Elizabeth is a gentleman's daughter, and as her father is in the room and has not objected to anything she has done, there is nothing for you to say. Miss Mary is waiting for you at the pianoforte, sir. I suggest you attend her."

Then without waiting for Mr. Collins's response, Mr. Darcy grasped Elizabeth's elbow and directed her to their previous seats on the sofa. Elizabeth did not look back at the man, so it was unclear to her what his reaction was, but she found that she did not concern herself with his opinion. The man was a buffoon; if Mary was actually induced to accept him, she would pity her sister.

"You are far too modest," said Lady Catherine when they had taken their seats. "It seems to me that you are quite talented, Miss Elizabeth. You play with a feel for the music which is rarely seen, and from my unpracticed eye, it seems like you have a very good notion of fingering."

"Your ladyship is too kind. I believe if I took the trouble to practice more I would be able to display my talents to greater effect. Alas, there are always so many other activities calling me that I rarely practice as much as I should."

"That I can understand," said Lady Catherine with a laugh. "I am always flitting from one pastime to the next, for there are so many things I enjoy, and so much to be done. My sister was a delightful performer."

Their attention was caught at that moment when Mary stumbled a little over the notes. Though Elizabeth had often thought Mary's playing was a little pedantic, she was technically proficient, and such a stumble was noteworthy. On the heels of this misstep, Elizabeth could hear her hiss: "Turn the page now, Mr. Collins!"

A quick glance at the pianoforte showed Mr. Collins clumsily turning the page, bumping into Mary as he did so, causing her to stumble again. "Only one!"

"A thousand apologies, my dear Cousin," came the tones of Mr. Collins. He reached across again, to turn the page back, and almost knocked her from the bench.

Mary glared at him. "Thank you, Mr. Collins, I believe I will handle the pages myself. You may return to the sofa."

Though he made some attempt to protest, Mr. Collins's words died on his tongue, and he stood, bowed, and returned to where the rest of them were sitting. Mary continued playing, and her efforts were much more creditable without Mr. Collins upsetting her balance. The man's distraction was soon revealed, for as soon as he took his seat, his gaze fell upon Elizabeth and lingered on her. It was clear he was not happy. It was also clear that his attention had been fixed on her while he sat beside Mary, and that was at least part of the reason why he had bumbled so.

"I see you practice much more diligently than your sister, Miss Mary," said Lady Catherine, ignoring the parson.

"Thank you, Lady Catherine," replied Mary. "I do enjoy practicing, though I think I would benefit from the instruction of a master."

"Perhaps you would, though I will say your playing is quite

pleasing. Maybe in the future you will be afforded the opportunity." Then Lady Catherine turned her attention to Mr. Darcy. "How does Georgiana get on, Darcy?"

"She practices constantly, Aunt, so in that at least she is superior to Miss Elizabeth." Mr. Darcy turned a tender smile on Elizabeth which quite took her breath away. "I believe she could do with some of Miss Elizabeth's feel for the music. She is improving in that respect, but I believe she would do better with an example."

"Surely your sister, who has had the advantage of masters and *practices diligently*, cannot be compared to my poor efforts!" exclaimed Elizabeth.

"Of course!" cried Mr. Collins. The sneer he directed at Elizabeth was followed by his spoken: "My poor cousin cannot hope to compete with a young woman of the superior breeding of Miss Darcy."

Mr. Darcy glared at the parson, and he subsided, though his dark look at Elizabeth never wavered. "No, in sheer execution, her abilities are superior to yours, Miss Elizabeth. But I believe your love of the music shines through in the way you express it. Your love of the music is evident every time you play. My sister, though she loves the music, has not quite learned how to express it yet. But she makes great strides, and I am certain she will become a wonderful performer as she matures."

"I am certain she will, Mr. Darcy," replied Elizabeth quietly.

"Write to her again and invite her," said Lady Catherine. "I would love to have her here with us, and I am certain she would benefit by an introduction to the Bennet sisters."

Miss de Bourgh snorted softly and Mr. Collins appeared as if he might almost contradict his patroness, but as both chose the benefits of discretion, Lady Catherine did not reprimand either. For her part, Elizabeth was touched at Mr. Darcy's praise. To declare her in some small way superior to his beloved little sister was a compliment Elizabeth could not ignore. There was something happening between them—something profound, and yet simple at the same time. It was still possible that nothing would come of it, but Elizabeth was rapidly coming to the conclusion that it would. And she could not wait to discover the fullness of whatever it was.

CHAPTER IX

*A*s matters between Darcy and Miss Elizabeth were becoming much more serious far more quickly than Darcy could ever have imagined, he determined to have an earnest conversation with her, one which he felt was long overdue. There were a certain number of items which might stand between them, and he wished to have them settled so he could continue with his courting without worry.

Miss Elizabeth was, as he had always known, an avid walker, and rare was the day she could not be found on the grounds of Rosings, skipping through the fields or running the paths, walking and twirling under the canopy of trees which towered over the hills of Rosings. With the patchwork of shade and sun Darcy could almost confess that Rosings was the equal of Pemberley in beauty, at least in certain locations. Almost. Pemberley was his home, and without equal, after all.

It was in the last attitude that he found her, two days after Easter. He watched, leaning against a tree trunk as she approached, and saw her turn and twirl twice, her arms extended out as she spun around, joy evident in her every motion. Never had Darcy felt so affected by the sight of her.

And suddenly he knew it: he was in love with her. She had stolen his heart without trying, without realizing she had done it. There were still impediments within his own mind to any sort of union with her, but the fact that he loved her opened up so many possibilities that simply had not existed before. Darcy felt almost drunk with the headiness of the feeling of utter love and devotion.

When Miss Elizabeth stopped spinning and turned toward the path again, she caught sight of him. Her eyes widened, and her cheeks turned the color of ripe strawberries.

"Oh!" exclaimed she. "I did not know you were here, sir."

"That much is evident," replied he. He stepped away from his tree and approached her, noting with pleasure that her eyes never left his. "I am very glad you did not notice me."

The skin between her perfect eyebrows creased, and she looked at him, the question written upon her brow.

"Why, if you had seen me, you would not have danced with such abandon. I was treated to a sight that I will not soon forget — the dance of a wood sprite."

"Is a wood sprite not a mischievous creature?" asked she, an impudent challenge in her tone.

"I believe I have prior knowledge of that," replied Darcy dryly. "As mischievous as can be, I would say. If you are amenable, this humble man would dearly love to walk with the wood sprite. Do you think she can endure his poor mortal person for a time?"

"Mortals are the bane of all faery creatures, Mr. Darcy," replied Miss Elizabeth. "I should fly away, lest you capture me, turn me into a novelty for all to see."

"Never, Miss Elizabeth. You are far too precious."

She flushed again, but she shyly nodded and took the arm he extended to her. They walked some distance down the path she had been traveling, Darcy too moved to speak, while Miss Elizabeth, he thought, was deep in her own thoughts. For a time, the silence was soothing, a calmness after a storm, or perhaps a quiet pause from the hectic pace of life. Her presence more than admirably filled any silence, rendering words unnecessary.

At length, however, Darcy, knew he needed to set such whimsies aside, and when they arrived in a small clearing where the path skirted the edge, he stopped and turned to face her.

"Miss Elizabeth, I believe I owe you an apology."

"Oh?" asked she. Her position at the edge of the clearing was such that the morning sun shone through branches of the trees above, painting her in dappled rays of sunlight and shade. She looked uncommonly pretty there, surrounded by nature where she belonged. If creatures such as sprites and nymphs existed, Darcy was certain she would be their queen, a veritable Titiana, to draw the love of mortal and immortal alike.

"Yes," replied Darcy, reminding himself of what he meant to say with difficulty. "For you see, when I reflect upon those few weeks I spent in Hertfordshire, I am convinced that my behavior was not the best. In particular, I recall a night soon after our arrival in which we attended a local assembly. I was not in the best humor that evening, and I did not put myself forward to dance with the ladies there. In particular, I remember grievously insulting a young woman who was in the unfortunate position of being the one singled out by Bingley's nagging."

Miss Elizabeth giggled. "He *was* nagging, was he not?"

"Always," replied Darcy with a grin. "I have no defense. I apologize unreservedly for those words and beg your forgiveness."

"It is forgotten, Mr. Darcy. It was forgotten long ago."

"That is a testament of your generosity, Miss Elizabeth, not my behavior."

Once again the woman enthralled him with her enchanting laugh. "Perhaps not quite so generous, sir. I related the event with great relish to my friend, Miss Lucas, and I will own that I was quite offended for some time. Hindsight, however, informed me that there was nothing to resent. Even if a man espoused such an opinion, what was it to me?"

"Again, evidence of your charity, Miss Elizabeth. Furthermore, you have my apology for my subsequent behavior. I was determined to be displeased by all and I was. But further reflection has informed me of the inadequacy of my displeasure. Have I not often decried London as a den of vipers, preferred country society to the debauchery found in those of so-called high society? Meryton is not so different from the society near my own home. I had simply forgotten it; wilfully forgotten it."

"As I said, sir, I have no injuries to resent. For my part, you are forgiven wholeheartedly, if you feel you require absolution. Let us think of it no longer."

"Thank you."

They turned and began to meander along the path around the clearing, and for a few moments, neither spoke. Darcy was contemplating the immense pleasure a pair of beautiful dark eyes instilled in him. He could not guess as to Miss Elizabeth's thoughts, but a moment's scrutiny told him that her recollections were more serious than his own. Thus, when she finally spoke again, he was forewarned and knew she had something of import to discuss.

"I wished to ask you, Mr. Darcy. You see, I..." She paused, struggling to find the words.

"You may ask anything you wish, Miss Elizabeth. It seems to me that you have something important in mind."

Miss Elizabeth shook her head with more than a hint of annoyance, he thought. "Jane would be vexed with me, I am certain. But her temperament is so calm and accepting, and she always sees the best in others. I, on the other hand, are more apt to remember transgressions, particularly those against my dearest sister. I should learn to forgive as she does, but though I try, I still wish to have an explanation."

Though her manner of speaking was halting, Darcy quickly understood what she wished to ask. "You would like to know of Bingley?"

She turned to him with a rueful shake of her head. "I should have known you would see through me so quickly, Mr. Darcy. You are correct. Mr. Bingley stayed in Hertfordshire almost to the end of November, paid my sister exclusive attention, and then one day after a ball he hosted, where he danced with her three times, he left Netherfield without visiting anyone and taking leave. To Jane his sister dispatched a letter, indicating that they would not return, and suggesting that it was the wish of everyone in both families that he marry your younger sister. These are not the actions of a gentleman."

Darcy shook his head; he had known something of Bingley's departure from the neighborhood and had heard a few crowing statements from the man's vulture of a sister, but he had not heard the full account of what had happened, as Bingley had been taciturn about it when asked, a trait unusual in him.

"I wish I could take back your sister's pain, Miss Elizabeth. Given what you have told me, how Bingley and his family acted was wrong. I have no knowledge of the exact sequence of events, and I have seen Bingley since I left Netherfield but rarely. But I can tell you a little of his character."

Darcy guided Miss Elizabeth to a nearby log. After inspecting it to make certain it was sound, he seated her on it while he paced and thought of what he should tell her. Miss Elizabeth watched him, her earlier mirth forgotten in favor of the solemnity of their current subject. He was grateful that she waited patiently for him to begin to speak, as he did not wish to blurt something out which would make her opinion of Bingley even worse.

"I would not have you think that Bingley is a man who would toy with a woman's feelings lightly, Miss Elizabeth. He is not, though sometimes he may give the appearance of it."

"Then how would you describe his behavior?"

"He is yet full young," said Darcy, running a hand through his hair. "His eye is easily caught by a handsome woman, and he confuses feelings of infatuation for that of love. I cannot say to what extent his infatuation with your sister progressed, but I do not think he intended to lead your sister on. He is not callous."

"So, by your reckoning, Mr. Bingley is thoughtless rather than cruel."

Darcy winced. Unfortunately, Miss Elizabeth's assessment of his friend was far more accurate than he wished to confess. But the sight of her sitting there, her eyes intent upon him, her brow furrowed in thought, meant that Darcy could not, in any way, prevaricate. With this woman, he must always be entirely open. His chances with her depended on it.

"Though it pains me to own to it, I believe you are correct in this instance, Miss Elizabeth. I will say, however, that I do not think any of his previous paramours were injured by his defection. This instance with your sister was unfortunate, but he does not set out to deliberately injure the feelings of young gentlewomen."

Miss Elizabeth sighed and her countenance softened. "I would not have suspected him of it, Mr. Darcy, unless he is the finest actor ever seen. For my part, though I do not absolve Mr. Bingley of his actions which led to my sister's heartbreak, I do understand what you are telling me." Miss Elizabeth paused for a moment, then she looked again into his eyes. "His sisters, on the other hand . . ."

She left the question hanging, and Darcy had no trouble filling in what she had left blank. "They are an entirely different matter. Miss Bingley, as I am certain you understand, was no friend of your sister, though she may have deigned to show her some favor. She undoubtedly discerned her brother's interest quickly, and befriended her in order to learn something of her to keep her brother from making, in her mind, a disastrous proposal. Mrs. Hurst, while not so vicious as her sister, is cut from a similar cloth. I tolerate them for Bingley's sake, but I have little desire to be in their company."

"I was aware of their characters the first night we met," said Miss Elizabeth. "It is one of life's ironies, for though Miss Bingley may have twenty thousand pounds to her name, Jane is the daughter of a gentleman. In terms of nothing more than standing, a marriage to Jane would be a step up for Mr. Bingley."

"It is even more ironic that Miss Bingley prefers town and disdains the country," replied Darcy. "She has visited Pemberley — my estate — once, and she was full of praise for it from morning to night. But she decries the country as savage and longs for the sophistication of town."

Miss Elizabeth shook her head and Darcy agreed with her — what an absurd woman! "I suppose she does not realize that most estate owners spend the summer months at their estates. I would be equally unsurprised to know that she has not the least idea of the work the wife of an estate owner must do with the servants, tenants, and all others who depend on the estate."

"The estate, and the monies it generates, are nothing more than a means for her to hold extravagant parties," said Darcy with a snort.

"I do not wish to further tear down Miss Bingley's character," said Miss Elizabeth. "But I feel you should know that Miss Bingley, in her final letter to Jane, intimated that there was an *expectation* of marriage between her brother and your sister."

Darcy frowned. "I will own that I have considered such a possibility, but even if it could come to pass, it would not be for several years now. Georgiana is only sixteen and very shy. *If* she loved him and he, her, I would give my blessing to such a marriage, but it would be on the condition that Miss Bingley not live with them if she is unmarried. Georgiana is not possessed of a forceful personality, and you are aware of Bingley's character. Miss Bingley would rule them should she live with them.

"Regardless, I have certainly *never* spoken with Miss Bingley about such a thing, nor would I, knowing how she would publish it far and wide. I believe I will need to speak with her and let her know in no uncertain terms that she is to hold her tongue." Darcy smiled tightly. "The Bingleys' status in London is due, in a large part, to my friendship with him. Though she does not like to acknowledge it, the withdrawal of my support would be devastating to her social ambitions. If I word it correctly, she would agree with any strictures I set out without hesitation."

"Especially since she wishes to be mistress of your estate," said Miss Elizabeth, a laughing undertone in her voice.

"Exactly," said Darcy, though with rolled eyes.

"But enough talk of Miss Bingley. Shall we?" Darcy gestured back toward the path, and when Miss Elizabeth nodded, he helped her up from the log on which she sat, and they began to walk again.

"Thank you for being so open, Mr. Darcy," said she. "I know it could be construed as none of my business. I appreciate your willingness to inform me of all these things."

"As it pertains to your sister, I do not think I could reasonably make the case it does not concern you." Darcy paused, thinking, before he once again said: "I hope you do not think ill of Bingley based on what I have said. He *is* an amiable man, and I count him among the best of my friends. But he is not perfect. I believe with maturity will come a more stable character."

"I have long suspected this of Mr. Bingley, so your recitation does not change my opinion. I will endeavor to consider him the amiable man we knew in Hertfordshire."

"Thank you," relied Darcy.

They continued their walk for some time, meandering through the woods, speaking of nothing of consequence. Darcy spoke to her of some of his movements since his departure from Hertfordshire in the autumn, mentioning his time with his sister, his Christmas visit with his uncle and aunt, and his subsequent return to London for the season. Her laughter, when he told her of some of the events he had attended, soothed his soul, and he soon understood that this woman, though she was comfortable in any kind of society, did not crave it. She was perfect for a man such as he, who *did* struggle in society. She could not be any more perfect for him than she was now.

In turn, she told him some little anecdotes of Meryton, of some of the people with whom he was acquainted. She was often playful in her descriptions, but she was so droll, her tone so affectionate, that there was no possibility of taking offense to her sometimes irreverent accounts. It was quite literally the most delightful time he had ever spent with a woman.

When they returned to the house, it was to the sight of an obviously angry Anne de Bourgh staring at them. She was tapping her foot with impatience, arms akimbo, and an expression on her face that could have curdled fresh milk.

"It seems, Miss Elizabeth, I must speak to you again about your behavior toward my intended" said she before Darcy or Elizabeth could speak. "Given your descent, I must attribute your highly forward and improper actions to your upbringing. Regardless, it stops now! You will leave Darcy alone!"

"You are quite mistaken if you think your childish demands will have any effect on *me*," replied Miss Elizabeth. Darcy was impressed all over again because of her confidence and determination not to be intimidated. "I have done nothing wrong. Perhaps you should turn your attention on some other man. If you should do so, you might wish to choose a man who is disposed toward you, if such a man exists."

The signs of an impending explosion were all there, and for a moment Darcy thought his cousin would fly at Miss Elizabeth with talons extended.

"Miss Elizabeth," said he, bowing to her and showing her with a grin that he was not upset with her, "perhaps you would be so good as to return to the sitting-room alone? I believe I must speak with my cousin."

Though Miss Elizabeth eyed Anne with more than a hint of contempt, she readily agreed and removed herself down the hall. Darcy watched her go, wondering what it would be like if she was never forced to leave him again. It was a heady thought, and one which he wished to explore to its fullest extent.

"I thought you would never come to your senses, Fitzwilliam," said Anne, breaking into his reverie. "Now, shall we repair to some other chamber where we may discuss our future together?"

Darcy turned to his cousin, filled with distaste for this task, which he had performed many times previously, but with negligible effect. "I believe where we are situated is quite sufficient for the task at hand."

The start of surprise from his cousin nearly prompted Darcy to roll his eyes. Even now, after all that had happened, all the many times he had told her, the disinclination for her company, and the attentions he was paying to Miss Elizabeth which were becoming ever more manifest, she could not understand. What was he to do to induce her to cease this objectionable behavior?

"I do not believe I wish to receive my proposal—finally—in the middle of a hallway near the entrance of my mother's house."

"Then you shall have your wish, for I will not propose.

Darcy began to pace, feeling the need to work off the excess energy which his anger at his cousin always produced. His only other option was strangling her, and Darcy did not think that would be acceptable.

"Anne, what can you be thinking of? Have I not told you repeatedly that I will not marry you? Why do you continue to hold to this doomed dream of yours?"

"My mother and yours agreed to our engagement when we were in our cradles," said Anne, her tone defensive.

"By the time *you* were in your cradle," said Darcy, his voice laced with sarcasm, "I was already riding my first pony."

"You are well aware of what I mean," snapped Anne. "When we were young, they planned our union. *I* was always meant to be the mistress of Pemberley *and* of Rosings, not some jumped up social climber."

"Enough, Anne!" growled Darcy. He stopped his pacing and stood directly in front of her, looking down on her, his affront almost beyond endurance. "You will not denigrate Miss Elizabeth. She is everything lovely and good, and I will not have her attacked."

"It seems I must censure her, as you will not!"

"Enough!" said Darcy, this time his voice descending into the lower registers. Anne started, and she stepped from him in alarm. Though Darcy should have been ashamed with himself for using his physical size to intimidate her, he found he could not. The woman was pushing him beyond all endurance!

"Our mothers' conversations were nothing more than idle speculations. My mother informed *me* of this, as has yours, and I have it on good authority that your mother also spoke with *you*."

"It was *not* idle speculation!" screeched Anne. She stamped her foot in annoyance, and with her diminutive size, it made her seem like a spoiled child.

"Are there any marriage articles signed?" asked Darcy. That brought her up short, and she looked at him with astonishment. "Did my father and yours draft our nuptial agreements? If they did, I have not seen them."

"It was our mothers' agreement."

"No, it was not! And even if it was, our *fathers* needed to ratify it to make it binding, and they needed to do so in writing. Even if it was, as you say, a tacit agreement between our mothers, neither one of us is in any way bound so long as it was not committed to paper by a solicitor.

"Heed me now, Anne, for this is the last time I shall ever repeat myself. I will not marry you. I am not bound to marry you. We do not suit, and I have no wish to have you as a wife."

"But you will have Rosings too! We will be among the richest families in all of England."

"That is nothing to me. I am not interested in owning Rosings. Find some other man who wishes to marry you. You should have no difficulty with this estate as your dowry."

With those words, Darcy turned on his heel and stalked away from her. He was not fit to join the others in the sitting-room, much though he wished to be in Miss Elizabeth's presence again, so he took himself to the billiard room to allow his emotions to cool. The clacking of the balls as he rapped them against one another was satisfying for a man who was on the verge of doing violence.

CHAPTER X

$\mathcal{L}$ady Catherine was uncertain where she had gone wrong and what she had done to deserve such an exasperating daughter. Despite her not knowing, there was no doubt she had one.

Though she had thought to enjoy a quiet morning in her rooms, her solitude was interrupted by the entrance of her only daughter and by the mottled hue of her countenance—her complexion often suffered when she was terribly angry—something had happened to infuriate her.

"Mama!" exclaimed she. "I must insist that the Bennets be thrown from the house this instant!"

"Oh, Anne," said Lady Catherine, wearily rubbing her temples, "what is it now?"

"Miss Elizabeth is determined to have Darcy! They were walking the grounds all morning together. She is using her arts and allurements to capture him. I know it!"

"I do not believe she intends any such thing, Anne. If there is any chasing being done, it is all on Darcy's part."

"No! I will not allow it!"

"There is nothing you can do, Anne," snapped Lady Catherine. "A man has a choice, and you know Darcy likes to have his way as much as any man. He will not be forced into marriage, as your antics from last week should have told you. Why do you want a man who does not want you in turn?"

"Because it will elevate us to the very highest levels of society."

"You do not even know what constitutes the highest levels of society. And if you did, you would not wish to go there."

"We will be one of the most powerful families in the kingdom."

It was all Lady Catherine could do not to sigh at her recalcitrant daughter. She beckoned for her to sit on the sofa beside her, which Anne did, though her mutinous glare never wavered.

"There is more to life than riches and status, Anne. If that is all that mattered, you might not exist."

Anne was suspicious. "Of what are you speaking?"

"You do not think I had other options when I married your father? I married him because we shared a mutual attraction and an honest affection with each other. But he was not the match your grandfather wished for. I *am* the daughter of an earl, after all, and I might have married one of equal status, had I chosen to do so.

"For that matter, neither of my father's daughters married as high as he wished. The Darcys, for all their wealth and their respected name, are *not* nobility, and your grandfather felt we could do better. But he gave his blessing because he knew we both wished it. You should think about that when you fix on Darcy as a marriage partner against his will. He *does* have a choice. He and you do not share the same ambitions. He is perfectly indifferent to status and power. Perhaps, if these are things which will make you happy, you should search for them elsewhere."

For a moment, Lady Catherine thought she had reached her daughter, as Anne appeared introspective. But it was not long before she huffed loudly and rose to her feet.

"Darcy simply does not know what he wants. I am determined to teach him."

Then she turned on her heel and flounced from the room. Lady Catherine watched her go, wondering what else she could do. Perhaps nothing was to be done. Anne would need to discover for herself that she and Darcy did not suit, and perhaps more importantly, that Darcy would not be forced into anything.

But perhaps their conversation had not all been for naught. Though Anne had remained stubborn until the end, it seemed to Lady Catherine that she had at least been thoughtful about what she had been told. There might be a way to use it later, to make her understand.

For her part, Lady Catherine was delighted by how matters were progressing. Fitzwilliam had taken to Jane Bennet from the very start, and it seemed like the girl had been equally responsive to his overtures. It was well that she had already recovered from her disappointment with Mr. Bingley by the time Fitzwilliam had come, or it might have been more difficult to induce her to give her heart over to him. Fitzwilliam was as constant as the tide, and Lady Catherine knew that he would never break the young woman's heart.

As for Darcy and Miss Elizabeth, if they were walking this morning, it was just the latest instance of it, for Lady Catherine knew they had walked out together—or met somewhere along the way—several times. There still might be some impediments from Darcy's side that she would have to help him overcome, but, in the end, she thought the attraction would be too strong for any objections he might have. Her nephew would be very happy.

Though she was correct about Darcy and Miss Elizabeth's propensity to walk out together, Lady Catherine did not know the extent of their meetings in Rosings' woods. Though it began as a sort of purposeful coincidence, soon they had begun to walk out together rather than meeting when they were already out. The privacy suited them both very well, indeed. Not only were they left to their own devices without jealous cousins to interrupt them, but it also allowed them to come to know each other better very quickly.

Unfortunately, on one of their walks, this was soon to change. On a day when the weather was warm and the wind kissed their cheeks as they talked and laughed, they strayed too close to the parsonage and found themselves walking a path close to the edge of the woods. Though there did not seem to be anyone in evidence, they found out soon that they had been observed by someone they would both prefer not to see.

They continued on the path which led further back into the woods, talking and laughing among themselves as was their wont. And the discussion soon turned to Mrs. Bennet's peculiar behavior.

"Can I assume, Miss Elizabeth, that your mother has quite a different idea of who is courting whom?"

Miss Elizabeth rolled her eyes and she laughed. "Unfortunately, you do have the right of it, sir."

"But I do not understand," said Darcy, feeling quite out of his depth. "I have never shown a hint of interest in Miss Bennet, and Fitzwilliam, though he is friendly with all, has never given you any particular notice. Does she not see this?"

"You have to understand my mother, Mr. Darcy." Miss Elizabeth shook her head. "She sees what she wishes to see. You are the man of greater consequence, so naturally you would be drawn to her most beautiful daughter. As for myself—well, she sees that Colonel Fitzwilliam is an amiable man, so she sees me as a good match for him, as we are alike in temperament. To be honest, I am a little surprised that she did not attempt to direct Colonel Fitzwilliam to Lydia, as she quite considers her to be superior to any of her other daughters excepting Jane."

"Then I must think she is blind. You are easily the equal of your sister, Miss Elizabeth."

To Darcy's delight, Miss Elizabeth's cheeks colored with pleasure, and she peeked at him shyly from behind her long lashes. The fingers which grasped his arm flexed, and Darcy irrationally wished he could touch her more openly than was presently acceptable.

"I thank you, sir, though I must wonder if you require spectacles. Anyone can see that Jane is more beautiful than any of us by far."

"You may hold to that opinion. Mine is different."

Miss Elizabeth turned a shade darker, but she immediately shook off her embarrassment. "Regardless, that is the way my mother thinks. Jane and I both have attempted to tell her the true state of affairs, but she will not listen. It will take irrefutable proof before she will see what is truly happening."

"Then I hope it will happen soon. For I do not—"

"Mr. Darcy! Mr. Darcy!"

The sound of a voice calling his name interrupted what Darcy was saying, and he turned to see Mr. Collins hurrying toward them. The man was quite obviously not used to running, for he puffed and wheezed, pulling in great gulps of air, and expelling them with great force. The sound of his steps along the dirt path revealed his gait to be nothing more than the stagger his drunken swaying proclaimed it to be.

He was on them as quickly as he could manage, and though he evidently meant to say something as soon as he had stopped before them, his attempts to catch his breath rendered speech impossible.

"What is wrong, Mr. Collins?" asked Elizabeth, though her smirk suggested to Darcy that she knew exactly why the man had hurried to catch them. "Surely everything is well at the parsonage."

"Of course . . . it is, C-Cousin," wheezed Mr. Collins. "I m-merely saw . . . you walking, and . . . wished to j-join . . . you."

"How . . . polite of you, Mr. Collins," said Darcy, looking at his lady love with a question in his eye. Miss Elizabeth shook her head.

"Then, shall we t-take . . . this way together?" asked Mr. Collins, as he began to regain his breath.

"Surely you have other things with which you must occupy yourself," said Darcy, unwilling to relinquish this time with Miss Elizabeth to this loquacious toad.

"On the contrary, sir. I am q-quite at my leisure, for I have . . . completed those tasks . . . set before me this morning."

"Very well, sir," said Elizabeth. "We were just about to turn in the direction of Rosings."

"Excellent!" exclaimed Mr. Collins. "I have some business — "

Unfortunately for the parson, Elizabeth and Darcy both turned at that moment, and they began to walk together, neither caring if the parson followed them. As they walked, Darcy listened for the sound of Mr. Collins hurrying after them, and for a few moments there was silence.

"Do you think we surprised him enough that he will simply leave us be?" asked Darcy.

Miss Elizabeth laughed. "I think you may be giving him too much credit, Mr. Darcy. I should think that he will be along any moment now."

True to her prediction, they soon heard scurrying footsteps, and within moments Mr. Collins was walking behind them. Darcy attempted to take the simple expedient of ignoring the man and concentrating on Miss Elizabeth. Unfortunately, the intimacy of their walk together was lost, with the man voicing his officious nothings behind them.

"Do you know, Mr. Darcy, that I am considering the subject for my sermon this Sunday?"

"I imagine that is a subject which occupies you with great frequency, Mr. Collins," said Darcy, attempting to inform the man with his tone that he was not interested.

"Indeed, it is, for you see, I must give a sermon every week. I set apart a certain amount of time during the week to write my comments out, and though my sermons often proceed from the inspiration of the moment, I still take the time to write down some little elegant words which I can insert at any time."

"That is interesting, Mr. Collins. If you will allow me to give you a little advice?"

"Of course, sir! I would be happy to hear anything you have to say."

"Then my suggestion is to write your entire sermon, sir. As a graduate of university myself, and one to whom speaking does not come naturally, I always found that my remarks made more sense, were less repetitious, and were always received better than when I simply spoke without writing anything down."

"I see. Well . . . Perhaps . . ." It was clear that Mr. Collins was not certain if Darcy had just insulted him. Miss Elizabeth seemed to understand that his words had been part censure—Mr. Collins had shown no talent for sermon making, and his delivery might be improved should he write his remarks out in full—and part advice. Regardless, they were able to speak for several moments unimpeded, while Mr. Collins attempted to work it through in his mind.

At length, however, he seemed to realize that their conversation had continued without his input, and he took steps to rectify it. But the actions he took to insert himself into the conversation nearly provoked Darcy to throw him into the dirt.

It must be understood that Miss Elizabeth was a diminutive woman, smaller in both height and weight than any of her sisters, and that Mr. Collins was, in fact, a large man, one who was made even heavier by the distinct paunch he carried around his middle. The first indication Darcy had that the man meant to interrupt was when he heard Mr. Collins's heavy footsteps approach rapidly. Then Miss Elizabeth gasped as she was pushed aside roughly and she stumbled, though she quickly righted herself.

All of this happened in an instant, and Darcy turned to see Mr. Collins standing directly beside him where Miss Elizabeth had previously stood. To his side a little apart, Miss Elizabeth was turning back to the parson, her affront ablaze in her eyes. But where Darcy thought she might flay him with the sharp razor of her tongue, she caught Darcy's eye, and in an instant her countenance changed and she shook her head, amusement written upon her brow. She smiled at him to let him know that she was unhurt, and she took her place by Mr. Collins's side, but Darcy was not about to allow this incivility to go unchallenged.

"Now, as I was saying—"

"Mr. Collins." Mr. Collins stopped speaking, his eyes wide at the icy displeasure in Darcy's voice. "What do you mean by pushing Miss Bennet out of the way? Are you a parson, or are you nothing more than an abuser of women?"

"I am no such thing," said Mr. Collins, drawing himself up, though his height was still made unimpressive by the hunching of his shoulders. "I merely wished to speak with you more closely."

"A man, Mr. Collins, does not shove a small woman aside so that he may take her place. One day, on the unhappy day that Mr. Bennet passes on, you will be a gentleman yourself, and yet you show little understanding of what exactly constitutes gentlemanly behavior."

"I am a parson, one of a noble profession, sir."

"Mr. Collins," growled Darcy. "Do you not know who I am?"

Perhaps it was beneath him to use his standing and connection to Lady Catherine to intimidate Mr. Collins, but it achieved Darcy's objective. The man's shoulders hunched even more, and the defiance bled from his countenance. He looked down at the ground, and his skin assumed a whiter hue.

"A thousand apologies, sir, I—"

"I am not the one to whom you should apologize, Mr. Collins. But before you do, I will remind you of this." Darcy stepped up to Mr. Collins and looked down at him, his contempt rolling off him in waves. Mr. Collins seemed to sense this, as he hunched down even further, making himself seem even smaller. "You will not ever behave with such violence toward Miss Bennet, or any other woman again. Miss Bennet is a diminutive woman, and you are a very large man. You might have injured her with your unseemly haste to walk beside me."

"Yes . . . yes, of course, Mr. Darcy," babbled Mr. Collins. "A thousand apologies, sir. I assure you—"

"Miss Bennet is there," said Darcy, gesturing toward the young woman. For her part, Miss Elizabeth was watching the scene with wide eyes, and Darcy had noticed at least once where she had put her fist in her mouth to prevent herself from laughing out loud.

Though it was with great reluctance, Mr. Collins turned to Miss Elizabeth and said: "Of course. I apologize for my clumsiness, Cousin."

Such a perfunctory apology could do nothing but stoke Darcy's ire, but the sight of Miss Elizabeth shaking her head prevented him from depositing Mr. Collins in the dust beside the path, sorely though he was tempted.

"Very well. Shall we?"

And Darcy extended his arm to Miss Elizabeth, and she took it, her eyes dancing in her amusement, and they began walking down the path.

"But, Mr. Darcy," cried Mr. Collins. "I wished to speak with you."

"Then speak, sir," said Darcy. "You may do so from where you walk as easily as you could if you were walking beside me."

Mr. Collins huffed but did as he was told. The man did not seem to realize that Darcy had, in fact, insulted him, but that was not surprising, as he had little understanding of anything implied rather than stated in a forthright manner.

Needless to say, Mr. Collins followed them like a puppy follows its master, and they were not able to speak without his interruption for the entire remainder of their walk.

It was not long before Elizabeth had become vexed with her relations — or two of them in particular — and she began wishing she could just ship them back to Hertfordshire so she would be left in peace. Mr. Darcy's objectionable relation was ever-present as well, but she seemed to have decided to step back and observe, though she was often there, an adder ready to strike.

Elizabeth's mother and Mr. Collins were the main sources of Elizabeth's ire, of course, as it seemed one or the other of them was constantly interrupting when most inconvenient or taking her to task to enforce their own vision of how they felt matters should be. At times, it was both, though it *was* amusing to Elizabeth how their opinions contradicted each other.

The day after Mr. Collins interrupted her walk with Mr. Darcy, the Bennet sisters staying at Rosings visited the parsonage. Elizabeth would have cheerfully forgone the pleasure, knowing that two of the three biggest threats to her sanity were residing there, but she was not allowed to do so.

"Mr. Collins did invite us to Kent," said Jane. "We should pay our respects to him and to our parents."

Elizabeth almost hated Jane for her reasonable words. "I suppose you have the right of it. Then let us go and be done with it."

All four Bennet sisters set out that morning, and soon they arrived. They were welcomed in, and Mrs. Bennet cheerfully guided them into the parlor — she *was*, after all, nominally acting as mistress of the house — and plied them with refreshments. Underneath her seeming good humor, however, Elizabeth detected more than a hint of calculation. Elizabeth sighed; she knew her mother would attempt to take them aside and impose her views upon them.

When it happened, Elizabeth felt vindicated, though she was still exasperated with her mother. Using the pretext of wishing to speak with them about certain matters, Mrs. Bennet led them into the garden, and there she proceeded to have her say.

"Girls," said she, her arms crossed and her eyes narrowed, "I am quite distressed by the manner in which your courtships with Lady Catherine's nephews are *not* proceeding. Do you know that her ladyship supports marriages between my eldest daughters and her nephews?"

"You have spoken to Lady Catherine?" gasped Jane.

"Of course, I have," replied Mrs. Bennet, as if conspiring with the daughter of an earl to commit matchmaking was a common occurrence. "Her ladyship understands her nephews, and furthermore, she understands how my daughters have been brought up in such a way that they may grace the homes of any man.

"It is fortunate, indeed, that we have come to this place at such a time, for it relieved her ladyship of the burden of having to search for wives for her nephews. With my two eldest, most eligible girls at hand, she may assure herself that they shall provide everything her nephews require, and I may finally marry my daughters to worthy gentlemen."

Elizabeth listened, aghast at such unguarded words coming from her mother, and the look she exchanged with Jane conveyed the same meaning. *Is this really happening?*

"Mama," said Elizabeth, "surely her ladyship's wishes for her nephews cannot take precedence over her nephews' own desires."

"Of course, Mr. Darcy and Colonel Fitzwilliam have their own wishes," said Mrs. Bennet. "But you must put yourselves forward and ensure that their desires quickly become that which you have to offer. And yet, I do not see anything in your behavior which would suggest that you are capable of doing so."

"Mama—" said Jane, but she was interrupted yet again.

"No, Jane, I shall speak and you shall listen. Jane, Mr. Darcy is the richest man we have ever seen, and he can easily care for all of us should your father pass on. He wishes for a quiet, demure sort of girl, one who will lend elegance to his house and a companion to his sister. You must put yourself in his company more, ensure he sees you as the fulfillment of his desires.

"And you, Lizzy, have not paid the attention you should to Colonel Fitzwilliam. He is a man of the world, gregarious, happy, and intelligent. Though he is not so rich as Mr. Darcy, I have it on good authority that he owns an excellent estate, one which will give you a comfortable life. Though I will own that I cannot understand why, it is clear he wishes for an intelligent wife, one who is at ease in society and may entertain his soldier friends. And yet I have not seen you put yourself in his company. That must change, so he can see you as the companion of his dreams."

What followed was long, often nonsensical, and at times completely improper. Mrs. Bennet exhorted and cajoled, and when that did not seem to be enough, she commanded. They were instructed to use their wiles to capture the man Mrs. Bennet had determined they should capture, and if that failed, she almost hinted at compromise to achieve their goals. At times her suggestions were so ludicrous as to cause Jane to pale, and Elizabeth was forced to keep an iron grip on her composure lest she burst out laughing.

"Now," said Mrs. Bennet at length, "do you see what you need to do? Heaven knows that with Mary the focus of Mr. Collins's attentions, I do not have time to watch you all the time to give you instruction. You are intelligent girls; surely you will know what to do."

"Mama," said Elizabeth, "have you not noticed that Jane is often with Colonel Fitzwilliam, and that Mr. Darcy pays more attention to me?"

"I am aware of that," snapped Mrs. Bennet. "And I put the blame on you, Lizzy. If you would curtail your loose tongue when in Mr. Darcy's presence, perhaps he would direct his attention to Jane where he should."

"But, Mama," wailed Jane, "I do not wish for Mr. Darcy's attentions."

"Of course, you do! He is a wealthy man, so tall and handsome. What young lady would not wish for him to make love to her?"

"Now, girls, no more discussion. You will do as you are told."

And with that, Mrs. Bennet turned and walked back to the parsonage. As she left, Elizabeth could hear her muttering as she walked. "Oh, to be cursed with such disobliging daughters. A mother's work is never complete."

Completely drained, Elizabeth looked at Jane, and she could not help the snicker that escaped at the sight of Jane's confusion. When Jane turned to her, the sight of each other caused them both to descend into laughter.

"I have often thought Mama to be ridiculous," managed Elizabeth, "but she has outdone herself this time."

"What can she be thinking?" demanded Jane, though her own peals of mirth never ceased.

"I suppose we shall simply have to prove it to her. Now, shall we return to Rosings?"

Unfortunately for Elizabeth, the absurdity still had not run its course. They stepped toward the front door, intending to collect their sisters and return to Rosings, when Mr. Collins stepped around the corner. He spotted them and approached.

"My dear Cousin, I have been searching for you, as I wish to take this opportunity to correct your behavior. Cousin Jane, you may leave—I wish to speak to your sister alone."

"There is nothing you can say that I would not share with Jane anyway," said Elizabeth. She looked longingly at the gate, but after the events from the day before, she found herself a little wary of Mr. Collins, and deemed it prudent to at least allow him to have his say.

"Very well," said he. "If you wish your humiliation to be witnessed by another, I have no objection.

"I wished to speak to you, Cousin, about your actions, particularly those concerning Mr. Darcy. I understand some females consider themselves elegant and suffer from the affliction of reaching for more than they should, but I am distressed that one of my own cousins could behave in such a manner. It almost induces me to wish I had not invited you here, for I am forced into the mortifying position of bringing a temptress, one intent upon catching her ladyship's own nephew into her presence.

"The time has come for you to cease this objectionable campaign to turn Mr. Darcy's head away from his rightful bride, Miss Anne de Bourgh. They are engaged to each other, and have been from the very cradle, and your attempts to capture him are not only in defiance of all decency and decorum, but are also doomed to failure. For what man could possibly turn his back on such a wonderful creature as Miss de Bourgh for a young miss who does not even know her place? It is in every way unfathomable, and I do not doubt that you are doomed to failure and ridicule if you persist."

"*If* you feel I am doomed to failure," said Elizabeth, her tone scathing, "I wonder that you would take the trouble to speak to me now. Should you not simply allow me to meet my fate?"

"I would, if it did not reflect poorly on me."

Elizabeth shook her head. Speaking with the man was a waste of her time and energy, but his words demanded response.

"Mr. Darcy is not engaged to his cousin. I have heard of the matter from both Lady Catherine *and* Mr. Darcy. It is a dream in Miss de Bourgh's mind only."

"I fancy that I, having known Lady Catherine longer, and being privy to all her intimate concerns, know more of the matter than you do, Cousin." Mr. Collins turned his ugly countenance on her, his manner almost petulant, and he stated his demands. "You will stay away from Mr. Darcy."

Elizabeth shook her head. Mr. Collins was not to be reasoned with. So, she took the simple expedient of making a promise she knew was irrelevant in any case.

"I can promise you that *I* will not pursue Mr. Darcy, sir. There, is that good enough?"

Though Mr. Collins eyed her, suspicion oozing off him in waves, he nodded once, curtly. Elizabeth curtseyed and led her sister away from the odious man, collected Kitty and Lydia, and departed from the parsonage. She determined that she would not allow anyone to talk her into another visit.

"You are aware that you promised him nothing," observed Jane as they walked.

"Oh, yes, Jane. But Mr. Collins, though he clearly suspects I did not give him what he wanted, still has no idea of what I just told him. It matters little. Mr. Darcy will put him in his place, should he continue to be a problem."

Jane shook her head, but she did not say anything else. For Elizabeth, she wished to forget even the existence of such an odious creature as Mr. William Collins.

CHAPTER XI

As time wore on, Lady Catherine saw enough of the couples' interactions to know that her plans were bearing fruit, and she could not be happier about it. Not only would her favorite nephews have ladies they loved and respected, but they would be happy in their lives, and bring much happiness to those around them.

Anne was still a problem, though she had been much less overt about her objections since the day she had vowed to change Darcy's mind, Nonetheless, Lady Catherine did not for an instant think that her daughter had abandoned all hope of marrying her cousin. If Darcy and Miss Elizabeth were to marry, it would also have the benefit of forcing Anne to recognize that she and Darcy were not meant to be. Maybe then she would open herself to other possibilities.

An event of great significance happened in those days, one which Lady Catherine was waiting for, but had not pushed, determined, as she was, not to stamp her authority on any of the young people. They had stayed at her house for a month complete by this point, and still formality was a barrier which separated them. It was not surprising, then, that it was Miss Elizabeth who finally broke through.

As she had promised, Miss Elizabeth accompanied Lady Catherine on her visits to the tenants on occasion, and one such morning, a beautiful day in which the buzzing of insects could be heard, and the warmth of the sun warmed their cheeks, they walked back toward the house, as the tenant cottage had only been a short distance away.

"These woods are lovely, Lady Catherine," said Miss Elizabeth. "I believe you are quite fortunate in the location of your estate."

"It is lovely," replied Lady Catherine. "Anne and I used to sit in a clearing not far from the back of the house. Anne, my sister, of course." Lady Catherine paused, the melancholic ache of her sister's absence still affecting her after all these years.

"You were very close?"

"As close as you and Jane. She would be so proud of her children. They truly are the best parts of her and her husband."

Though she had not done so in many years, the thought of her departed sister brought up a well of longing in Lady Catherine's heart, and she felt a tear slip from her eye, to trickle down and leave a wet trail on her cheek.

"I cannot imagine losing Jane," said Miss Elizabeth, her voice subdued.

Lady Catherine smiled through watery eyes. "I hope you do not experience that pain for many more years."

"Oh, Lady Catherine," said Miss Elizabeth, throwing all caution to the wind and herself into Lady Catherine's arms. "I am sorry for your loss. You speak of her with such devotion that I feel like I know her."

"She would have approved of you, I am sure," replied Lady Catherine, her tears flowing now in earnest. "She wished for nothing more than for her children to be happy, and it is clear that you make Darcy very happy, indeed."

Shyness descended over Miss Elizabeth, and she pulled away, hugging her arms around herself as if to ward off a chill. "I did not think highly of him in the beginning."

"I believe you have already told me, dear girl," said Lady Catherine. "But it seems to me those feelings have changed."

"They have," replied Miss Elizabeth quietly. "He is so much more than I ever imagined. I—" She stopped, and then she gazed up at Lady Catherine shyly. "You approve?"

"How can you doubt it? I knew you would suit him from the moment I met you."

Miss Elizabeth laughed and she wagged her finger. "No matchmaking, if you please. If Mr. Darcy and I are to be together, we must find our way to each other."

"I would never dream of it," murmured Lady Catherine. It was true—she needed to do nothing else but watch events play out. Of course, it might be necessary to ease Darcy's concerns, but she did not truly see that as matchmaking so much as simply opening the boy's eyes. Fitzwilliam was the easy one—he was enamored of Miss Bennet, and he had enough experience in the army to know that the content of one's character was more important than one's descent. Darcy still clung to notions of marriage for standing and fortune, although those considerations were becoming weaker as Miss Elizabeth proved herself to be worth more than the price of rubies.

"I would be pleased if you would call me Elizabeth," said her companion. "Or even Lizzy. Tis what all my friends and family call me."

"Very well," said Lady Catherine, delighted that they had taken that step. "At present, it would not be proper, but sometime in the future, I hope you will be able to address me as 'Aunt Catherine.'"

Once again the girl colored and she turned shyly away. "Perhaps. We shall simply have to see."

Delighted as she was by the way the conversation had gone, Lady Catherine only agreed with her and led her back toward the house. She had never been more hopeful in her life that things would proceed exactly as she wished.

Of course, not all was proceeding as she had designed, but she decided with a philosophical bent that life was not perfect. Mrs. Bennet was a particularly exasperating factor those days. Lady Catherine attempted to tell the woman repeatedly that she was wrong in her expectations, but Mrs. Bennet would not listen. Had she any doubt as to the strength of the two couples' attachments, she might have been cross with Mrs. Bennet. But as they appeared to be playing their parts perfectly, she could simply look on Mrs. Bennet with amused tolerance, waiting patiently for the spectacle which would ensue when the woman learned the truth of the matter.

Or perhaps the courtships were not proceeding quite perfectly, as she found out. A few days after becoming closer with Elizabeth, Lady Catherine happened to be in the sitting-room alone when Darcy stepped inside. He surveyed it once, looking for Elizabeth, Lady Catherine thought, before bowing and turning to leave. Then he seemed to think twice of it, however, and he entered and sat nearby. Intent as she was upon his every expression, Lady Catherine thought he was a little pensive.

"My mother, Lady Catherine—" said he suddenly before breaking off, casting about for the words he wished to say.

"Yes, Darcy? You wished to ask me something about my sister?"

Darcy heaved a frustrated sigh and sat back on the sofa. "She died when I was young, so I was denied the opportunity to know her as an adult. I think—I believe I know what she wished for Georgiana and me, but I am not certain."

"Surely you are not on the verge of falling in with Anne's desires," said Lady Catherine in a teasing tone.

Though startled, Darcy soon made a face and shook his head vigorously. "No, I am not. I know mother did not wish for a marriage with Anne unless it was my own choice."

"No, she did not." Lady Catherine paused and laughed. "You know, I was always more forceful on the subject than she was. For a time, I quite had my heart set upon it. But your mother . . ."

For the second time that week Lady Catherine felt the emotions welling up within her.

"Your mother," continued she, and she could hear the roughness of emotion in her own voice, "though she was sweet and complying, possessed a stubborn streak without equal. She persuaded me that it was foolishness to attempt to dictate your lives.

"The answer to your question, Darcy, as that your mother wished for the best for you. She wished for you and Georgiana both to be happy—nothing more, and nothing less."

"Do you think . . ." Darcy paused, once again considering his words. He was such a careful, sober man; Lady Catherine was excessively fond of him. "Do you think mother would approve of Miss Elizabeth?"

"There, was it truly that difficult?" asked Lady Catherine.

"What do you mean?"

"Why, confessing your interest in her."

Darcy scowled, but Lady Catherine just waved him off. "It was obvious, Darcy, from the moment I saw you together.

"Yes, your mother would love Miss Elizabeth as if she were her own daughter. You need have no concerns on that score."

A nod, though distracted, was Darcy's answer, and for a moment he sat quietly. Lady Catherine once again allowed herself the luxury of losing herself in remembrances of her sister and the love they had shared.

"The earl will not approve," said Darcy, drawing Lady Catherine's attention back to him. "The last time I saw him, he spoke of strengthening some alliance or another in the House of Lords."

Lady Catherine only rolled her eyes. She was intimately acquainted with her brother's character.

"Hugh is full of himself—that is true. He might wish for an alliance by marriage, but he will never insist on it. In the end, he will accept what he cannot change, and I dare say that by the end he will love Elizabeth as much as the rest of us do."

Clearly bemused, Darcy turned to Lady Catherine and raised an eyebrow. "Love her like the rest of us do?"

"Indeed," said Lady Catherine. "You cannot think that I do not love the girl—she is as dear to me as my own daughter, and of late, far less aggravating."

A laugh escaped Darcy's lips, though he tried to hide it in favor of a censorious scowl.

"She is a breath of fresh air," continued Lady Catherine. "Yes, I am prodigiously fond of her. Jane, too, is everything that is good and delightful, though much quieter, as you know. I am fond of her as well, though I will own that Elizabeth has a special place in my heart. And even the younger girls, with a little guidance, will turn out to be good girls, I am certain." Lady Catherine paused, then grinned at Darcy. "I will own that Miss Lydia needs more than a *little* guidance."

"Guidance you plan to offer?"

"I already have been," said Lady Catherine with a shrug. "They will need some maturity before they can join society, and I will not allow them to embarrass you and Fitzwilliam. You will both be required to endure some scrutiny for your choice of wives; Kitty and Lydia will excite gossip and scandal the way they are now."

"True," said Darcy, apparently deep in thought. "But before you begin planning the weddings, I suggest you practice prudence. Nothing has been decided, and nothing may yet come of it."

"I am always prudent, dear boy," said Lady Catherine, rising to her feet. She brushed her hand across his cheek, a feather-like touch, before turning to leave the room. "I simply know what I have seen, and I am convinced that both you and Fitzwilliam will soon decide you are unable to live without your chosen Bennet sister."

With those impudent words, Lady Catherine departed from the room, leaving Darcy to himself. He supposed he should be annoyed with her. She had masterminded all this, he was certain. From the invitation to the Bennet sisters to stay at Rosings to skillfully maneuvering them into positions where they could be in each other's company, she had manipulated events to her liking. It was because the events were also to *his* liking that Darcy had not allowed his annoyance to be known. It had all worked to his benefit, after all.

Sighing, Darcy stood and looked about the room. He had been searching for Miss Elizabeth when he had come across his aunt. Perhaps he should now find her.

But before he could do anything more than stand, the door opened and the housekeeper entered and announced the arrival of Mr. Collins.

"Mr. Darcy," said he, with a low bow. "How fortunate it is that I have come across you."

"Mr. Collins," said Darcy. He was still cross with Collins for his clandestine attack on Miss Elizabeth and was not interested in bandying words with the man. He bowed to excuse himself.

"I will send the housekeeper to find Lady Catherine. If you will wait here a moment, I am certain she will come directly."

"I did come to speak with my patroness, but if you would, I have a few words to say to you.

"You see, Mr. Darcy," said he before Darcy could do more than direct a pointed glare at him, which he ignored, "I am aware of what has been happening under your aunt's roof, and I am certain that she is as distressed by the matter as I am myself. She has been all that is gracious and amiable to my family, and yet she has been repaid with treachery and dishonesty.

"I would not, of course, accuse you of any such devilry, Mr. Darcy. Indeed, I am aware of the lengths to which my cousin will go in order to achieve her aims and capture a wealthy man. I was almost inclined to pursue her as well, you understand. But I was able to withstand her siren call, and I am certain that you shall be able to do so as well, if you are presented with the right encouragement."

About the only thing Darcy was encouraged to do at this very moment was to pummel Mr. Collins until he begged for mercy.

"Mr. Collins," said Darcy, fighting for the control he knew Miss Elizabeth would wish him to exercise, "I will warn you not to speak to me or Miss Elizabeth on this matter again. I will not repeat myself."

Shocked, Mr. Collins made to interrupt, but Darcy held up a hand. The man subsided, however sullenly.

"It is none of your concern, Mr. Collins. I am my own man, and I will pursue the woman I see fit to pursue. As for Miss Elizabeth, her father is her guardian, and as such, you can have nothing to say. You have not only insulted her by attributing to her the worst of motives, but you have also insulted me, by suggesting I do not know my own mind. I will not hear another word of it from you."

Darcy turned on his heel and stalked from the room. To stay would be to give in to his desire to call the stupid man out.

The meddling was becoming a serious distraction, and though Elizabeth was determined to meet it all with good humor and patience, it had begun to wear on her. Her mother had been taking every opportunity to berate her daughters, instructing them on the best way to catch *her* chosen husband for each, and though Mr. Collins had nothing to say to Jane concerning her behavior, he was not much better when it came to Elizabeth. At least they did not live at Rosings. Miss de Bourgh, after a period of relative quiet, was once again her obnoxious self, inserting herself on Elizabeth's notice whenever she came near Mr. Darcy. Before long, Elizabeth was almost ready to scream out her frustration.

"Then let us depart the estate for a time," said Jane in her most reasonable tone. "I believe we could all use a distraction from the chaos which surrounds Rosings."

"Oh? And what would you suggest?" asked Elizabeth of her peacemaking sister.

"A picnic?" asked Jane. "If we arrange it so that it is only you, Mr. Darcy, Colonel Fitzwilliam, and me, we could obtain a much-needed rest from our troubles. We could go to a secluded spot and not have to worry about the interference of our relations."

Elizabeth chewed her lip, thinking about her sister's suggestion. "If we are not able to leave without Miss de Bourgh or Mr. Collins seeing us, we will be forced to endure their interference again."

"Yes, that is exactly it. If we ask Lady Catherine for assistance, I am certain she will be pleased to assist."

"I dare say she would!" said Elizabeth, remembering her conversation with the lady.

"Then with her ladyship's assistance, I am certain we can make our escape."

In the end, it was absurd how easy it was to slip away. Miss de Bourgh was detained by her companion by a trivial matter—Elizabeth did not even know what it was—and Mr. Collins was called in to a meeting with Lady Catherine. As the man would never gainsay his patroness, his absence was guaranteed. If Mrs. Bennet even knew of the outing, Elizabeth was certain she would approve, though not likely of the pairings. Lady Catherine was happy to assist as they had expected, and as Elizabeth and Jane were leaving the room, she could not allow them to leave without one final comment.

"I expect you both to return engaged, my dears."

Jane blushed and could not respond, but Elizabeth gathered her courage and said: "Should we be the ones doing the proposing, then?"

With a laugh, Lady Catherine waved them from the room. "Go. Enjoy yourselves. I will ensure no one can intrude upon your solitude."

And so they did. Mr. Darcy had chosen the location, a wooded area near a small stream, with wildflowers sprouting, their waving petals lending riot of colors to the scene. Each lady, with her chosen partner beside her, walked gaily along the path, and Elizabeth, in particular, swung her arms, joyful to be out of the oppressive atmosphere which seemed to have settled over Rosings of late, or at least whenever any of her tormentors were near.

"I see the sprite has again made an appearance," observed Mr. Darcy.

Elizabeth turned to him, noting the soft smile on his face, and she turned and skipped down the path. "One thing to remember about sprites, Mr. Darcy," said she over her shoulder. "You must catch them!"

Elizabeth heard Mr. Darcy's growl, followed by his footsteps. Laughing with abandon, Elizabeth raced ahead, daring the man to truly chase after her. She looked back to see him laughing along with her, and he did not seem to be chasing her with any true intention of catching her. But there was a gleam in his eye which suggested retribution when they were next together.

They all arrived at Mr. Darcy's chosen location only a few moments later, and they stood, each with their chosen companion, looking at the scene with interest.

"Is this not where Anne fell into the stream when we were children, Darcy?" asked Fitzwilliam.

"No, that was a little downriver from here," replied Mr. Darcy. Then he turned to Elizabeth and regarded her with mock severity. "Would your mother not consider your little exhibition to be less than ladylike?"

"My mother considers much of what I do to be unladylike," said Elizabeth with airy unconcern.

"I sometimes think that Mama is a little hard on my sister," said Jane, though timidly.

"She simply does not understand me," replied Elizabeth. She was a little uncomfortable with the conversation and wished to end it. "I am the daughter who is least like her and the one most likely to flout her instructions. She does not know what to make of me. Now, shall we eat our luncheon? I am starving."

This suggestion was agreed to by all, and for a few moments they busied themselves with preparing for their meal. The baskets which had been carried by the gentlemen were opened, and they produced two blankets which were spread upon the ground. Elizabeth and Jane emptied the baskets of their bounty and placed the food out in preparation for their enjoyment. Elizabeth looked at what they had brought, filled with appreciation for the thought which had been taken in selecting their meal. There were light sandwiches of all kinds, crispy fruits, cold meat, cheeses, and a carafe of wine for their consumption.

"I believe Lady Catherine took a hand in these preparations," said Elizabeth, directing an amused grin at Mr. Darcy. "If we had allowed you gentlemen to choose the menu, I believe Jane and I would have been forced to wait while you caught fish, skinned them, and cooked them over a campfire."

Colonel Fitzwilliam turned a lazy eye on his cousin. "Perhaps we should do that for our next outing."

Elizabeth laughed and wagged her finger at him. "Indeed, you shall not. If you wish to catch fish, then go to it, but I believe Jane and I will watch from a distance. No campfires, if you please."

"You take all the fun out of life, Miss Elizabeth," said he, showing her a pout.

"I merely do not wish to be near when fish are divested of their scales and other sundry slippery parts. It seems like a nasty business."

It was with animated discussion such as this that they ate their lunch, though there was far too much food for them to eat it all. Elizabeth had never felt so happy—perhaps it was the absence of the trouble with their relations or the contentment of the moment, but she felt almost like she was being lulled to sleep by the pleasure. Such moments had been too few lately, and she longed for uninterrupted time with Mr. Darcy.

To distract herself with such thoughts, Elizabeth turned to Colonel Fitzwilliam. "You have been here for some time, sir. Will you be required to return to your regiment soon?"

"You wish me gone, do you?" asked the colonel.

"Of course. I must protect my sister's sensibilities from you."

They all laughed, though Jane exclaimed: "Lizzy!"

The colonel, however, directed a tender look at Jane. "I believe, Miss Elizabeth, that I am quite ready to give up my commission. Though it has been on my mind for a time, recent events have made it almost a certainty."

Jane blushed, but Elizabeth only beamed at the man with pleasure. "By all means, sir. I believe we would all be relieved if you took up a much less dangerous profession."

"You do not know how truthfully you speak," said Colonel Fitzwilliam with a mournful frown. "These new recruits do not know one end of a rifle from the other. I am in far more danger from them than I would be from legions of the French!"

Again, they all laughed. Elizabeth found herself content. Her dearest sister would be cared for by a good man who would protect and love her. There was nothing more for her to wish.

"Shall we, perhaps, walk toward the river, Miss Elizabeth?" asked Mr. Darcy, pulling Elizabeth from her reverie. "I believe a walk would do me good after that excellent lunch."

"I should think so!" teased Elizabeth. "I believe you ate enough for any two men."

"It is nothing unusual," said Colonel Fitzwilliam with his usual insouciance. "I have never seen a man with as healthy an appetite as Darcy."

"You should not speak," said Jane in the teasing tone she sometimes used with Elizabeth. "I have it on good authority that you ate enough for *three* men."

They all laughed, though Colonel Fitzwilliam pouted at such a characterization. Elizabeth agreed with Mr. Darcy's suggestion, and she was helped to her feet. They wandered for some time, stopping near the river where Mr. Darcy cast smooth stones out onto the water, skipping them several times before they sank into the watery depths. Elizabeth tried her hand herself, laughingly managing a few skips of her own.

"It is much easier on a still pond," said Mr. Darcy. "Moving water skews the results of the throw, and this river is much too small to do skipping stones any real justice."

"Where did you learn to do it, Mr. Darcy?"

"My father showed me. There is a small lake in front of Pemberley which is perfect for a young boy to learn such essential skills." He grinned at her. "I hope to someday teach my own sons to skip stones."

Such a brazen suggestion should have caught Elizabeth by surprise, but she found that his attentions these past weeks, the laughter and happiness they had shared, had led to a greater understanding. She knew that Mr. Darcy would eventually propose to her, and she now knew what her answer would be. It was only a matter of time before it was resolved to their mutual satisfaction.

The sight of Mr. Darcy, standing in the shade of the large tree beside the stream, his wavy locks ruffled by the slight breeze touched something deep within Elizabeth, and she sighed and leaned back against the tree's large trunk. *This* was what true love was supposed to be: two lovers focused on nothing more than each other, worries and concerns far away, and the promise to love and cherish each other forever more. The cares of the world would inevitably intrude, but she knew she would have this moment, and many others like it to sustain herself in the years to come.

"What has prompted your sigh, Miss Elizabeth?" said Mr. Darcy. He approached her, his eyes never leaving hers, his hand braced against the tree above her head as he continued to study her.

"I was just thinking of how perfect this is." Elizabeth's hand sought out his, and they clasped their hands together, fitting together so perfectly that she had no idea of how she would ever let go. "It is a shame we are required to return to Rosings."

"Could we not simply stay here?"

A giggle escaped Elizabeth's lips. "Perhaps we could. But the night will undoubtedly be cold, and it might not be so much fun when our food is exhausted."

"There is always the stream. I am certain Fitzwilliam and I could feed us with nothing more than fish."

Elizabeth laughed and swatted his hand. "That still does not solve the problem of the cold nights."

Mr. Darcy echoed her sigh, an exaggerated show of regret at that. "Then there is nothing to be done. We shall have to return.

"But before we go . . ." Mr. Darcy's eyes dropped to Elizabeth's lips, and she felt a fluttering in her midsection. "I believe I should like to claim a kiss."

"How shocking!" murmured Elizabeth, unaccountably wishing he would get on with it. "I am a maiden, sir. Do you think I would allow just any man to kiss me?"

"Not any man, but I am sure you would allow me."

"I think you are —"

Mr. Darcy's head lowered and his lips brushed against hers, and Elizabeth suddenly could not remember whatever teasing remark she was just about to make. And then it did not matter; nothing did, except for the warmth of Mr. Darcy's lips on hers, the feeling of his breath fluttering on her cheek, and the deep musk of his cologne. Elizabeth was not quite sure how it happened, but soon her arms were around his neck, and she held him to herself tightly. It was long before they separated.

Back in the clearing, Jane and Colonel Fitzwilliam watched as Mr. Darcy and Elizabeth disappeared into the trees. Jane shook her head as she watched her sister with amusement. They were as different as two people could be, but there was no one in the world Jane loved more than Elizabeth. She truly was one of the most remarkable people Jane knew.

"You are very close to her."

Jane turned and smiled at the colonel. Well, perhaps there was now one she loved as much as Elizabeth, though her shyness urged her to hide it to protect herself. But Jane Bennet had learned something from her ill-fated romance with Mr. Bingley. She had always thought it improper for a woman to put herself forward, and to behave such as Miss Bingley had with Mr. Darcy would have been improper, indeed. But Charlotte Lucas had also been correct: a man might fancy himself in love but never act upon it if a woman did not encourage him. Jane did not intend to make the same mistake again.

"She is my dearest sister. She makes me laugh, and she lends me some of her confidence to make my own. I love her more than I can possibly say."

"It is clear she returns your devotion." The colonel grinned. "I do not doubt I would find myself called out if I should ever dare hurt you, and I am certain my life would be in grave danger should she set her sights on me."

Smiling, Jane nodded and said: "I dare say you are correct."

Feeling more than a little daring, Jane allowed herself to lean back against the tree which the colonel was already resting against. The moment her back touched his shoulder, he gathered her to him, his hand about her shoulders. Jane sighed—never had she felt more cherished than she did at this moment. But it was nothing compared to when the colonel turned her head and pressed his lips against hers.

All was right in the world. Jane knew she would have all she ever wanted, and if the journey to this moment had been rocky and she had known heartbreak along the way, she knew it had all been worth it.

CHAPTER XII

*M*ary Bennet was the sister most unlike any of the others, a fact she had always keenly felt. Though Jane and Elizabeth often tried to include her in their friendship, she had, at times in the past, rebuffed their overtures. She had always felt ugly in their presence, the awkward, plain, ungainly sister, beside the acknowledged beauties of the family. Jane and Elizabeth had never made her feel this way—in fact, Elizabeth had often pointed out that Mary was pretty in her own right, and at times, when Elizabeth had induced her to display her charms with more appropriate clothes and hairstyles, she had felt pretty, indeed. But they had such a profound relationship that Mary had not wished to intrude, and she had often gone her own way for that reason.

Of course, there was no reason for Mary to attempt to become close with Kitty and Lydia, as they were so unlike her and had tendency to be cruel to her anyway. Mary responded by scolding them for their behavior, though she could confess that was likely not an effective way to mold them into proper ladies. In the end, simply ignoring them had been much easier.

Coming to Kent and being the unexpected recipient of Mr. Collins's attentions had given Mary a bit of confidence. She did not know how the man had come to fix his attentions upon her, but Mary had always thought that she would be suited to be a parson's wife, and she accepted his attentions willingly. It did not escape Mary's notice that Mr. Collins was not a suitor of which a young woman dreamed. He was not intelligent, had not the slightest idea of how to behave, and was ponderous and dull. Moreover, she had no expectation of much in the way of companionship should the courtship eventually lead to marriage. But even with these things, she thought he might be an acceptable suitor to a young woman who did not expect much from marriage.

In the past few weeks, however, that had changed. In the beginning, Mr. Collins had paid her a great deal of attention, and though Mary often found his society irksome, it still felt good to be the object of a man's admiration. But lately, Mr. Collins had largely been absent, both from the parsonage and from the act of courtship. And his concentration appeared to be on Elizabeth, not because he wished to have Mary's older sister for himself, but because he wished to prevent her from being Mr. Darcy's object. That did not sit well with Mary.

On a morning when only Mary and Mr. Bennet were sitting at the table at the parsonage, she found herself the recipient of her father's attention.

"Why the heavy sigh, Mary?" said he, startling her from her thoughts. "Is this courtship your mother has contrived suddenly not to your taste?"

Though Mary was aware of her father's propensity to tease, she thought there was an element of seriousness in his tone. She smiled at him and shrugged. "I always knew that Mr. Collins was not the most intelligent of men or the most acceptable suitor. But I thought I could get on with him well enough."

"Obviously, that has changed."

A hint of anger welled up in Mary's breast. "You are not as unmindful of us as you pretend, Father. You have seen what is happening."

But her father continued his maddening act of ignorance. "And what is that?"

"The fact that Mr. Collins is more interested in interfering with Lizzy than he is in making love to me."

"That does seem to be an accurate statement."

Mr. Bennet put his paper aside and gave Mary his full attention—it made her uncomfortable, so rarely had it happened in the past.

"I will own, however, that the thought of Mr. Collins *making love* to anyone is likely to give me nightmares."

Mary could not help but giggle at her father's words, though she quickly suppressed it. Mr. Bennet only smiled at her; it seemed like his observation was designed to induce her to laugh and put her more at ease.

"If Mr. Collins's behavior is objectionable," said Mr. Bennet, "then why do you put up with it?"

A shake of her head indicated she did not wish to speak of it, but her father's raised eyebrow told her he was having none of it. Mary sighed.

"I know I am not pretty like my sisters, Papa. I know I do not receive the attention they do. Should I not grasp the opportunity for marriage, even if the man is not exactly what I wished for?"

"First, let me correct you," said Mr. Bennet. "You say you are not pretty like your sisters, but I have personal knowledge that you are pretty enough for any man when you take the trouble to be so. Second, I would not wish you to accept a suitor simply because he is eligible, especially when the man is a fool."

Mr. Bennet sighed and reached a hand out to Mary, which she instinctively grasped. "I know I have not been the best father to you all. But I would not wish for my girls to be unhappy in their marriages, merely because they feel they cannot attract another man. I believe that you would be surprised at what you can do if you put your mind to it."

At that moment, Mary almost believed him. But there was another problem, one she did not relish confronting.

"Mama will not be happy if I do not accept Mr. Collins."

A snort told Mary what her father thought of that. "With all due respect to your mother, it is not *her* prerogative to approve or deny requests for her daughters' hands. If you do not wish to marry Collins, then reject him should he propose. You may be assured of my support."

"But what if I am never able to attract another man?" wailed Mary. She had never thought much about being married, but the thought of being denied it now that her hopes had been raised was almost unbearable.

"I believe Lizzy has the right of it," said Mr. Bennet softly. "It would be better to remain unmarried than to be tied to life with a partner you cannot love or respect, and I cannot imagine Mr. Collins inspiring anything other than contempt. Do not throw your life away on such things, Mary — you never know what may be waiting for you around the next corner."

And there it was in a nutshell. She had no need to rush, considering her still tender age and not knowing what might come her way. And perhaps of far more importance, Mary had long known that her father was not happy with her mother, and as such, his advice was perhaps the most apropos she would ever receive.

"Thank you, Papa. I will consider your words if Mr. Collins does propose."

"Good." Mr. Bennet paused and looked at her critically. "I believe you have resisted your elder sisters' efforts to display your charms to their best advantage. Perhaps it is time to give in and allow them to assist you."

"Perhaps it is," replied Mary shyly.

Mr. Bennet grinned at her. "And perhaps it is time to turn your attention to subjects other than Fordyce? I have long thought you might enjoy Shakespeare. Shall we read one of the comedies together?"

Warmth suffused Mary's being. It was possible that the prospect of losing his favorite daughter as an intellectual partner had prompted her father to extend this invitation. But whatever the reason, Mary was still grateful.

Mrs. Bennet was at her wits' end. Nothing was proceeding as she and Lady Catherine had planned, and worst of all, the woman appeared to be unconcerned about what was happening, leaving Mrs. Bennet to fend for herself. And attempt to cope she did, but neither Elizabeth nor Jane—who was always so obliging and dutiful—heeded her instructions. It was as if they did not wish to be married, though the thought beggared belief. Mrs. Bennet might be inclined to blame the entire debacle on Elizabeth, had not Jane been so unreasonably contrary. If they did not obey and oblige her, the worst of Mrs. Bennet's fear might even come to pass and *both* courtships come to nothing . . . .

For a brief moment, Mrs. Bennet considered the possibility that Lady Catherine had been toying with her in suggesting possible marriages between her daughters and the lady's nephews. But as soon as the notion occurred to her, Mrs. Bennet rejected it. The lady had been all friendship and affability, and besides, why would she bother with such a subterfuge? It simply did not make sense.

"I do not know what to do," said Mrs. Bennet, pacing in the parsonage parlor while her husband read his newspaper. That the infernal paper was a week old did not seem to bother him.

"I am sorry, Mrs. Bennet," said he. "What did you say?"

Mrs. Bennet looked skyward, wondering what she had done to deserve such a disinterested husband. It was not enough that the man had not given her a son, allowing his cousin to be his heir, thereby putting his wife and daughters at risk to poverty, but he did nothing to assist her in ensuring their future. How was such betrayal ever to be borne?

"I said, I do not know what to do," replied Mrs. Bennet, one of the rare times she had used such an acid tone with him. Her pique had caused it, and she could not repine how she spoke to him.

She might not have concerned herself, for Mr. Bennet took no notice. "What to do? I do not follow your meaning."

Frustration mounting, Mrs. Bennet threw her hands into the air and stalked to the other side of the room. "Jane and Lizzy! Neither will listen to me, and I begin to wonder if the situation is salvageable."

"Are your daughters ignoring you again? Perhaps I should bend them over my knee, remind them of the respect they owe you."

"Do not be silly!" snapped Mrs. Bennet. "They are both women full grown."

"Yes, but if they do not give you your due, then they are naught but wayward children and should be punished. Call them to Hunsford and I shall attend to it directly."

"Oh, Mr. Bennet! How you do trample on my nerves. Is the matter of your daughters' future security nothing but fodder for your wit?"

"No, indeed, Mrs. Bennet. In fact, I wish for nothing more than security for them. But I wish them to find it on their own terms, in ways which will make them happy."

"Their happiness is bound up in their security!" exclaimed Mrs. Bennet. "How can it be otherwise? Would they be happy to reside in the hedgerows once you are gone?"

"Mrs. Bennet, we must think of better things and not allow ourselves to be overcome by such thoughts. For all we know, you might predecease me and never know the hedgerows as intimately as you now fear."

If Mrs. Bennet had not heard her husband joke in such a way so often, and had she not been consumed with worry over her daughters, she might have taken offense at his words. But she could not. There were much more important things afoot than to be angered at her husband's usual efforts to be clever.

"I believe I must go to Rosings," said she, though she had not meant to speak out loud.

"You spend a significant amount of every day there, Mrs. Bennet."

Mrs. Bennet looked skyward. "Of course, I do, for I must, Mr. Bennet. If I did not, there would be nothing left to salvage."

"Please sit, Mrs. Bennet," said her husband. He motioned her to a chair, and though Mrs. Bennet was not inclined to cease her pacing, she huffed and threw herself into it. But Mr. Bennet only looked on with amusement, further souring her mood.

"My dear," said Mr. Bennet, "I know you worry yourself excessively about the situation with your daughters, but perhaps if you stepped back and tried to understand what is happening you would not be so concerned."

"I cannot imagine what you mean, unless you think that losing the two wealthiest and most eligible men we have ever met to be nothing more than a game."

"I do not think they are lost. But I do not think that matters will be settled in the manner in which you expect."

"What do you mean?" Her husband teased her so often that she could not trust that he was not trying to do so now.

"That matters are not lost at all. In fact, I think if you watched them, you would be heartened."

"Tell me what you mean."

But her husband, rather than acceding to her demand, only regarded her with a cheeky grin. "I find it far more diverting to allow you to come to the realization yourself, my dear."

"Then there is nothing for it. We must go to Rosings."

"We have not been invited."

"Yes, we have. Lady Catherine has told me that we may remove to her estate at any time convenient. Well, I mean to make it convenient right now."

Mr. Bennet only waved her away. "That will be fine. I will be quite comfortable wherever we reside."

Though Mrs. Bennet attempted to induce her husband and daughter to stay at the parsonage, Mr. Bennet was having none of it. Mary's opinion, which he canvassed not long after Mrs. Bennet had determined to go to Rosings, only confirmed his own desire to leave the parsonage.

"Would you prefer to remain here, Mary?" asked Mr. Bennet. For an instant, he was worried that Mary would act contrary to his expectations and desire to stay.

"I believe I would be much more comfortable with my sisters, Papa. I would have thought *you* would wish to stay."

Mr. Bennet chuckled. "At one time, you might have been correct. But not only is Mr. Collins's peculiar brand of silliness beginning to bore me, I will not stay at the parsonage and miss the fun that is certain to unfold at Rosings."

"Oh, Papa," said Mary. Bennet was oddly pleased that his daughter had become so comfortable with him so quickly that she was willing to voice her disapproval, much like Elizabeth often did.

"Either way, I do not doubt we shall be much more comfortable at Rosings than we are here. Let us go with your mother. Perhaps we can do something to keep her from ruining your elder sisters' courtships."

And so, they were decided to go. Mrs. Bennet wrote a note to Lady Catherine, stating their intention to remove to Rosings, and true to her prediction, the lady returned her letter immediately, confirming the invitation. Their trunks were packed and they readied to depart. The only issue was the opinion of Mr. Collins, who was not at all pleased that his captive audience was about to depart, though he truly had not been paying Mary much attention of late.

"But, Miss Mary," said he when he was told of their intentions, "were you not happy to be here and so readily available to accept my continued overtures?"

"It was, indeed, convenient, Mr. Collins," replied Mary. "But I cannot allow it to continue in this manner. It is not proper for a man to be courting a woman in his own home, so I must respectfully restate my wish to depart for your patroness's house to remove the temptation from us both."

Bennet was so amused that he almost laughed aloud, both at the sight of Mary stating her case with nary a hint of a smile—he was convinced that Mary had decided against Mr. Collins and now only wished to get away from him—but also because Collins appeared to be a child denied a jam tart.

"Well, I suppose if you put it that way, that is how it must be," said Mr. Collins.

"I do put it that way," was Mary's crisp reply. "Considering how often you visit Rosings, I dare say it shall be as if we were never parted. These coming days will feel no different from the previous."

Again, Bennet bit his tongue to keep from laughing. Mary was showing a predilection for, if not quite Elizabeth's brand of saucy comments, then at least her own. It was a side of his daughter he had never seen before. It *almost* made the prospect of losing Lizzy to Mr. Darcy bearable.

* * *

Though Darcy was certain that Mr. Bennet and Miss Mary, at the very least, were eager to see the last of the parsonage, he lamented the coming of Mrs. Bennet. Though her attempts had been ineffectual at best, her desire to separate him from Elizabeth was irksome, and restraining his temper had become much more difficult in recent days.

"Breathe, Mr. Darcy," said Elizabeth to the man sitting by her side.

Chagrinned that she could see through him so easily, Darcy turned his gaze on her, only to find her smiling at him. "I am sorry, Miss Elizabeth. I should be more tolerant of your mother."

"So should I, Mr. Darcy. But you are not displaying any frustration the rest of us have not displayed on occasion."

"Perhaps not." Darcy paused and looked around. Most of the rest of those in the sitting-room were engaged in their own conversations, though Anne was watching them, much as she always did. Mrs. Bennet was looking back and forth between Darcy and Miss Elizabeth, and Fitzwilliam and Miss Bennet, as if trying to solve some particularly tricky puzzle. "You do not suppose anyone else saw my displeasure?"

"I am certain my mother, at the very least, did. But you may rest assured that she will assume that *I* said something to annoy you, so there is nothing to fear."

"Lizzy!" cried Mrs. Bennet right on queue. "What are you saying? I hope you are not rattling on, offending Mr. Darcy with your constant clever comments."

"Of course not, Mrs. Bennet," said Darcy. "I could never find Miss Elizabeth anything other than charming."

"That is very good of you to say so, sir. But my daughter is sometimes intent upon speaking when she would best be silent, and I would not wish for you to be offended."

"Thank you, Mrs. Bennet, though I assure you that your daughter cannot offend me. I am quite sure speaking when one should remain silent is an affliction which besets us all, at times. It is no more particular to Miss Elizabeth than to anyone else."

Both Miss Elizabeth and her father smiled and looked away, and Darcy was keenly aware they knew what he had *not* said, but as neither seemed affronted, he could not repine his words. For her part, Mrs. Bennet watched him as if wondering if he was mad.

"Lizzy, I think it would be better if you came and sat beside Mary. Your sister may take your place."

"Leave your daughters be, Mrs. Bennet," said her husband. "I am certain Lizzy is quite well where she is, and if you do not wish to provoke an impromptu session of musical chairs, perhaps in the future you should be clearer about which of your daughters to whom you refer."

"I do not understand you, Mr. Bennet."

"Only that if you mean for one of your daughters to take Lizzy's place, you should specify which you mean. You *do* have four other daughters, after all."

"Oh, Mr. Bennet! You know precisely to which daughter I refer."

"I thank you for the compliment, Mrs. Bennet, but I am afraid you have quite mistaken the matter. I possess no ability to read your mind."

As the Bennets kept bickering back and forth, Darcy watched them with more than a little disapproval. Mrs. Bennet was ungovernable and unintelligent, and he had no doubt that living with the woman would be a punishment, but Mr. Bennet's continued propensity to make sport of his wife was not admirable by any means.

"I fear your expression, Mr. Darcy."

The sound of Miss Elizabeth's voice broke through his thoughts, and he turned to her askance.

"The expression with which you were regarding my parents suggested disgust, sir."

Darcy carefully schooled his features and cursed himself for his tendency to display his revulsion. A quick look at Miss Elizabeth showed that she was uncertain of him, which he thought was because of uncertainty of his ability to tolerate her family rather than any concern over his feelings for her. Darcy sighed and leaned forward, speaking softly so that only she could hear.

"I will own that there are times when I do not approve of your family's behavior."

"There are times when *I* do not agree with it," was her wry reply.

With a nod, Darcy decided that not only was this not the best time to have this conversation, but, in the end, it truly did not matter.

"It seems that I sometimes possess a tendency to . . . for my facial expressions to be taken as disapproval, Miss Bennet. I tend to be of a serious disposition, and though I often *appear* to be disapproving, that is not always the case. With your assistance, perhaps I can overcome this deficiency.

"Regardless, whatever meets with my endorsement or not, there is nothing that will induce me to change my mind about *you*. A thousand silly relations would not affect me."

Miss Elizabeth watched him carefully, her eyes searching his for the truth of his words. Darcy, sensing that she required this reassurance, opted against speaking again—she required more than his verbal assurances. She needed to see into his heart.

"Then perhaps we shall assist each other," said Miss Elizabeth at length, an impish smile spreading over her face. "After all, I do not believe that I am the only one who possesses a ridiculous relation."

Her eyes darted to where Anne sat watching them both like a hawk, and Darcy's composure was sorely tested. "Touché, Miss Elizabeth. Touché, indeed."

When they rose to go to dinner, inanity once again ruled, for when the announcement was made, Mrs. Bennet rose to her feet and crossed to her two daughters. "Come, Jane, Elizabeth, let us go into dinner together."

Though reluctant, both girls rose together to attend their mother, and they proceeded to the dining room, Mrs. Bennet directing them and whispering urgent instructions in their ears. Darcy's eyes caught those of both Fitzwilliam and Mr. Bennet, and while Fitzwilliam smirked at him, Mr. Bennet only shook his head and chuckled to himself. Darcy still was not pleased with the man's behavior at times, but he wondered what he might do if he was in Mr. Bennet's position—had he married Anne, for example. Anne was more cognizant of proper behavior than Mrs. Bennet was, but she was more wilful and assured of her position above such considerations. Would Darcy have reacted in the same way?

He could not imagine that he would have, but the thought gave him a little more insight and tolerance toward the behavior of his beloved's father. There were many paths one could take in dealing with an unhappy marriage, and perhaps Mr. Bennet had chosen one which was not so bad as some—he was not seeking comfort in the arms of other women, for example. Darcy decided that he would avoid judging the man. He had his own faults to worry about and no time to concern himself with others'.

In this unconventional manner, they proceeded to the dining room, but when Darcy was looking for a means to avoid having his cousin as a dinner partner, Lady Catherine intervened.

"You may sit here, Lizzy," said Mrs. Bennet, pointing to a chair near the foot of the table where her ladyship had been escorted by Mr. Bennet. "And if he will . . ." continued the Bennet matron, casting about for Colonel Fitzwilliam, Darcy thought.

But then her words died on her tongue, for she noted Lady Catherine's expression of clear disapproval, and she faltered. The sight provoked Darcy to action. He approached swiftly and bowed to Mrs.

Bennet.

"I thank you for thinking of me, Mrs. Bennet."

Then he pulled out the chair beside the one he was about to take and motioned her to take her seat. With a grin, Fitzwilliam also approached and took Miss Bennet's hand.

"And if you will follow me, Miss Bennet, I have a pair of seats waiting for us."

With nothing left to do but accede, Mrs. Bennet allowed Darcy to seat her, after which he took his own between the woman and her daughter. Miss Elizabeth's beaming smile spoke volumes.

"Very smooth, Mr. Darcy," said she in a soft voice once the soup had been served.

"I rather thought so myself," replied Darcy.

Dinner proceeded without further incident, and though Darcy was often distracted by Mrs. Bennet's chatter, he nevertheless responded with equanimity, for Miss Elizabeth was on his other side and commanded much of his attention. When they retired back to the music room after dinner, Darcy and Fitzwilliam both simply stayed by their chosen partners, not allowing Mrs. Bennet to scheme to separate them. Miss Elizabeth and Miss Mary both played for the company, and Darcy turned pages for both. When he was finished assisting Miss Mary, receiving shy thanks for his attention, he returned to Miss Elizabeth without hesitation, again denying Mrs. Bennet the ability to interfere.

Throughout the course of the evening, Mrs. Bennet watched the two couples, frowning, her brow furrowed in thought. Enlightenment never came, and though Darcy thought it was because the woman could not conceive of him preferring Miss Elizabeth to her elder sister, he was content to allow her to discover the matter in her own time. At present, he was too engaged in paying attention to Miss Elizabeth to worry about her mother.

CHAPTER XIII

With all the players of the comedic farce now present at Rosings—except for Mr. Collins, who inserted himself into their notice at every opportunity—Elizabeth was certain that it was only a matter of time before the tensions erupted into a conflagration of prodigious proportions. Not much changed in the few days after her parents decided to come to Rosings, but as Mrs. Bennet, Mr. Collins, and Miss de Bourgh continued to attempt to obstruct Elizabeth's courtship with Mr. Darcy, and Lady Catherine often pushed back against the three, tensions seemed to be rising. She could not think these tensions would not eventually be released.

Mr. Darcy, dear man that he was, controlled his temper admirably, though it was obvious at times that he was displeased with them all. His attentions were ever more ardent as time wore on, and Elizabeth found her breath quite taken away whenever he turned those dark eyes on her or when they managed to steal a few kisses.

On a day in early May, Elizabeth had finally had enough of those meddling influences in her life. Mr. Collins's coming had been delayed by some matter of the parish, and as Mrs. Bennet was focused on Jane, Elizabeth took the opportunity to slip from the room. A significant look at Mr. Darcy informed him that she expected him to find some way to escape as well.

A swift walk through the house led her out the east door, confident that she would not be observed, as it was the least used part of the house. She walked quickly east, and then turned to the south toward the woods, soon escaping into the haven of the trees. And there, comforted by the peaceful surroundings of nothing more judgmental and inhibiting than trees, she allowed herself to slow and glory in the scenes she so loved.

It was not long before she heard footsteps approaching, and she turned toward them, seeing Mr. Darcy appearing from in between the trees. He did not hesitate in the slightest, walking toward her, his long gait eating up the distance between them, and when he had drawn near, he swept her up into his embrace, kissing her with abandon. Elizabeth gasped with the pleasure of his lips upon hers — she thought she might die if he stopped. Then again, she might die if he did not!

This pleasurable activity continued for some time, until Mr. Darcy drew away, but only a little, continuing to bestow light, nipping kisses on every inch of her face. For her part, Elizabeth pressed closer to him, burrowing her hands under his coat and waistcoat, and caressing his broad back with her hands. Mr. Darcy moaned and stepped up his assault of kisses on her face.

"Do you suppose all this interference has made us all the more obstinate, Mr. Darcy?"

Chuckling, Mr. Darcy pulled away and looked into her eyes. "In what way?"

"Just that we were more determined to have each other than we might have been had so many others not been doing their best to deny us."

A rumbling laugh built up in Mr. Darcy's breast, and he lifted his head and allowed his mirth release. "Are we truly so obstinate?"

"I cannot speak for you, but I am known to be as immovable as a mountain when my mind is made up."

"I have often said that my good opinion once lost is lost forever," replied Mr. Darcy. "So perhaps I am a match for you in this regard.

"But I believe that we could have found our way to each other without all this drama." Then Mr. Darcy smirked at her. "There have been some interesting benefits to the situation. Had we not been so frustrated, I doubt we would be this . . . ah . . . free in showing our affections."

"Hmm . . . Perhaps you are right." Elizabeth paused and a sudden thought came to her, prompting a giggle. "I believe my mother would be mortified to see us like this, sir. And perhaps even your aunt."

Mr. Darcy shook his head. "I doubt Lady Catherine would feel anything other than triumph were our tryst made known to her. You have not missed her efforts at matchmaking, I am sure."

"I have not," replied Elizabeth. She leaned forward and rested her head on his chest, feeling like she might purr like a cat should he continue to kiss her hair and caress her back. "I will state, in your aunt's favor, that she has managed to merge her matchmaking and desire for our union with a laudable ability to let us come to our own conclusions. She made some comments in the beginning of our acquaintance, but she has been most circumspect since."

"Unlike your mother?" asked Mr. Darcy.

Elizabeth could not help but roll her eyes. "Completely unlike my mother. I am positive that they colluded in the beginning, but I cannot understand how they managed to misunderstand each other so thoroughly."

"I would have thought Lady Catherine would take her aside and explain the situation."

"I believe she likely has. But I am not the only person in my family who possesses a predilection for obduracy. My mother could outwait the tide, if she so chose."

They laughed together again, but when Mr. Darcy quieted, she noticed that he was looking at her with a tender expression such as she had rarely seen on his face.

"You have made me so happy, you know," said he. "I had not realized how lonely my existence was until I met you."

"How could you be lonely?" teased Elizabeth. "You have Lady Catherine, your sister, Colonel Fitzwilliam, your other Fitzwilliam relations, and, most importantly, Miss de Bourgh to keep you company."

"Ah, but I had not the companionship of a lover. Had I recognized your worth when I was in Hertfordshire last year, we would already be married and would not have had to endure these past weeks. I believe it is time to rectify that oversight."

But rather than propose, which she was certain he had been on the verge of doing, he reached down and claimed her mouth again.

A yell rang out from the woods around them.

In a similar piece of derring-do, Jane and Colonel Fitzwilliam had managed to escape from the confines of Rosings for their own assignation in the woods. They walked the path together, hand in hand, unaware of the presence of her sister and his cousin nearby.

Jane was different from her sister. Elizabeth burned bright with passion unfettered, the rush of a swiftly flowing river over the rocks in the middle of a stream. She would then, necessarily, be more fervent in all her doings, and that would spill over into her courtship with Mr. Darcy, who, Jane was certain, was of an equally passionate, but quieter, nature.

For Jane herself, she was of a much milder character, steady, calm, and dependable, a slow-moving river flowing placidly to the sea. Colonel Fitzwilliam, *her* beloved, was for all his outer joviality and playfulness, much the same as she was. His time in the army had taught him to be prudent and rational, and Jane was certain that he would prove to be a conscientious father, one who was involved with his wife and children, teaching, loving, providing protection and support. And that was what she wished for, though she did not think a little passion would go amiss.

They had taken liberties themselves, though Jane did not think they gone as far as Elizabeth and *her* lover had. He had kissed her, gentle kisses which satisfied and even thrilled her, and she had leaned against him whenever she had the chance. These things were enough for Jane, and she reveled in the feeling of being loved and cherished by a good man.

This was why the man's actions when they were out of sight of the house astounded Jane, and for a moment left her bereft of all sense. For with a growl of longing, Fitzwilliam stopped walking, and Jane only had a confused moment of seeing his lips descend toward hers before she was swept up in his ardent attentions.

The man invaded her mouth as if he were on a cavalry horse, spearheading a thrust toward some foreign army, his breath hot upon her face, and when he put his arms around her and lifted her up against him, her feet dangling a few inches above the ground, she thought she might expire from the pleasure.

When they finally separated, sharing murmured endearments and little nips and pecks, they once again began to walk slowly through the woods, content in each other's company. Jane could not imagine such bliss as she was feeling now.

Could she have felt this way with Mr. Bingley in the colonel's position? She could not say for certain, but the thought did not make much sense. On the surface, Mr. Bingley and Colonel Fitzwilliam were similar men—both amiable and open—but underneath there was a significant difference between the two. Jane could not quite state exactly what it was, but she thought perhaps it was the difference in their experience, both in life and in age. Whatever the case, she now found herself grateful that Mr. Bingley had left without a word.

"There seems to be some gravity to your thoughts, Miss Bennet."

Jane could not help but smile, and she looked up at her companion. "Nothing so weighty. I was just thinking of how I came to be here. There were many times, many things which, had they changed even slightly, I might not be here right now."

"You are referring to Mr. Bingley."

"In part," said Jane, shaking her head. Then she shot Colonel Fitzwilliam a teasing grin, much as her sister might have done. "Did you know a young man wrote poetry for me when I was fifteen?"

"And did he steal your heart with his verses?" replied the colonel in like manner.

Jane laughed. "No. In fact, it was atrocious. But Mama was determined that he was going to propose and that I was going to accept him."

The colonel appeared intrigued. "What happened?"

"It turned out that he had not a penny to his name, and Mama withdrew me from consideration."

"That is quite convenient for me," murmured the colonel

Then he stopped and turned toward her, and Jane could immediately tell that he was much more serious than he had been before. A shiver of excitement raced up her spine, and she wondered if this was the moment for which she had been waiting.

"I would like to know, Miss Bennet . . ." began Colonel Fitzwilliam, before he fell silent, far less self-assured than Jane had ever seen. Then he squared his shoulders and looked directly at Jane. "I merely wish to ascertain your feelings for Mr. Bingley."

"Mr. Bingley?" asked Jane, feeling stupid at the unexpected question.

"Yes," said Colonel Fitzwilliam. He ducked his head and gave a little helpless shrug. "The evidence of my own eyes and heart should be enough, do you not think? And yet I find that I wish to know if you have any tender feelings yet for Mr. Bingley."

At first, Jane wondered if she should be affronted at Colonel Fitzwilliam's questions concerning Mr. Bingley. Then she realized that he had a right to know, especially if he was considering proposing, as she thought he was. Perhaps his eyes should have informed him, not to mention how passionately she had just returned his kisses!

"Mr. Bingley is an amiable man," said Jane, looking into his eyes so he could see the truth of what she was saying. "But though he did pay me ardent attentions, he has been gone from me these last six months. If I reflect on the time I spent in his company, I cannot honestly say that I was ever in love with Mr. Bingley. In fact, I cannot say that Mr. Bingley ever felt anything more for me than the infatuation of the moment."

Jane smiled and ducked her head in embarrassment. "I believe I may also say that I was more in love with the prospect of being in love. I am not used to being the subject of an eligible man's attentions."

Though he had been silent, listening to her intently, it was clear he could not help but protest. "Surely not! I cannot imagine that you are not the focus of attention of every man within range of your smile!"

"I *do* receive plenty of attention, sir," said Jane, shaking her head. "But we do not have many *eligible* men in Meryton. Receiving the attentions of a man who cannot afford a wife, or who has no intention of marrying, is gratifying, but it tends to be playful, rather than serious. Mr. Bingley was the first truly independent man to make me believe he might offer for me."

"He is a fool for letting you go," averred Colonel Fitzwilliam.

Jane laughed and touched his face with affection. "Perhaps he was, perhaps not. I cannot say." Jane paused and then, feeling mischievous, said: "You remind me of my sister, sir. Lizzy is always the first to take my part. Have you been colluding with her?"

"It is only that we are both very intelligent. We recognize excellence when we see it, and we are not afraid to promote it."

Jane laughed. "I am not so special."

"I beg to differ, Miss Bennet." He paused. "I am sorry for speaking as if I do not trust you."

"I understand, sir. In fact, it seems to me that it was more for my benefit than for yours."

"Yes, that is it exactly! If you believe it is so, then I must agree!"

They laughed together, but it was quickly replaced by a renewed earnestness in the colonel which made Jane's heart flutter once again.

"Then there is nothing to do but to state my affections for you, Miss Bennet. I love you, and even though we have not known each other long, I know that nothing would make me happier than if you would be my wife."

"Of course, I will," said Jane, her eyes misting over in her pleasure. "I would be honored."

The kiss they exchanged on the occasion of their engagement was more playful and sweet than passionate. But there was the promise of so much more. And Jane knew she would experience it with her dearest Fitzwilliam.

They walked again for a time, meandering without thought of any destination, simply enjoying each other's company. Their conversation was inconsequential, the words exchanged of no real interest to anyone other than the two involved. The only thing of any import which passed between them was a short conversation concerning her sister and his cousin.

"Do you think Elizabeth and Mr. Darcy will come to an understanding?" asked Jane, her thoughts on how happy it would make her to see her sister equally happy.

"Darcy can take care of himself," replied Colonel Fitzwilliam. "He is capable of managing his own affairs."

Jane turned a look of mock severity on him, and he grinned. "Oh, very well. I have never seen Darcy so animated or intense as he is in his admiration of your sister. I would not be surprised if he was asking Miss Elizabeth for her hand at this very minute."

Whatever Jane was going to say in response went unsaid, for at that moment a loud yell interrupted their discussion. Surprised, Jane turned in the direction of the voice, but the foliage was thick and there was nothing to see.

"What do you suppose that was?" asked she.

"I do not know, but perhaps we should investigate."

Then taking her hand, Colonel Fitzwilliam led her away down the path as it curved away to the right. As they walked, the sound of loud voices soon reached them, one of them Elizabeth's. Sharing a concerned look with her newly betrothed, Jane hurried her steps until they burst upon the scene unfolding in front of them. Mr. Collins was there, speaking in a loud voice, berating both Mr. Darcy and Elizabeth.

Startled by the loud yell, Elizabeth drew back from Mr. Darcy, a feeling akin to guilt oversetting her at being caught in such a compromising position. Mr. Darcy was in little better condition, as he looked about them wildly, trying to locate the voice.

Out of the corner of her eye, Elizabeth caught sight of a large form charging toward them, and out of instinct she stepped back to protect herself. When she had finally managed to gather control of her faculties, the sight which assaulted her was of a visibly angry Mr. Collins bearing down on them.

"Cousin Elizabeth!" thundered the man. He hurried up to her and put his heavy frame in front of her, as he loomed over her, his posture intending to intimidate. "How dare you attempt to seduce Mr. Darcy! Are you no better than a common woman of the night?"

If Elizabeth had not been so affronted at her cousin's indictment, she might have been amused. "Mr. Collins, are you mad? Did it seem like I was the only one involved in what just happened?"

Mr. Collins's nostrils flared with anger, and he leaned forward, forcing her to retreat. "I never could have imagined that I was inviting a viper into the very bosom of Lady Catherine's home. Well, it is a mistake I may rectify, for you shall return to Hertfordshire immediately."

With a swiftness of motion she would not have thought him capable, Mr. Collins's hand darted out toward her wrist, but Elizabeth pulled her hand away before he could capture it. Then Mr. Darcy was there, inserting himself between the enraged parson and Elizabeth, though Elizabeth, angry as she was, only shouldered her way forward to stand by his side.

"If you so much as attempt to lay a hand on her again," snarled Mr. Darcy, "I will not be responsible for my actions."

"Mr. Darcy, I understand this temptress is attempting to seduce you, but I abjure you to remember your duty! What of your fair cousin? Will you leave her broken-hearted and bereft?"

"For the final time, Mr. Collins, I am not engaged to my cousin!"

"She—"

"Anne is delusional! I have never been engaged to her, and I never will be!"

"It is none of your concern, Mr. Collins."

As one, the three combatants looked toward the sound of the voice, and they saw Colonel Fitzwilliam and Jane approaching at a quick walk. Elizabeth did not miss the fact that their hands were clasped as if they never intended to let go.

"But Colonel! Miss de Bourgh herself has told me this is the case. How can she be doubted?"

"It is none of your concern, sir," replied the colonel. When he stepped up to Mr. Collins, Jane released his hand and stepped close to Elizabeth, grasping her sister to her, feeling the need for the support of a beloved sister. "You seem to have a high opinion of yourself, sir, to be attempting to take Darcy to task. If you do not wish to be out of favor with your patroness, I suggest you be silent about matters which do not concern you."

"But it *does* concern me," replied Mr. Collins, a haughty tone, akin to Miss de Bourgh's rebuking them all. "I am Lady Catherine's spiritual advisor, and I am privy to all her concerns. She would not wish for me to allow this travesty, and I shall not."

"I do say, Mr. Collins," said Elizabeth, her tone scalding, "you are quite possibly the stupidest man I have ever met."

Mr. Collins's complexion took on the hue of a ripe tomato, and he growled at Elizabeth. But he was prevented from reaching for her by the combined presence of Colonel Fitzwilliam and Mr. Darcy, who both stood menacingly over the man in case he should attempt something.

"You will not touch her, Mr. Collins," said Mr. Darcy, his tone icy and menacing. "If you ever attempt violence with her, I shall return your actions upon you tenfold!"

"I abjure you, Mr. Darcy," said Mr. Collins, his tone descending into petulance, "do not fall prey to this temptress. She is nothing. Miss de Bourgh is the lady meant for you. Do not throw that all away!"

"Come, Darcy, Miss Elizabeth," said the colonel, though his dark look at Mr. Collins suggested he would prefer to beat the man to a pulp. "There is no reason to stand and listen to this vermin. Let us return to the house."

"Excellent suggestion, Fitzwilliam," replied Mr. Darcy.

He turned and gathered Elizabeth's hand, placing it in his arm, and began to walk back toward the house. By his other side, Colonel Fitzwilliam walked with Jane, while Mr. Collins followed behind them, his whining continuing as they walked.

"Mr. Darcy! Colonel Fitzwilliam! You must listen to me!"

With an abruptness that surprised Elizabeth, Mr. Darcy suddenly stopped and turned, confronting the man. Mr. Collins almost fell to the ground in his attempt to avoid running into Mr. Darcy.

"Do not say another word, Collins. Be silent, worm!"

"I cannot make you out, man!" said Colonel Fitzwilliam. "You protest Darcy's attentions to Miss Elizabeth as if the fate of the very world depended on it, and yet you say nothing of my attentions to Miss Bennet. What do you hold against Miss Elizabeth?"

"Other than her improper, impertinent ways, I care nothing for her." The sight of Mr. Collins's sneer, which made him appear more than usually ineffectual, almost set Elizabeth to laughing. "But though I would not advise you to lower yourself to marry my cousin, at least you are not engaged already. Mr. Darcy is, and he simply cannot betray his fair betrothed in such a way."

"For the last time, I am not engaged to Anne!" Mr. Darcy clenched his fists, seeming to use the rhythmic motion to prevent himself from throttling Mr. Collins. "How many times must I say it to be believed?"

"I flatter myself that I understand what is happening here, sir," said Mr. Collins, his tone more than usually unctuous. "I am not unaware of the lengths to which young ladies will go to attach themselves to a man of fortune. Though I would not injure you by suggesting you do not know your own mind, it is clear that my cousin has beguiled you and led you astray, confusing you and pulling you away from your duty.

"As I have said, Mr. Darcy," said Mr. Collins with a smile likely intended to be commiserating, but which struck Elizabeth as being fraudulent, "I myself almost succumbed to my cousin's siren call. There is no shame in falling prey to an unscrupulous woman, sir. The best thing to do is to separate yourself from her immediately, so you may begin your recovery. I am sure Miss de Bourgh is waiting for you and will extend the balm of forgiveness without hesitation. Shall you not come away?"

It was clear to Elizabeth that the only reason Mr. Darcy did not respond immediately was because he was fighting to control his temper. Elizabeth could well understand his feelings—Mr. Collins was enough to try the patience of a saint! The longer he was silent, the wider Mr. Collins's smug grin became, and it was not long before Mr. Collins started shooting triumphant glances at Elizabeth. Elizabeth only smirked back at him, knowing the odious man was destined to be disappointed. She did wonder, however, about Mr. Collins's apparent virulent dislike of her. It made little sense, though she supposed that since the man himself was not blessed with sense, it could not be helped.

"Mr. Collins," said Mr. Darcy when he had finally mastered himself, and in a tone which made Mr. Collins visibly jump, "you reach too far above you. I will not hear another word from you, on this matter or any other."

"But, Mr. Darcy!" wailed Mr. Collins.

"Not another word!" thundered Mr. Darcy. "Your opinion is not needed or wanted. If you do not wish your life to become very uncomfortable, you will not say another word!"

Then Mr. Darcy gathered Elizabeth's hand in the crook of his arm and began leading her back toward Rosings, with Colonel Fitzwilliam and Jane following. Behind them all, Mr. Collins fluttered and fretted, his continued protests akin to the squawking of a crow, though none of them paid him any heed.

This was what it felt like to have a protector, Elizabeth thought. She found that she rather liked it, though she hoped Mr. Darcy did remember that she was a capable and intelligent young woman. They would need to find a proper balance. For now, she found that ceding their response to Mr. Collins was quite agreeable.

CHAPTER XIV

$\mathcal{M}$r. Bennet's favorite room in Rosings was, not surprisingly, the library. Though Lady Catherine's library was not as eclectic as his own, it was still a light, spacious room, held plenty of material to hold his interest, and with a ready supply of Lady Catherine's port and her books to read, Bennet felt himself to be quite content. There was, of course, a steady correspondence between himself and Mr. Hill, his butler and the man who was caring for Longbourn in his absence, but it was not too onerous, and Bennet found he was rather enjoying himself. There were benefits to living in a large house, for even if Kitty and Lydia did cause a ruckus, unless it was in the next room, Bennet could not hear it. And with his wife as thick as thieves with Lady Catherine, well, he was not bothered by her either.

One further interesting point about the library was the fact that it allowed the person within a fine view of the back gardens, all the way back to the woods some distance behind the house. On the day in question, Mr. Bennet was ensconced in the library as usual, and when he happened to look up, he saw, coming from the east toward the formal gardens, a rather motley crew. Mr. Darcy and Elizabeth led the way, with the colonel and Jane following. But what interested him the most was that Mr. Darcy's stride was stiff, his pace was such that Elizabeth needed to hurry to keep up with him, and Bennet's jackanapes of a cousin was following behind, looking like he was worrying at them like a vulture at a corpse.

"Look, Mary," said he to his daughter, who was sitting close by with Lady Catherine's copy of *Julius Caesar* in her hands. "The storm approaches."

Mary lifted her eyes up from her book—which, to her credit, appeared to have held her interest—and took in the scene. Her lips thinned, and the familiar disapproval overtook her features—it was much the same as the look the girl usually wore when confronted with Lydia and Kitty. Bennet concealed a smile at the sight; he would not lose his suddenly close daughter to Mr. Collins.

"What do you suppose that is?" asked she.

"I believe that we are about to be treated to more of Mr. Collins's absurdity."

With a sigh of exasperation, Mary turned to him and said: "Why do you find amusement in this, Papa? I know Elizabeth is very frustrated with Mr. Collins."

"Because, my dear Mary," said Mr. Bennet, affecting a pompous tone, "one must take amusement whenever he can. So much of life is serious that the chances to laugh are scarce."

"Perhaps we should repair to the sitting-room, so that we may be of use to Lizzy."

"An excellent suggestion, my dear," said Bennet, grinning at her.

Mary only rolled her eyes. "I wish to be of use to Lizzy, Papa. I have no desire to simply laugh at her frustration."

"I would not dream of doing that, Mary. I promise you that I will do my utmost to protect Lizzy from Mr. Collins, but I rather think that Mr. Darcy has the matter well in hand."

The only further response he received from his daughter was a grunt before she stood and watched him with imperious impatience. Bennet rose with alacrity and offered her his arm. He was almost certain they would arrive in the sitting-room first, though given the pace of Mr. Darcy's stride, it might be close.

The noise, as soon as the party burst into the sitting-room, was almost deafening, and Mrs. Bennet wished they would all be silent, for they were giving her a headache. For a long moment she could hardly understand what they were saying.

Mr. Bennet and Mary had arrived a few scant moments before Mr.

Darcy's party and quickly took their seats, Mary with her customary disapproval displayed for all to see, while Mr. Bennet showed his usual diversion.

Then came the warring parties. Mr. Collins, whom Mrs. Bennet was rapidly coming to think of as "that odious man" again, she could hear from well down the hall, but the others could also be heard, especially Mr. Darcy, who snapped several rebukes at the man, as did Colonel Fitzwilliam. Elizabeth was glaring at Mr. Collins as if he were an insect, and even Jane—*Jane!*—was looking at him with disapproval. Though she would prefer to have retired to her rooms to rest her nerves, Mrs. Bennet forced herself to listen to them and understand what they were saying.

"I do not wish to hear it again," said Mr. Darcy, almost growling at Mr. Collins in his anger. Mr. Darcy guided Elizabeth to a chair and saw her seated before turning to confront Mr. Collins, and Mrs. Bennet was surprised to notice that he seemed very solicitous of her comfort. Strange that she had not noticed it before.

"Stop, man, before I am forced to act against you!"

"My position as rector of this parish will not allow me to step aside, sir. You must be brought to see sense."

"The world is backwards," said Colonel Fitzwilliam, but though his tone was jovial, his glare was harsh. "A stupid man possessing not a hint of sense wishes to teach it to one of the most intelligent men I know."

Mr. Collins glared at Colonel Fitzwilliam, but he sniffed and turned to Mr. Darcy. "I cannot allow this travesty to take place! I will not allow it."

"*Allow it!*" Mr. Darcy looked as angry as Mrs. Bennet had ever seen him. "How dare you presume to allow *anything*? You are a fool, Collins! I have half a mind to call you out!"

"Half a mind is more than this worm possesses," said Colonel Fitzwilliam.

"You may insult me as you will, but it will change nothing for me. I will do what is right, regardless of your rudeness toward me, *or* of your threats of calling me out. I am a servant of Lady Catherine, and she takes precedence in this matter."

"You are a servant of God, man! Even if my aunt did wish you to pursue this matter so stringently, though she quiet obviously does not, it is your duty to the church and your flock which take precedence."

"And my actions will not offend either. But it will assist my patroness. All I wish for is to be of use to her."

"You are *not* being of use to her by insisting on pursuing this!"

"I will. Miss Elizabeth is leading you astray. Can you not see this?"

"Lizzy!" exclaimed Mrs. Bennet, latching onto the name of her daughter. "Lizzy, what is the meaning of this?"

"Mr. Collins is objecting to Mr. Darcy's attentions to me," said Elizabeth. It was the first time the girl had spoken since they had entered the room, strange, as it was usually more difficult to keep her silent.

"Madam," said Mr. Collins, turning his affronted glare on Mrs. Bennet. "I caught your Jezebel daughter seducing Mr. Darcy in the woods. She was in his arms, kissing him most ardently."

Later, Mrs. Bennet would wonder exactly what happened to her in that moment. It seemed like the world had ground to a halt. In Mrs. Bennet's mind, all she could think of was the unlikely thought of Lizzy caught up in Mr. Darcy's arms. How could such a thing have happened?

They were all ruined.

Ruined!

"Kitty! Bring me my salts! Your sister has ruined us!"

Pandemonium erupted in the room. Kitty caught up the bottle of smelling salts, which Elizabeth noted that her mother had not actually used in some time, and rushed to her side. Lydia watched the scene, laughing at the absurdity, and Elizabeth thought to herself she would dearly love to join her sister in laughter.

And speaking of laughing, her father also was making no attempt to disguise his own mirth, though by his side, Mary looked on with disapproval and more than a little disgust. Even Jane was angry at Mr. Collins. And anger did not even begin to describe the frightening fury with which Mr. Darcy and Colonel Fitzwilliam regarded the parson.

"A passionate clinch, is it?" asked Mr. Bennet into the din.

Mr. Collins, seeming to realize for the first time that Mr. Bennet was in the room, turned expectant eyes on the man and sneered at Elizabeth, expecting him to reprimand her.

"It was nothing so dramatic, Papa," said Elizabeth, though inside she winced at the lie. It most certain *had* been intense.

"Oh?" asked Mr. Bennet. Though Mr. Collins's grin grew wider, Elizabeth, who knew her father better than anyone else, knew he was only toying with the parson, though he likely was not exactly pleased that they had been kissing.

"You have my apologies, Mr. Bennet," said Mr. Darcy, his manner abrupt rather than contrite. "I will come to speak to you, so we can resolve the matter."

"That is likely for the best," said Mr. Bennet, still affecting his sternness. Mr. Collins, as a result, appeared a little less sure of himself.

"But in the interim, allow me to congratulate you most sincerely, sir." Mr. Bennet grinned, which turned to smugness when he looked at Mr. Collins. "I have known for some time that you and Lizzy would suit, but I wondered if you yourself would finally come to the point."

"Mr. Bennet," gasped Mr. Collins. "Your *daughter* was caught in a most compromising position with one of the most illustrious personages in all the land. Will you not censure her for it?"

"Are you suggesting the episode was at Elizabeth's instigation and that Mr. Darcy was not complicit in it? You will forgive my skepticism, sir, but I have learned throughout the course of my life, that one cannot kiss oneself." Colonel Fitzwilliam snickered and even Jane smiled. "You will forgive me for saying so, but it seems unlikely in the extreme that a young woman of impeccable reputation and character—not to mention a dainty size—should be able to force Mr. Darcy, a large and capable man, with a spotless reputation of his own, into a kiss. Especially when I know my daughter and understand she would never allow such liberties without a good reason."

Mr. Collins was at a loss for words, the first occasion Elizabeth had ever seen him thus afflicted. Would that he was affected so permanently! He was silent for some moments, though his mouth worked, and he appeared to be trying to say something. When he was finally able to speak, his words took everyone in the room by surprise.

Had Mary not already decided against Mr. Collins, his next words would have sealed her disgust and disinclination for any continued attentions.

"Then you must marry me, Cousin Elizabeth."

"What?" asked Elizabeth.

"Yes, you must marry me. That is the only way I may be assured that you will not influence Mr. Darcy or stand in Miss de Bourgh's way."

Elizabeth flayed him with a harsh laugh. "I cannot imagine anything in this world that would induce me to accept a marriage proposal from you, Mr. Collins. It is in every way repulsive."

But Mr. Collins seemed like he had not heard her. "Of course. I cannot think of why I did not think of the solution before. I do not wish for you as a wife. Indeed, I find your impertinence deplorable and your lack of respect intolerable. But I may change that in a wife, if it is required. You are comely enough and will bear me the children I require, I have no doubt. Yes, that is the answer."

"Mr. Collins," said Mary, interjecting before Elizabeth could shred the man with her tongue, "were you not courting *me*? How do you propose to suddenly jilt me for my sister when she cannot even stand the sight of you?"

The parson regarded Mary with lofty unconcern, and his hand waved in the air ineffectually, as if brushing aside a gnat. "Surely, as a servant of God yourself, Cousin Mary, you must understand that some things take precedence. In this case, though my heart tells me to marry according to my inclination, there is clearly a higher calling which beckons, and that is to prevent your sister from ruining a longstanding arrangement between Miss de Bourgh and Mr. Darcy. You shall be sister to the woman who will be mistress of Longbourn. Surely this is enough for you."

"Whether you marry my sister or not, sir," said Mary, "I will tell you now that you will *never* marry *me*. I would not have you were you the last man on earth."

"I can see you are still disappointed. I understand it will take some time before you are able to overcome your distress. Do not be alarmed—I am sure you will recover tolerably once you have thought on the matter."

"It has nothing to do with thought or lack thereof," replied Mary. "Your behavior has been abhorrent, and I have come to believe you are no fit mouthpiece of God. This is just the last confirmation I required to know that it would be a mistake to accept you. Thank you for making it so clear."

A muffled chortle sounded from beside her led Mary to glare at her father. But his mirth-filled eyes told her that his amusement was reserved for her cousin, and Mary was forced to acknowledge that there was more than a hint of humor in the situation.

"Good for you, Mary," said Mr. Bennet, and Mary felt warm all over to be the recipient of his approbation.

"It is nothing more than your loss," said Mr. Collins.

The man turned away from Mary and faced Elizabeth again. Though she did not feel like laughing as her father had done, Elizabeth was relieved that she would never share a closer relationship with this oaf than she did now. Even Mr. Collins as a brother by marriage would be far too close for comfort.

"Now, Miss Elizabeth," said the parson again, "we must plan for the announcement of our nuptials. The banns will need to be read in Hunsford and your home parish, of course. I believe the marriage should take place as soon as possible, or you may take advantage of the situation and attempt to compromise Mr. Darcy more thoroughly."

"You may make all the plans in the world, Mr. Collins," replied Elizabeth. "But I have not agreed to marry you, and I never shall. You may go to the altar, but I will not be waiting for you."

"Of course, you will," replied Mr. Collins. His manner was distracted, and he appeared to be pondering his plans to the exclusion of much else in the room. "Of course, you will bring little to the marriage, which is regrettable, though Miss Mary would not have brought any more. And I must plan to curb this impertinence of yours which is so unseemly. But a husband may correct a wife's behavior, by force, if necessary, so I must only wait until you are my wife in fact to begin to educate you."

"All the more reason not to marry you," said Elizabeth, finally drawing his attention to her. "I would not wish to marry a man who plans to abuse his future wife."

"Correction is what you require, and that is what you will receive."

"I swear, Mr. Collins," snarled Mr. Darcy, "if I hear one more word pass through your lips, I will not be responsible for my actions!"

"And I will hold you down while my cousin beats you senseless," added Colonel Fitzwilliam.

"It is for your own good, sir," said Mr. Collins, though his wide eyes told Elizabeth their threats had finally managed to penetrate his thick skull.

"I was on the verge of accepting a proposal from Mr. Darcy." Elizabeth looked at Mr. Collins like he was an insect. "Even if Mr. Darcy did not propose, I would never marry you. You are repugnant, sir—in every way contemptible."

"And I was just about to propose," added Mr. Darcy. "In fact . . ."

Mr. Darcy turned and walked resolutely toward Elizabeth, and she watched him approached with heightened anticipation. Surely, he could not mean to propose in such a scene in front of everyone!

"Miss Elizabeth," said he, "I must be allowed to tell you how ardently I love and admire you. From the first days of our acquaintance I have felt there is something different about you. Your *joie de vivre*, your intelligence and compassion, your beauty and gentleness are traits I could not resist if I tried. Though some have called you impertinent and abused your manners as improper, I find your playful archness intoxicating, and I beg you to relieve my suffering and consent to become my wife."

Mr. Collins gasped and attempted to interject his opinion, but Colonel Fitzwilliam stepped forward and stood menacingly over him, the threat written in his stance. To the other side, Kitty, Lydia, and Mrs. Bennet gasped almost as one, while Mary and her father looked on with interest. Even Jane, dear sister that she was, seemed to be shocked that Mr. Darcy had actually proposed to her in such circumstances.

All these concerns, however, were extraneous, as Elizabeth looked into the eyes of her beloved. The fire and determination she so loved were burning deep within them, mixed with the depth of love for her which left her breathless and speechless. But then she focused on the half smirk which he directed at her, and the frustrations of the past days welled up within her, and she responded in a way she could not have predicted. She laughed.

It began as a giggle, which escaped when she could not hold it in, soon turning to a chuckle, and then finally an open laugh. For Mr. Darcy's part, though he was confronted with the sight of a woman laughing after he had proposed, he was not offended — in fact, nothing could be further from the truth. Soon he was laughing alongside her, and within moments the entire company was following suit.

Except for the odious and affronted Mr. Collins, of course. The man must have suspected that they were all laughing at him, for his face turned beet red, and he sputtered and stammered in his outrage. Soon, however, he managed to work his way around Colonel Fitzwilliam, and he confronted Elizabeth.

"Bedlam is too good for you, Cousin. To laugh at the proposal of an illustrious man such as Mr. Darcy is beyond the pale, and this after your professed desire to entrap him. Have you suddenly raised your sights? Has Colonel Fitzwilliam's brother, the viscount, now become your target? Will your avarice never end?"

"You would never understand why we laugh, Mr. Collins," said Elizabeth from between giggles which still escaped her lips. "Your performance here is proof that you would not understand. I can only inform you that I am glad Mary has rejected you, for I believe your brand of stupidity would have served her very ill, indeed."

"You will not talk to me in that way! You will accept my proposal, and I shall teach you how to behave, if it is the last thing I do."

"Mr. Darcy has proposed and I will accept him."

"He cannot propose. Every good thing revolts against such a connection!"

"I can and I have done so," growled Darcy.

"You have already proposed to Anne!"

"I have had enough of this!" said Darcy and he grasped the parson by the lapels. "Fitzwilliam, help me take this trash out where I will thrash him within an inch of his life!"

"What is the meaning of this?"

As one, the company turned to the door. There stood Lady Catherine, with Miss de Bourgh standing beside her. The mistress of Rosings had finally come.

CHAPTER XV

*I*t had started as a low buzz in Lady Catherine's ears, akin to the sound of a bee happily going from flower to flower, or perhaps a housefly lazily winging its way around a room. Though she had invited the Bennets to her house of her own free will and enjoyed their company, at times they were a little much for her equanimity. She and Anne had lived alone at Rosings for so long, she supposed it was not surprising that the intrusion into their domain had brought disadvantages. Thus, Lady Catherine had retired to another, smaller parlor, one to which she had not invited any of the Bennets and to which she retreated when she required distance.

But the room was central enough in the house that she was still able to hear what was happening, and at times she could hear the giggling of Miss Kitty and Miss Lydia—though thankfully there was less of that than there had been—or the murmur of conversation. What she heard that afternoon, however, was far beyond the murmur of conversation. Once she became aware of it, she thought she could hear loud voices raised in anger.

Such sounds were uncommon at Rosings, and Lady Catherine stood and walked to the window, thinking to investigate what it was. But there was nothing to be seen in the garden—everything in her domain appeared to be calm and peaceful. With a frown, Lady Catherine turned to the door and opened it. That was when she could hear it again quite clearly. It was coming from down the hall toward the sitting-room.

Determined to discover what was happening in her home, Lady Catherine walked down the hallway, noting as the sound seemed to turn to laughter. So intent was she on what she was hearing, Lady Catherine almost bumped into her daughter, who had appeared from the entrance hall.

"What is it, Mama?" asked she.

"I am not certain, Anne," replied Lady Catherine. "But you may be assured that I intend to find out."

The footman stationed outside the door to sitting-room bowed as they approached, and Lady Catherine's keen eye noticed that he winced when the volume suddenly increased and sounded angry again.

"Who is within the sitting-room?"

"I believe everyone other than your ladyship and Miss de Bourgh."

"And this loud argument has been going on how long?"

"Since Colonel Fitzwilliam and Mr. Darcy returned, some five or ten minutes gone. They were escorting the two eldest Bennet sisters, and Mr. Collins was chasing behind them."

Why Mr. Collins would be following the two couples, Lady Catherine had not the slightest notion. It was likely the man had misconstrued something—he was not the most intelligent specimen. Lady Catherine had thought his behavior of late had been odd, even for him, but she could not imagine what had incited this strangeness in her house.

Lady Catherine motioned to the man, and he opened the door, and the noise spilled out of the room, a great wave pouring out into the hallway. Lady Catherine would not have been surprised had the loud cacophony of voices been heard all the way to Hunsford! But what shocked her the most was that Darcy—who had never become violent, even when confronted by the sins of that libertine Wickham—was holding Mr. Collins by his jacket and threatening bodily harm.

"What is the meaning of this?" asked Lady Catherine in a loud voice.

All at once, the noise ceased, and the occupants of the room all turned to stare at her. For a moment, no one spoke.

"Once again I ask: what is the reason for this argument? I might have thought this room was inhabited by a horde of common rowdies, all intent upon destroying my sitting-room."

"Lady Catherine," said Mr. Collins, incongruously the first to regain his wits, "I am grateful you have arrived, for I have a matter of great import to share with you. Though I would not injure yourself or your excellent nephews, a grave miscarriage of justice is occurring under your roof, and I am ashamed to say that members of my own family are complicit in this travesty. I beseech you to make your opinions known to all, so that this perfidy might be brought to a halt before the situation becomes irredeemable."

The parson's long-winded and interminable speech brought Lady Catherine's already fraying temper close to the breaking point, though she managed to swallow her annoyance with difficulty. The glare she directed at Mr. Collins instantly had the man bowing and scraping, and she could see beads of sweat forming on his forehead.

"Mr. Collins," said she, "unfortunately, since you have not seen fit to inform me of the nature of this travesty, as you call it, I have no idea what I must say to prevent it. Might I ask you to be more explicit?"

The stupid manner in which the parson stared at her for moments after she spoke made her wonder what she had been thinking to offer him the living at Hunsford. She had known he was quite possibly the densest man to whom she had ever been introduced, but she had trusted in her own ability to mold him into something better than he was now. It was apparent her confidence had been nothing more than hubris.

"Explicit?" asked Mr. Collins after some hesitation.

"Yes, Mr. Collins," said Lady Catherine, her annoyance beginning to spill into her tone. "You have informed me of a travesty under my roof, but you have yet to state what it is. If you wish me to act, you must be more forthcoming. Now, what has got you so worked up?"

Out of the corner of her eye, Lady Catherine saw Elizabeth covering her mouth attempting to hold in a laugh, and her father was in the same straits. Most of the others were looking at Mr. Collins with either amusement or disgust, though Kitty and Lydia were the only ones not attempting to hide their mirth. Darcy appeared ready to skewer the parson where he stood.

"Of course, your ladyship," said Mr. Collins, bowing low several times, reminding Lady Catherine of a chicken pecking at the ground. "How silly of me to have forgotten. I was so caught up in my righteous indignation that I completely forgot that I have not yet made you aware of what has been happening. I had thought several times to speak of it, but I was assured of my ability to handle the matter, and furthermore—"

"Now, Mr. Collins!" snapped Lady Catherine, her patience gone.

"It is all my cousin's fault!" screamed Mr. Collins. He turned and pointed at Elizabeth, his tone and gesture wild. "She persisted in chasing after your nephew in defiance of all that is good and right, and nothing I said could induce her to desist."

"Miss Elizabeth pursuing my nephew?" asked Lady Catherine incredulous. "Whatever can you mean? As far as I was aware, Darcy was doing the pursuing."

The way Mr. Collins's eyes bulged from their sockets, Lady Catherine wondered if they would pop right out of his head. "Surely not! I know that Mr. Darcy is destined for your wonderful flower of a daughter, Miss Anne de Bourgh. He could not possibly prefer my cousin when such a delicate ornament is before him."

"You think Darcy is engaged to my daughter?"

"Of course! I am aware of all the particulars, and so are the Bennets. And yet Miss Elizabeth has refused to give up her hopeless pursuit of him!"

"Mr. Collins!" said Lady Catherine. "Where did you get such a ridiculous notion as this? Darcy and Anne are not engaged."

If Lady Catherine had been concerned for the man before, now she wondered if he might expire right before her eyes. He watched her, vacuous surprise flowing from him in waves. His mouth moved, but nothing was issuing forth from it. She might have thought he was suffering from an apoplexy.

Mr. Collins was hopeless, so Lady Catherine turned to her daughter, noting the guilty color which had risen in her cheeks. So that was what had happened.

"You spoke with Anne, and she told you of this engagement?"

The man appeared incapable of speaking, so he nodded his head in a vigorous fashion. Lady Catherine wondered if his head might detach itself from the neck due to the abuse it was suffering.

"And because of this intelligence, you have tried to separate Darcy from Miss Elizabeth?"

More nodding ensued. Darcy only glared at the man and growled: "He has taken it upon himself to interfere with us whenever we are in company. Then he attempted to suggest that Miss Elizabeth *must* marry him to preserve me for Anne."

"I would never marry such a toad," said Elizabeth, her glare impaling Mr. Collins. For his part, Mr. Collins stared back at her, and Lady Catherine was surprised at the virulence of his apparent antipathy for her.

"I would not expect you to," said Lady Catherine, nodding at Elizabeth. "There is a man in the room with whom you are well suited, and it most certainly is not Mr. Collins."

"But Lady Catherine—"

"Be silent, Mr. Collins," snapped Lady Catherine, thinking of the mess before her now. "Did you not think to come to me to confirm what Anne told you?"

"But she is your daughter!" wailed Mr. Collins. "Should I not expect that her heart and mind would be as one with yours?"

"Apparently not." Lady Catherine turned to Anne, who had taken a nearby chair and was pouting. "Anne, what can you mean by this silliness? It is bad enough that you pine for Darcy when he does not wish to marry you, but then you involve Mr. Collins in this mess when you know what will likely happen."

"I mean to marry Darcy," said Anne, her back straight and defiant.

Lady Catherine only shook her head. "Anne, Darcy is not engaged to you. My conversation with my sister was nothing more than idle speculation between two sisters. We agreed on nothing, and we did nothing legal to seal the match.

"My sister, you see, wished for her son to be happy, and she was certain that happiness would come with the choice to find his own wife. I would never do anything to frustrate my sister's wishes. Her children are as dear to me as you are.

"It is time for you to relinquish this fantasy, Anne. Darcy is not for you."

"But, Mama—" protested Anne.

Lady Catherine interrupted her daughter, though not unkindly. "No, Anne. You may not force your wishes upon your cousin. It is clear he has decided on another, and if I may say so, I have known you suit each other ill, indeed, for many years now. It is time for you to attain a little more maturity and set your sights on another who is more receptive."

Though Anne sulked, Lady Catherine thought she was finally reaching her daughter. A thought occurred to her, and she decided to voice it, though she suspected Anne would not take it in the manner she might wish. "Consider this, Anne: you are the scion of not only the house of an earl, but also a baronet. Perhaps you might wish to consider looking for a spouse in a different sphere. Perhaps you might even consider restoring our line to the nobility, for Rosings is an attractive dowry, as you know."

A slow smile came over Anne's face, as Lady Catherine had suspected it would. "A viscount or maybe even an earl?" asked she.

"Perhaps," replied Lady Catherine. "Fortune and standing *are* important, Anne, but of more importance, I would see you happy. If these things bring you happiness, then I would not disapprove."

"Very well," said Anne, and with a haughty look at Darcy, she continued: "I shall marry someone of higher standing, then. Darcy may have his country miss."

"Thank you, Anne," said Darcy, "for your magnanimous blessing. Please believe me when I say I wish you equal felicity in marriage as I am sure I will have."

Lady Catherine did not think Anne recognized the sardonic edge in Darcy's voice, for she only smiled and nodded regally at him before turning away altogether. For her part, Lady Catherine heaved a sigh of relief—she had despaired of ever reaching Anne and ending this hopeless infatuation of hers. Now, perhaps, she would turn her attention to finding a husband, though Lady Catherine knew she would need to keep a close eye on her daughter to ensure she did not attempt to choose anyone objectionable.

"Then if your daughter is not to marry Mr. Darcy," spoke Mr. Collins, "he should search for someone of greater standing."

Elizabeth turned her attention to the parson, and she noted the intense dislike the man had somehow developed for her. As she could not say that it was not returned in full, she decided she did not care for his opinion.

"Surely there is no cause for him to bring such degradation on his noble line as he would by marrying Miss Elizabeth," continued Mr. Collins. "I am sure your ladyship would prefer a more eligible match for your nephew."

"And you would be incorrect, Mr. Collins," said Lady Catherine shortly, her patience with her parson almost exhausted. "After all the trouble I went through to ensure they were afforded the chance of falling in love, you cannot think I would disapprove at this late stage."

Mr. Collins went a deathly shade of white. "Lady Catherine! Surely—"

"Be silent, Mr. Collins," snapped Darcy. "I do not understand this unreasoning hatred you possess for Miss Elizabeth, but I will not hear another word against her."

"I believe I can tell you," said Elizabeth, her own look spearing the parson. The man returned it with equal ferocity. "He resents my intelligence and the fact that I am able to talk circles around him at any time of my choosing. I think he also despises my liveliness, when his life is all dullness and ponderous nothings."

Mr. Collins glared at Elizabeth, but Lady Catherine could not help but wonder if she was not correct. Though it was of no consequence, Lady Catherine thought Mr. Collins did not understand himself why he disliked her. He truly was a dense, foolish man.

"I am sorry, but if I may?"

The entire company turned to Mrs. Bennet, who had spoken, and Lady Catherine was amused to see the woman so unsure of herself. She had a good heart, which was what had drawn Lady Catherine to her, but she was not much cleverer than Mr. Collins.

"Of course, Mrs. Bennet. What do you wish to say?"

"I only wish to ask . . . That is to say . . . I would like." Mrs. Bennet stopped and visibly gathered herself before saying: "You intended for my *Lizzy* to capture Mr. Darcy?"

"I did not intend for *anyone* to be caught, Mrs. Bennet."

"Though that is essentially what happened," said Mr. Darcy quietly. The way that he and Miss Elizabeth were looking at each other made it obvious to them all how they felt about each other.

"Perhaps," said Lady Catherine, delighted to be proven correct. "But yes, I thought that Darcy and Miss Elizabeth would suit very well, indeed, and I believe my point has been amply demonstrated, has it not?"

Mrs. Bennet licked her lips. "But I had thought you meant to promote my Jane to Mr. Darcy and Elizabeth to Colonel Fitzwilliam."

"I have nothing against your second daughter, Mrs. Bennet," said Fitzwilliam, "but I am much more attracted to your eldest. With her quiet fortitude and reticence to temper my garrulity, I think we shall do fine together."

"Why did you think Jane and Darcy would suit, Mrs. Bennet?" asked Lady Catherine.

"Well . . ." The woman's eyes darted toward her daughters. Her reasons were clear to Lady Catherine — and likely to Jane and Elizabeth too, if not most of the room. But Lady Catherine had no interest in humiliating her in front of them all.

"It appears we have suffered a miscommunication, Mrs. Bennet. As I said before, I merely wished to give these young people a chance to become better acquainted and learn whether they were compatible for themselves. Had Jane preferred Darcy and Elizabeth, Fitzwilliam — and their sentiments been returned, of course — they would have found their ways to each other, and I would have been proven incorrect."

"We all know that is simply not possible—" said Mr. Collins, though a look from Lady Catherine silenced him. She had no patience for his groveling at present and even less for any attempt to once more worm his way back into her approval.

"I am as fallible as anyone else, Mr. Collins," said Lady Catherine, her stern glare informing him that further comment would not be welcome. For once, the man took the hint.

"Mrs. Bennet, did you not note how your daughters were often to be found in their current attitude? Did you not notice the attentions Darcy paid to Elizabeth, and how Fitzwilliam made love to Jane?"

"I—" But the woman could not say any more. She had been too busy trying to arrange things in the way she thought they needed to be, rather than simply allowing them to come to their own understandings.

"It was clear to me," said Mr. Bennet. He turned a sternness on Darcy and Fitzwilliam, which was belied by the twinkling in his eyes. "Of course, neither of these young men have deigned to approach me for permission, and since I assume proposals have been tendered, that is a serious oversight. Is it not?"

"I have proposed and Jane has accepted," said Fitzwilliam. "It was, however, just this afternoon, so I may defend myself. You may expect a visit from me as soon as this farce is concluded."

Mr. Bennet grinned and saluted Fitzwilliam. "I shall be waiting for you, Colonel."

All eyes then turned to Darcy, but rather than be made uncomfortable by the scrutiny, Darcy only turned to Elizabeth and raised an eyebrow at her. "It seems to me that I have asked the all-important question, but I believe Miss Elizabeth was interrupted before she could reply. How say you, Miss Elizabeth?"

The girl seemed to find the situation amusing, for she giggled, prompting another dark look to be thrown her way from Mr. Collins.

"I believe it was my own doing, Mr. Darcy," said she. "But since you have been so good as to prompt my memory, I will favor you with a response. Yes, I would be happy to accept your proposal."

Darcy grinned and grasped her hand. He turned to Mr. Bennet and said: "It appears that I, too, have been accepted. You may expect my own visit after Fitzwilliam's—or before, if I can beat him to it."

"Not on your life, Darcy," replied Fitzwilliam easily. "Not only was I first, but as the elder, marrying the eldest daughter, I believe I have precedence."

"If it will prevent fisticuffs," said Mr. Bennet, "perhaps you could attend me together?"

The company laughed at his quip, relieving some of the tension. Lady Catherine noted that even Anne chuckled at Mr. Bennet's joke, though Mr. Collins still glared at Elizabeth with distaste.

"Two daughters engaged!" cried Mrs. Bennet. "How am I to ever bear the happiness?"

"I hope you are not disappointed, Mrs. Bennet," said Fitzwilliam.

The lady smiled at him, a hint of shyness coming over her. "I am not, Colonel Fitzwilliam. Though I misunderstood what was happening, I could not be more pleased. My girls deserve this to have husbands who love them. I am certain they will be very happy with you both."

"You may be assured of that, Mrs. Bennet," said Darcy with a bow. "It will be my lifelong task to ensure Elizabeth is as happy as I can make her."

"Come, Mr. Darcy, that would not be any fun," said Elizabeth, mischief in her every word. "I am fond of a good argument, you know. I absolutely insist we have at least one argument a month."

"Lizzy!" cried Mrs. Bennet, even as the rest of the company laughed. The Bennet matron was startled, then appeared a little shamefaced as she understood her daughter's tease.

When the mirth had died down, Mrs. Bennet once again spoke. "I do hope you will make an attempt to respect your husband, Lizzy. Though it appears that Mr. Darcy does, indeed, prefer a lively wife, his position in society demands that you bring honor to his family."

"I believe you have no need to concern yourself with such things," said Darcy. "I am certain Elizabeth shall bring great credit to my family name, and I have no doubt she will confound any naysayers with her usual éclat."

"And I will be there to guide both of your daughters, Mrs. Bennet," added Lady Catherine. "I have been presented and I am well-known in society. I shall sponsor their curtseys to the queen and ensure their introduction is a success."

It was clear that Mrs. Bennet was overwhelmed with the thought of such lofty considerations, so Lady Catherine let the matter rest where it was. She turned her attention to Mr. Collins, who was still displaying his sourness for all to see. Though the conversation became animated, Mr. Collins looked at all with sullenness, and at his cousin with something akin to hatred. It would behoove her to rein the man in before Darcy took offense and called him out.

Catching his eye, Lady Catherine motioned to her side, a chair which was situated close to the one she usually used. His petulance forgotten at once, Mr. Collins eagerly made his way thither, exclaiming upon his arrival:

"Yes, Lady Catherine? You have need of me?"

"After a fashion, Mr. Collins," said Lady Catherine. The stern look she directed at him immediately set him to mopping his brow as he often did when he was nervous. "In fact, I require you to cease this objection to the match between your cousin and my nephew. The matter has been decided and will be official as soon as Mr. Bennet gives his consent, which I am assured he will deliver with alacrity."

The sourness once again came over Mr. Collins, and he shot a sullen glance at Elizabeth. "Your nephew is capable of aspiring to so much more."

As a final gasp of defiance, it was rather pitiful. It was also fortunate, for though Mr. Collins had not noticed, she had seen Darcy's reaction to even that much, and it was clear he was not amused.

"In matters of fortune you may be correct," replied Lady Catherine. "However, on a personal level, I cannot think of anyone who is more suited for Darcy than Elizabeth, and it is clear that they love each other. *That* is the most important concern."

Mr. Collins turned his dull eyes on her. "I would not have thought you to be a romantic, Lady Catherine."

A laugh escaped her lips, though she had not intended it. "I dare say there are many things you do not know about me, Mr. Collins. My husband and I shared felicity in marriage, and I could not wish for anything less for my child, or for the children of my siblings. Regardless, I like to think I understand that I do possess a certain measure of influence, but in some things—especially matters of the heart—I am powerless, not that I would presume to take the happiness of these good people from them.

"You would do well to take my advice and cease any and all objections to these matches. Society may very well look on them with the same opinion you possess, but it is truly none of your concern. Furthermore, you are on the verge of seriously displeasing Darcy, and it would not do to earn his enmity."

The man glanced at Darcy, and his carriage became less certain as he noted Darcy's challenging glare. Unsurprisingly, it was Collins who looked away.

"I believe you may be correct, your ladyship."

"I do not understand you, Mr. Collins," said Lady Catherine, leaning back in her chair and regarding the man with confusion. "You have proclaimed a vociferous opposition to Elizabeth's match with Darcy, declaring it to be beneath him, but you have said nothing about Jane's attachment to Fitzwilliam. It is strange, as Fitzwilliam is the son of an earl, whereas Darcy is just the nephew of one, and yet the Bennets are sisters."

As Lady Catherine suspected, Mr. Collins was unable to answer her question, and for once he did not attempt to do so amid flowery language which would make little sense to anyone but him. Lady Catherine allowed him to squirm under her sharp gaze for a few moments before she relented.

"Very well. Take my advice to avoid angering Darcy, Mr. Collins. He is an implacable enemy, one you would not wish to make."

Then assured that Mr. Collins would behave himself, Lady Catherine allowed the man to retreat to lick his imaginary wounds in silence. During their discussion, the rest of the room had descended into conversation, and Lady Catherine thought that the two couples were sharing accounts of their courtships. It was not surprising that most of the sharing was being done by Elizabeth and Fitzwilliam, as each were the more vocal of the couples. But Lady Catherine also did not miss the fact that Darcy held Elizabeth's hand tightly, seemingly disinclined to let go, and Fitzwilliam was doing the same with Jane. Perhaps it was not quite proper, but after all the interference they had endured, Lady Catherine could not find the heart to reprimand them.

It had all turned out as she had expected. Lady Catherine felt the warmth of being right well up within her breast. Her nephews would be happy, she did not doubt, and perhaps Anne would learn to be happier too. Lady Catherine loved being of use.

Chapter XVI

Though Elizabeth would have preferred otherwise, Lady Catherine extended an invitation to Mr. Collins to stay at Rosings for dinner that evening. Elizabeth would choose never to be exposed to the man again. But she understood the lady's situation as well; the living had been given and could not be rescinded, so she had little choice but to make the most of the situation.

It was fortunate for all involved—especially the parson himself, given Mr. Darcy's dark looks—that Mr. Collins paid no attention to Elizabeth. It resulted in a peaceful evening for the most part. Elizabeth basked in her newfound happy situation, as did Jane, and the sisters spent some time in happy conversation with their intendeds, the chaos of the past days forgotten in favor of their happiness. Several toasts were raised in honor of the newly engaged couples, and conversation and laughter flowed long. To some of the company, however, vexation still prevailed.

Elizabeth felt for her sister Mary, for Mr. Collins seemed to feel that her regard was unaffected by his energetic opposition to Elizabeth's engagement to Mr. Darcy, though his method of lovemaking was as curious as everything else about him.

"I have decided," Elizabeth overhead Mr. Collins say in his usual weighty voice, "to forgive you for the words you spoke to me earlier and extend the benefit of my attentions once again. I am sure you can have no objection, for it is clear that should I not propose, you may never receive another offer, your close connection to the Darcy and Fitzwilliam families notwithstanding. Perhaps once we are married, you will learn the proper respect, and that my authority is not to be challenged."

A few short weeks ago, Elizabeth might have thought that Mary would ignore his words, no matter how offensive they were. This Mary, however, seemed to have matured and gained a measure of confidence, and though she did glance at her father, his smile and nod seemed to instill her with resolve. Thus, when she turned back to Mr. Collins, it was with coolness the parson could not fail to understand.

"I thank you for that civility, Mr. Collins," said she. "But that will not be necessary. I have no intention of accepting your attentions, to say nothing of your proposal."

The look which Mr. Collins bestowed on Mary was for the briefest moment dumbfounded, though he soon recovered, and it changed to knowing. "Ah, I am familiar with this facet of maidenly comportment, I believe. You wish to punish me for objecting to your sister's match by withholding your affections. There is no need to resort to such stratagems, Miss Mary, for what I did was nothing more than in the service of my patroness. I am certain you can understand this."

"My understanding or lack thereof is not at issue, Mr. Collins, nor is the infamous way in which you treated a beloved sister. I have been the recipient of your attentions, and I have found them wanting — it is as simple as that."

Mr. Collins frowned. "I have explained my reasons for objecting to your sister's match, so there is no reason to act in such a way. There is also no reason to continue to attempt to punish me. You may expect me tomorrow morning when we may continue our courtship."

"You may come, but I will not receive you," said Mary. "As I stated before, I simply am not interested in anything you might offer. Please find some other young lady who wishes to receive you."

"Miss Mary, this is unseemly," said Mr. Collins. "You should remember my previous words and that it is unlikely you will ever receive another offer of marriage. Would you throw this chance away when it may be the only one you ever receive?"

"Better that she remain unmarried than to see her married to you, Mr. Collins," interjected Mr. Bennet. Elizabeth, who had been following the conversation, had not noted her father's increasing displeasure.

"What do you mean, Cousin?" asked Mr. Collins, a hint of alarm in his voice.

"Just what I have said," was Mr. Bennet's short reply. "I am certain Mary will have ample opportunity to meet other young men, given who her brothers will be. Her response to your inept attempts at lovemaking only spares me the effort of rejecting your application should she have accepted you." Mr. Bennet turned a smile on his middle daughter, which she returned warmly. "It seems Mary has grown in confidence these past months. I am happy that she has seen the imprudence of accepting your proposal."

"Imprudence!" exclaimed Mr. Collins. "What imprudence do you call it? I am the rector of this parish, a very valuable living, I might add, and heir to your estate. Would you not wish for your daughter to be cared for?"

"Her physical needs you can meet, but everything else is beyond your reach." Mr. Bennet's glare at the man was brimming with contempt. "I am aware of my failures as a father to my children, but do you think I could countenance ever marrying one of them to a man who would mistreat them?"

Mr. Collins sputtered, but nothing coherent came out of his mouth.

"Do not think I did not understand your meaning when you spoke of 'correcting' Elizabeth's behavior, Mr. Collins. I have no respect for a man who would beat his wife. You will not have Lizzy, as she has made a match with a fine man, and you will not have Mary, as she has rejected you. You may as well put any thoughts of my youngest daughters from your mind, as I will not approve any applications for *them* either. I will not see any of my daughters married to a fool."

"But, Cousin—"

"Enough, Mr. Collins! I will hear no more of it."

Elizabeth had the distinct impression that Mr. Collins might have continued to protest, but he happened to look up and see the twin looks of displeasure Mr. Darcy and Colonel Fitzwilliam were giving him, not to mention the warning look from Lady Catherine. Thus, he subsided, though not with any grace. For the rest of the meal the man was mercifully silent, pouting by the side of the table.

It was not until after dinner that Elizabeth had the opportunity to speak briefly with her father, as she was curious about two things. "I am wondering, Father," said she. Across the room, Mr. Collins was sitting by himself glaring at them all, sulking in silence. "I thought you rather enjoyed Mr. Collins's company or, at the very least, his foolishness. I would have thought you wished to keep the connection."

"Of some foolishness, Lizzy," replied he, "a little goes a long way. Yes, I have enjoyed the man's absurdity these past months, but I find that I have had my fill of it. His comments about you and correcting your behavior told me that he is, at the very least, capable of enforcing his ideal of behavior on a wife with his fists. I have no wish to maintain a connection with a man who is capable of such things."

A complex man, her father surprised her to a certain extent. Elizabeth had not missed Mr. Collins's references herself, but they had not affected her as she would never have accepted him and had been confident of Mr. Darcy's regard. But her father—though he had never been a violent man, she might have thought he would reprimand the man and then ignore him, turning back to his enjoyment of Mr. Collins's foolishness.

"And Mary?" asked Elizabeth. "It seems to me you have come to a new understanding with my sister these past weeks."

"I had to replace you in some fashion," replied Mr. Bennet, the familiar twinkle which appeared when he was teasing shining in his eyes. "Since your Mr. Darcy is about to take you away from me and spirit you off to Derbyshire, I am about to lose my companion."

"Oh, Papa!" said Elizabeth. "Do not speak so. You will hurt Mary's feelings if she overhears you."

"I believe you have misjudged your sister, Lizzy. Mary has grown much, and though she still scolds me when I tease too much, she has learned to accept it. She would not be offended."

Mr. Bennet smiled, though to Elizabeth it seemed like a wistful sort of gesture. "Mary is not the same as you, Lizzy. She does not possess the sense of humor you share with me, though she has learned to laugh a little. My relationship with her will be different from that which I share with you, but change is a necessary part of life, do you not think? I find that I am anticipating the debates I shall have with her. They will be different, and I think I will enjoy confounding her much more than I did you."

"I am glad you have reached this understanding with her, Papa," said Elizabeth. "Perhaps she will take a greater interest in life outside Fordyce."

"I have not even seen that book in days," replied Mr. Bennet with a wink.

Elizabeth laughed and excused herself to return to the side of her future husband. Mr. Darcy welcomed her, though the look in his eye told her he would much prefer to have her in a secluded grove where he might express his appreciation in a more animated fashion.

"All is well?" asked he.

"It is, Mr. Darcy. In fact, for the first time in quite some time, I am hopeful for the future of my family. Our association with your aunt has done much to improve many things, even beyond the benefits I myself have received."

"And what benefits might those be?" asked Mr. Darcy.

"Do you not know?" asked Elizabeth, arching an eyebrow at him. "Why, the benefit of improved society and entrance into her ladyship's company. And I must not forget how Mr. Collins's constant harangues have curbed my impertinence. Indeed, I must be grateful to Mr. Collins above all others."

"Minx!" exclaimed Mr. Darcy. "I can see Mr. Collins was right about one thing: that insolence must be curbed. I shall need to see to it directly when we are married."

"Then do your worst, Mr. Darcy."

And he did, though it was clear to anyone who cared to look that Mr. Darcy had no interest in dampening Elizabeth's spirit. It was that which had attracted him in the first place, and he encouraged it rather than the reverse. The Darcys were married alongside the Fitzwilliams, and they all retired to Derbyshire and their estates there. If their happily ever after was at times beset with rough patches, they decided with philosophy that it was the fate off all to end that way. Both couples had their share of happiness, their own measure of vexations and grief, their triumphs and defeats. But as Lady Catherine predicted, they were well suited and very much in love, and that was enough to keep the world at bay.

The inevitable meeting between Jane and Mr. Bingley took place not long after the weddings, and in the highly public arena of Covent Garden. As it was their first foray into society, the entirety of their new family had turned out in force, with Lady Catherine and her daughter, the earl and countess and their children, as well as other sundry more distant relations. In accordance with Lady Catherine's prediction, the earl had not been particularly pleased with his nephew and his son's choice of wives. However, he had accepted them in favor of family unity and had quickly come to appreciate them. Elizabeth, who was standing and speaking with her aunt and uncle Gardiner, who had also attended, had been in a position to see what happened with the additional benefit of not being noticed.

"Darcy, my friend," said Mr. Bingley, approaching with hand

extended. "It has been some time, has it not?"

"Indeed, Bingley," replied Mr. Darcy—or William, as Elizabeth now called him. "How have you been?"

"Quite ill, indeed," interjected Miss Bingley. The woman had followed her brother and was eyeing William as if he were a particularly fat side of beef. "We spent some months in York with our relations, and it was a most tedious time. I cannot be happier that we have returned to London and its superior society."

"And did you find them well?" asked William of Mr. Bingley, ignoring Miss Bingley's exaggerated ennui.

"Yes, thank you," replied Mr. Bingley. His irrepressible good humor was unaffected by his sister. A little farther away in the press of those gathered in the lobby stood Mr. and Mrs. Hurst, but while they watched the scene, they did not approach.

"And how is your dear sister, Mr. Darcy?" asked Miss Bingley, stepping forward and laying a coquettish hand on his arm. "I dare say her playing has grown so exquisite that all of London must be waiting in anticipation of her coming out." She turned a sly look on her brother. "Charles has spoken much of her. I believe he is as eager as I to once again make her acquaintance."

A giggle escaped Elizabeth's lips, drawing the attention of her aunt. "Do you find something amusing, Lizzy?"

"Only the antics of Miss Bingley," said Elizabeth, gesturing at the woman. "She is about as subtle as a herd of stampeding horses."

Both her aunt and uncle turned to view the scene. It was clear that William was disinclined toward Miss Bingley's company, and equally clear that she could not see it. He spoke with Mr. Bingley, who did his best to take part in the conversation, while Miss Bingley did *her* best to speak over him at every opportunity.

"Is Mr. Bingley not the man who left our Jane heartbroken last year?" asked her uncle.

"He is, indeed," replied Elizabeth. "He is an amiable man, but as you can see, his sister is a gorgon. Though I would have been happy for Jane had she married him, I cannot but think it has turned out for the best."

The Gardiners watched the Bingley siblings for a few moments, before Mrs. Gardiner nodded her head. "I agree, Lizzy. With a sister such as Miss Bingley, I doubt Jane would have been comfortable."

At that moment, William was joined by Lady Catherine. Elizabeth, who was by now familiar with the lady, noted the gleam in her eye and the slight smirk on her face and was certain that her ladyship was up to something mischievous.

"Mr. Bingley," said she, prompting a bow from the man. "How agreeable it is to see you again."

"And you, your ladyship," replied Mr. Bingley. "I hope you have been well."

"Tolerable, yes," replied Lady Catherine. The conversation continued for the next few moments, and Elizabeth could not help but notice Miss Bingley's eagerness and impatience to be introduced to her ladyship. In a remarkable bit of restraint, she held her tongue as was proper, waiting for the higher ranked to request an introduction. After the fact, she probably would have preferred to remain unintroduced.

"I believe this is your sister, is it not, Mr. Bingley?" asked Lady Catherine. Again, the haughty and knowing tone of her voice almost brought Elizabeth to laughter.

"It is, your ladyship."

"She seems a pretty, fashionable girl, though a little too forward for the daughter of a tradesman. Perhaps you will be so good as to introduce us?"

Though Elizabeth could see William almost choking on his tongue, incredulous at his aunt's words, and Miss Bingley's eyes almost bulged out of their sockets, they all managed to maintain their composure. Mr. Bingley obviously had never seen this side of Lady Catherine before, but he did as requested with alacrity and introduced them.

"I am pleased to make your acquaintance," Miss Bingley was quick to say once her brother had finished speaking. "I have long wished to be known to you, for you are quite obviously highly regarded by your nephew. Our connection is so close to Mr. Darcy that I almost feel like we have known each other for years."

"Does the woman have no shame?" asked Aunt Gardiner as Elizabeth was busy stifling her laughter.

"I almost thought she was going to claim that they were already family," replied Elizabeth.

Mrs. Gardiner shook her head, but neither wished to miss the conversation, so they continued to listen.

"That is an interesting point of view, Miss Bingley," said Lady Catherine. "I had not known you were so deep in Darcy's councils."

"We have been to Pemberley, and my brother has been his friend for years, Lady Catherine," said Miss Bingley. The self-congratulatory note in her tone was unmistakable, as was her brother's mortification. "I dare say there are few as close to Mr. Darcy and his sister as we are."

For a moment, Lady Catherine did not say anything in return, and the scrutiny seemed to make Miss Bingley uncomfortable. "Then you should feel grateful for my nephew's attentions," said she at length. "For he belongs to one of the most prestigious families in the kingdom."

"We do, indeed," said Mr. Bingley, apparently eager to interrupt his sister's embarrassing display.

Lady Catherine nodded once, regally, and turned to William. "I believe it is almost time to go in, Darcy."

"Shall we not all sit together?" interrupted Miss Bingley. "It has been an age since we were in each other's company."

This time Lady Catherine's displeasure was unmistakable. But William seeming to sense that she was about to castigate his friend's sister, said: "I am afraid we cannot, Miss Bingley, for our boxes this evening are quite full."

"Yes, quite," said Lady Catherine with a sniff. Then she turned back to Darcy. "Where is Elizabeth, Darcy? I hope to sit beside her, for I believe her observations of the night's entertainment will be vastly amusing."

"Elizabeth?" gasped Miss Bingley. Several unpleasant emotions crossed her face at once, and she seemed to have a premonition of what was about to occur.

"She is speaking with the Gardiners," replied William, and he turned and held out his hand, beckoning Elizabeth to his side. She went readily, though it was a trial to keep the grin from her face.

Miss Bingley's first sight of her caused her eyes to widen impossibly wide. "Miss Eliza Bennet!" blurted she. "I had no expectation of seeing *you* in such a place as this."

"I am happy to see you too, Miss Bingley," said Elizabeth, her tone purposely dry. "But I must correct you on one point: I am no longer Miss Bennet—I now go by the name of Mrs. Elizabeth Darcy."

An expression of sheer horror came over Miss Bingley's face, and she gaped at Elizabeth for several moments. Then, in desperation, she blurted: "You have married a cousin of Mr. Darcy's?"

Elizabeth laughed and leaned into William's side, and he responded by pressing his hand to the small of her back. "No, indeed," said she. "In fact, I am Mrs. *Fitzwilliam* Darcy. We have been married these past three weeks."

If the woman was not so reprehensible, Elizabeth might have pitied her when her face appeared to crumble. All her pretensions toward becoming the next Mrs. Darcy had been laid bare as nothing more than vain ambitions. But she quickly recovered, and turned a smile on Elizabeth which was just short of a sneer.

"I am all astonishment. How ever did you manage such a thing, Miss Eliza?"

Both William and Lady Catherine's countenances darkened at the insinuation in her tone, but Elizabeth only laughed. "In the usual manner, I would expect, though I have no other experience with which to compare it. Mr. Darcy proposed and I accepted, after some weeks of courtship, of course."

"I could never have imagined that a man such as Mr. Darcy would have had any admiration for you. I had thought his tastes were more sophisticated, though I do remember having heard something about fine eyes."

Amused at the woman's venom, Elizabeth looked up at her husband, noting the playful quality in his returning gaze. "That was only when I first knew you, my dear, and it was far short of the mark. It has been many months since I have considered you to be the handsomest woman of my acquaintance."

Outrage colored Miss Bingley's countenance, though Elizabeth could not imagine why she would be offended for a husband's obvious appreciation for his wife.

"And we count ourselves fortunate to have her," said Lady Catherine, interrupting when Miss Bingley appeared ready to unleash her vituperation again. "I cannot imagine a better wife for my nephew, I assure you. They are quite happy together.

"Of course," continued Lady Catherine in a casual tone, "given Elizabeth's background as the daughter of a gentleman, there can be no question of the eligibility of their match. I am certain any naysayers are intelligent enough to hold their tongues, as the entire Fitzwilliam family stands behind them."

Mr. Bingley, who had stood by stupefied, found his voice—it was just in time, Elizabeth thought, for Miss Bingley appeared on the verge of making some further social faux pas.

"I extend my congratulations." He turned to William, a question in his eyes. "I had no idea you had renewed your acquaintance with the Bennets, Darcy. You left Hertfordshire long before I did."

"We became reacquainted when I visited Lady Catherine in Kent at Easter," replied William. "Elizabeth and her family were visiting a relation of theirs at the same time."

"And it was to our benefit," asserted Lady Catherine. The stern countenance she presented to Miss Bingley appeared designed to quell any attempt at incivility or cutting comments. It appeared to work, as Miss Bingley held her tongue, though her eyes blazed.

"Indeed, it was," said William, bestowing a soft look on Elizabeth. "I cannot be any happier with how everything has proceeded."

Bile appeared to rise in Miss Bingley's throat, for she turned green. For his part, Mr. Bingley appeared more than a little confused, but his confusion soon turned to consternation.

"And your family, Miss Bennet?" asked he, turning to Elizabeth, his eyes pleading. "Your parents are well? And *all* your sisters are still at Longbourn?"

For a moment, Elizabeth watched Mr. Bingley, wondering how she should handle this situation. He was not a bad man, she thought, just one who was too easily led. Yes, his departure had caused Jane grief and had left her the target of gossip, but she knew that Mr. Bingley had not meant to hurt her, and Jane would not wish for him to be unduly hurt in return. Miss Bingley was a reprehensible creature in Elizabeth's estimation, but Mr. Bingley was not. That knowledge tempered her response.

"My family is quite well, sir. I thank you for asking. My younger sisters are at Longbourn, though I believe Lady Catherine will host Kitty and Lydia again soon. But Jane is here tonight, as she has been recently married to Mr. Darcy's cousin, the former Colonel Fitzwilliam."

"Married?" asked Mr. Bingley in a faint sort of voice.

"Yes," replied Elizabeth, "in the same ceremony in which Mr. Darcy and I were joined."

A pallor settled over Mr. Bingley's face, but he could not say anything more as Jane and Fitzwilliam approached at that point, and he was faced with the previous object of his affections.

"Mr. Bingley, Miss Bingley," greeted Jane. "How pleasant it is to see you again."

Though Mr. Bingley appeared like he could not think of anything *less* pleasant, he readily agreed. Then, proving himself to be a good and amiable man, he shook Fitzwilliam's hand and bowed over Jane's, saying: "I offer my congratulations. I believe you will be very happy with Fitzwilliam, for I know him to be a good man."

Elizabeth had known that Fitzwilliam had wondered about his first meeting with Mr. Bingley after his marriage, and his response was determined by Mr. Bingley's reaction. As such, he only nodded his head warmly at the other man and said: "I intend to make her very happy, Bingley. I thank you for your felicitations."

A nod from Mr. Bingley and he turned back to his sister. "I believe we must find our seats, Caroline, for the first act is about to begin." He shook William's hand again, saying: "I am eager to hear all that has happened to you these last months, Darcy. I have no doubt the story will be fascinating."

"We will invite you for dinner," said Elizabeth, smiling warmly at the man. "I am certain Mr. Darcy will be happy to renew your acquaintance."

Mr. Bingley beamed and then turned away, leading his brooding sister back to the rest of his party. Elizabeth watched them go, feeling compassion for Mr. Bingley. She did not know if he had possessed any true love for her sister, but such a meeting must have been a shock for him.

"He is an amiable man, Darcy," said Lady Catherine, "but the sister is intolerable."

"You have stated my opinion quite succinctly, Lady Catherine," replied William.

Mr. Bingley was, indeed, invited to dine with the Darcys soon after. And though Mr. Darcy would have preferred otherwise, Elizabeth convinced him that they should at least attempt to come to some sort of accommodation with Miss Bingley, if for nothing else than to preserve Mr. Bingley's reputation in society. Unfortunately, it was not to be, for Miss Bingley came to dinner determined to find fault with Elizabeth and voice her displeasure in a way which could not be mistaken. As Lady Catherine also attended the dinner, sparks soon flew between the two women, resulting in a blistering set down which left Miss Bingley sullen and silent for the rest of the evening.

Though the invitation was not repeated and Miss Bingley never set foot across the threshold of any house the Darcys owned again, Mr. Bingley maintained his friendship with Mr. Darcy for the rest of his life. His attachment to Jane was soon revealed as nothing more than infatuation, and when he finally did marry to a woman connected and possessing a healthy dowry—and *not* Georgiana Darcy—it was clear that matters had worked out for all involved. On the other hand, Miss Bingley's schism with the Darcy and de Bourgh families soon became known, and she returned to York where she spent the remainder of her life. Elizabeth never knew nor cared if the woman eventually married, and Mr. Bingley did not inform them, knowing that she had become a persona non grata to them.

As for the other Bennet sisters, Mary did, indeed, become a new favorite of her father's, often leading Mrs. Bennet to say that her middle daughter had become as incomprehensible as Elizabeth. This did not bother Mary in the slightest, for her desire to be noticed in the family was realized with her relationship with her father. When some years later she met a young man who could not live without her, Mr. Bennet gave his permission, though with as much reluctance as he had with her elder sisters. But she was happy, and that was what counted. Thereafter, Mr. Bennet took to visiting all his daughters—including the youngest when they finally married—often when not expected, though he was always welcome.

For their parts, Kitty and Lydia, after their sisters' marriages, stayed as often with their new relation by marriage, Lady Catherine de Bourgh, as they did with their elder siblings or parents. There, they were often joined by Georgiana Darcy, who overcame her fear of Lady Catherine and became close friends with the youngest Bennets. Under Lady Catherine's tutelage, all three girls improved until they too found young men of their own and joined their elder siblings in the state of matrimony. Lady Catherine was known to say quite often that the three young girls were her proudest achievement—Kitty and Lydia because of their previous wildness and Georgiana because of her shyness. They were a great comfort to her, especially after Anne married and moved into her own home.

And Anne did, indeed, marry, though perhaps not in quite the way she had expected. She did not catch the eye of an earl, as she had expected, but a year or two after her pursuit of Mr. Darcy ended, she found a baronet who met all her expectations of happiness, and followed in her mother's footsteps. Whether she was disappointed in not being able to find a man of higher rank, she never said, but as Lady Catherine was reasonably assured of her daughter's comfort, she found no cause to repine.

Mr. Collins, unfortunately, was never to find the same felicity in marriage as all his cousins did. Whether it was because word of his behavior toward Elizabeth was circulated or because his comments of amending her behavior became known, he never found a wife and did not marry. Thus, though he did inherit Longbourn on the passing of Mr. Bennet, it was after many years as the parson of Rosings, for Mr. Bennet lived to a hale old age. And having no children of his own, the entail, which was to continue one more generation, was broken, and Jane's second son inherited the estate.

As for Lady Catherine herself, she also lived to a ripe old age. She found much joy and contentment in being a grandmother to Anne's children, as well as great aunt to her nephews' children and those of the other Bennet sisters. Her exploits were legendary, as were her actions in arranging matters so that her younger relations could find joy. The Darcys and the Fitzwilliams were often found at Rosings visiting, and laughter rang through its halls. Elizabeth and Jane ever after considered her to be a dear friend and aunt, for they were sensible of how she had brought them together with their husbands by insisting they stay at Rosings that eventful spring.

The End

Wisteria was much as Terrace remembered. She was heavyset, though not quite overweight, with the brown hair and eyes of her people, and though her younger sister was delicate and slender, Wisteria was rather like a battering ram in comparison. She was not unattractive, but Terrace knew many men would be put off by her plainer features and the contemptuous curl of her lips. If, indeed, they had not already been put off by her domineering manner and poisonous tongue. With some interest, Terrace noted a few pockmarked scars on Wisteria's face, including one—quite deep—just under her left eye. Terrace wondered whether she had been in a battle of some kind.

There were a number of noble men and women standing by in the room, gazing on Terrace, as though wondering what she would do. Wisteria held her hand out to a nearby servant, who placed a goblet in her hand, backing away deferentially, almost genuflecting before the woman.

Terrace watched this scene with shock. Groundbreathers had never required such strong obeisance from their subjects. Most of those who lived in the castle were Groundbreathers themselves, descended from the same people who had originally been blessed by Terrain. Tillman's requirements for respect had been almost perfunctory in nature, though Sequoia had always been more stringent. But even *that* imperious woman, who Terrace knew to be a good person at heart, had not acted the way her oldest daughter did. The girl almost seemed to think that she was Terrain himself.

"Welcome, Aunt," Wisteria said, her contemptuous amusement not hidden when she paused to drink deeply from the goblet that had been provided to her. "To what do I owe the honor of this unannounced visit?"

"I am sure you understand exactly why I am here, Wisteria. I wish to know what happened to my brother, and I want to know what you have done with River."

Wisteria cocked her head to the side. "You were informed, were you not?"

"I was. But I would hear it from you nonetheless."

Wisteria shrugged. "It is as you were told. There was an attempt to take over the castle, and my father was an unfortunate casualty."

"You speak of him as if he was nothing more than a Groundwalker," Terrace spat. "He was *king* of our people!"

"You had best moderate your tone," the chamberlain said. "Your niece is to be addressed with the respect she deserves and referred to as 'Your Majesty.'"

"I changed her soiled linens when she was a child and swatted her bottom when she misbehaved," Terrace snapped. "You had best mind your manners, or my niece will need a new toady to do her bidding."

The man stiffened at the insult, but Terrace's glare must have been fierce enough that he knew better than to speak any further. The sullen glare he directed at her, however, informed Terrace that she had made an enemy. But she did not fear what a man who kissed her niece's feet could do, and she turned her stony gaze back on Wisteria.

"Well, Wisteria?" Terrace prompted. "I am waiting for your answer."

"I do not make light of my father's death," Wisteria responded. "I mourn his passing as much as anyone, but as *I* am the eldest and the leadership of our people must be maintained, I have put my personal feelings aside for the good of the people and so that I might act in obedience to Terrain."

Terrace glared at her niece. Wisteria had rarely been obedient to anyone, and Terrace had always thought her devotion to the earth god to be little more than superficial.

"Where is River?" Terrace asked, deciding a different tack was required. "Where are Sequoia and Tierra?"

Watching for Wisteria's reaction as she was, Terrace was not surprised when an expression of almost insane revulsion crossed the young woman's face. Wisteria had always hated Tierra with an antipathy so deep that Terrace suspected Wisteria would not shed a tear if Tierra fell over dead.

"My mother disappeared in the chaos," Wisteria replied, though her short tone indicated her patience was being exhausted. "As for River and *Tierra*, they are safe at present. That is all you need to know."

"River is my daughter, and I demand—"

"You are in a position to demand nothing!"

Aunt and niece glared at each other, neither giving an inch. Wisteria stared with cold eyes, her gaze almost seeming to bore through Terrace as though she were not even there. Belatedly, Terrace realized that this woman now held absolute power over the castle and its surrounding environs. These strange Iron Swords guaranteed that.

Wisteria would not be loved by her people. She did not have the ability to inspire such loyalty. Rather, she would rule by fear and her implacable will. Judging by the atmosphere in the throne room, she had already made a start down that path.

It was time to take greater care. Terrace could not do anything from the inside of a cell, and Wisteria would have no compunction about incarcerating her own aunt if her displeasure grew too great.

"I am merely concerned over my daughter," Terrace said. Her attempt at a conciliatory tone was likely an abject failure, but Terrace thought Wisteria would care more about outward respect than inner feelings.

"I know you are concerned," Wisteria replied, her grating attempt at a soothing tone nearly causing Terrace to grimace, "but at present, you must trust me. River will be returned to you, and I promise you she has not been harmed."

Terrace did not miss how Wisteria did not even attempt to mollify her concerning the fate of Tierra. "And when will that be?"

Again, Wisteria's composure cracked, though she controlled her tone. "That is yet to be determined. I will keep you informed of her status. At present, I believe it would be best to return to your home."

Though it galled Terrace to be forced to retreat in such a manner, there was nothing more to be done. "Very well. But I must insist you inform me the moment there is any news."

Terrace inclined her head in farewell and turned to leave, but she was arrested by the sound of Wisteria's voice.

"Aunt, I am afraid I must ask you to remember that my father is dead . . . and *I* am now the queen. My father's reign was marred by laxness, not only in the manner in which his subjects were allowed to behave, but also in . . . other matters that he championed before his death. I have restored the order of our kingdom now. I require all my subjects to behave properly, as our god would require it. I will not hesitate to enforce my dictates. Am I understood?"

Once again, Wisteria and Terrace stared at each other, Terrace searching for any hint of weakness. If there was any, it was well-hidden, for Wisteria's expression was unreadable. It appeared Tillman was correct after all. He had often mentioned his concerns over the fitness of his daughter to rule when he passed away, and Terrace could see nothing before her but the realization of those fears. Wisteria was not to be trifled with, and if she were not stopped, then she had the potential to become the worst despot in the history of their people.

"Perfectly," Terrace replied.

"Excellent! Then we shall see each other anon. Changes are coming,

Aunt, and we must do our part to bring about our god's designs."

Terrace nodded and turned to leave the room, her retinue trailing behind her. She did not understand what Wisteria meant concerning Terrain, but she feared it nonetheless. It was at times like this that she wished Heath was still with her. He had always known what to do, and he had possessed an instinctual ability to read others and determine their motivations with a single glance. Terrace missed him; she had loved and cherished him, and theirs had been a marriage of the hearts.

But there was no point in dwelling on her loss. Terrace had to take action. First, Terrace needed to try to find Sequoia. She was the key. If Terrace could find Sequoia, then Tierra and River could be located afterward.

But first, Terrace needed to involve Basil. As it was his fiancée who was missing, Basil had a direct interest in the matter, and Terrace would not leave him out of it.

And so Terrace departed the castle. But it would not be for the last time. She was now convinced that Wisteria had played a part in Tillman's demise. Terrace meant to find out what had happened to her brother. Wisteria would be held responsible, even if she had only failed to act to save him.

FROM ONE GOOD SONNET PUBLISHING

http://onegoodsonnet.com/

For Readers Who Enjoyed
Chaos Comes To Kent

Coincidence
Fitzwilliam Darcy finds Miss Elizabeth Bennet visiting her friend, Mrs. Collins, in Kent, only to realize that she detests him. It is not long before he is bewitched by her all over again, and he resolves to change her opinion of him. Though she only wishes to visit her friend, Elizabeth is soon made uncomfortable by the presence of Mr. Darcy, who always seems to be near. As their acquaintance deepens, them much learn more about each other in order to find their happiness.

My Brother's Keeper
When Fitzwilliam Darcy accompanies Charles Bingley to Netherfield, he is accompanied by George Wickham, a friend of many years. At first, Darcy does not see Elizabeth Bennet for the jewel she is, but his eyes are soon opened to her true worth. As Darcy and Elizabeth grow closer and love begins to blossom between them, the actions of a scoundrel threaten their happiness.

The Angel of Longbourn
When Elizabeth Bennet finds Fitzwilliam Darcy unconscious and suffering from a serious illness, the Bennets quickly return him to their house, where they care for him like he is one of their own. Mr. Darcy soon forms an attachment with the young woman he comes to view as his personal angel. But the course of true love cannot proceed smoothly, for others have an interest in Darcy for their own selfish reasons…

The Mistress of Longbourn
When the Netherfield party arrives in Hertfordshire, the family they find at Longbourn is small, composed only of Elizabeth and her younger sister. A change in the circumstances of the entail has left Elizabeth Bennet as the mistress of Longbourn, beholden to no one. But the challenge before Elizabeth is to recognize a deep and abiding love when it finds her.

For more details, visit
http://www.onegoodsonnet.com/genres/pride-and-prejudice-variations

ALSO BY ONE GOOD SONNET PUBLISHING

THE SMOTHERED ROSE TRILOGY

BOOK 1: THORNY

In this retelling of "Beauty and the Beast," a spoiled boy who is forced to watch over a flock of sheep finds himself more interested in catching the eye of a girl with lovely ground-trailing tresses than he is in protecting his charges. But when he cries "wolf" twice, a determined fairy decides to teach him a lesson once and for all.

BOOK 2: UNSOILED

When Elle finds herself practically enslaved by her stepmother, she scarcely has time to even clean the soot off her hands before she collapses in exhaustion. So when Thorny tries to convince her to go on a quest and leave her identity as Cinderbella behind her, she consents. Little does she know that she will face challenges such as a determined huntsman, hungry dwarves, and powerful curses . . . .

BOOK 3: ROSEBLOOD

Both Elle and Thorny are unhappy with the way their lives are going, and the revelations they have had about each other have only served to drive them apart. What is a mother to do? Reunite them, of course. Unfortunately, things are not quite so simple when a magical lettuce called "rapunzel" is involved.

If you're a fan of thieves with a heart of gold, then you don't want to Miss . . .

THE PRINCES AND THE PEAS
A TALE OF ROBIN HOOD

A NOVEL OF THIEVES, ROYALTY, AND IRREPRESSIBLE LEGUMES

BY LELIA EYE

An infamous thief faces his greatest challenge yet when he is pitted against forty-nine princes and the queen of a kingdom with an unnatural obsession with legumes. Sleeping on top of a pea hidden beneath a pile of mattresses? Easy. Faking a singing contest? He could do that in his sleep. But stealing something precious out from under "Old Maid" Marian's nose . . . now that is a challenge that even the great Robin Hood might not be able to surmount.

When Robin Hood comes up with a scheme that involves disguising himself as a prince and participating in a series of contests for a queen's hand, his Merry Men provide him their support. Unfortunately, however, Prince John attends the contests with the Sheriff of Nottingham in tow, and as all of the Merry Men know, Robin Hood's pride will never let him remain inconspicuous. From sneaking peas onto his neighbors' plates to tweaking the noses of prideful men like the queen's chamberlain, Robin Hood is certain to make an impression on everyone attending the contests. But whether he can escape from the kingdom of Clorinda with his prize in hand before his true identity comes to light is another matter entirely.

About the Author

Jann Rowland

Jann Rowland is a Canadian who enjoys reading and sports, and dabbles a little in music, taking pleasure in singing and playing the piano.

Though Jann did not start writing until his mid-twenties, writing has grown from a hobby to an all-consuming passion. His interest in Jane Austen stems from his university days when he took a class in which *Pride and Prejudice* was required reading. However, his first love is fantasy fiction, which he hopes to pursue writing in the future.

He now lives in Alberta with his wife of more than twenty years and his three children.

For more information on Jann Rowland, please visit:
http://onegoodsonnet.com.

50449077R00115

Made in the USA
San Bernardino, CA
23 June 2017